# THE
# TRANSFORMATION
## *Of Life*
# TO LEGEND

# THE TRANSFORMATION *Of Life* TO LEGEND

Arlene Cotterell

ISBN:    978-1-63795-749-3    (Paperback Edition)
ISBN:    978-1-63795-750-9    (Hardcover Edition)
ISBN:    978-1-63795-744-8    (E-book Edition)



**Book Ordering Information**

Phone Number: 315 288-7939 ext. 1000 or 347-901-4920
Email: info@globalsummithouse.com
Global Summit House
www.globalsummithouse.com

Printed in the United States of America

According to the historical books of the pale one's prior to their turning when they were still human they held onto their society for a bit longer than was just spoken about, things deteriorated even more and eventually next would be world war two which was from 1939 to 1945 and was considered to be a global war and involved more conflicts than world war one involving many more conflicts. World war two involved massacres, genocide, strategic bombing, and the use of nuclear weapons for the first time but in strategic areas not world-wide, starvation and disease played a part in this war also. Since world war one there were a lot of advances in technology and warfare, casualties and war crimes were at an all-time high. This war made Adolf Hitler a common household name for centuries until the end of time as the humans had known life to be within normal limits which was until the third and final world war. According to legend of the dinosaur tail the third world war which came too soon as it started in February of 2925 when North Korea and the United States both launched their nuclear missiles at one another which bled out into the other areas of the world leaving practically nothing left to identify, it was a miracle that the few humans that were left in Las Vegas Nevada were still there and they believed that it was simply the will of God that they survived. You see, when the United States launched their great missile, they also sent out submarines, ships, plains, stealth bombers, and the likes to assist in destroying the North Koreans and anything that stood in the way as North Korea had followed suit to a point but instead of targeting strategic places both sides were aiming at destroying the entire portion of their enemies world. According to human records Nostradamus made some reference to the world events and was quite accurate in his account of how things would unfold and what it would be like just before and after the events were over according to his supporters, he had many who did everything they could to disprove his parables though the parables here were proven to be correct as in his other parables. There was no reference for events past the year 2050 from Nostradamus but the end of life as humans had known it was imminent for them however, how many years or decades did eminent have to be before it was to be upon the humans was yet to be prophesied or proven at that time. This is where The legend of the dinosaur tail comes into play where it was now seen that in the year 2925 the nuclear war or should we say world war three had suddenly started and just as swiftly ended and left only approximately three hundred individuals alive in a clump known as Las Vegas, Nevada where one hundred of the three hundred living there just happened to be in their smart houses when the toxins filled the air and turned the once smoggy yet clear air blood red and made it go from smog filled to radioactive and lethal to anything requiring oxygen to survive. The society was set up for a security system in the event that the nuclear war should occur and there would be some survivors which was not likely but extremely hopeful. The security system allowed for robotics to come alive when their sensors were tripped by a certain level or higher of radiation and if there were no humans alive than there would only be robotics alive and no harm nor loss. No one else in the world had a set up like Las Vegas did with the smart houses and preparedness supplies with extreme training as well as ways to get around and live an almost normal life. Sure, things were needing to be altered a bit but again no harm no loss actually only gain.

The adults would take the children who were older and start cross training them in medical, engineering, and everything necessary to be self-sufficient and run their little society alone if necessary. All the children went to school to learn the basic skills of reading, writing, the history of how they and their society got to where they were as well as the local history inside their little community for there were hidden secrets in the mole hills that laid halfway between their homes and the local school house called Dobbins Memorial. The hidden secrets were taught little by little as age appropriate so the children were not frightened too much because it was even horrifically fear-provoking to the adults and the more the adults knew the more alarmed they were, it was a good thing only a few adults knew the whole story because the facts were nearly driving them to the brink of irreversible shock. Prior to the third world war there was prophesied to be great earthly natural disasters and there were a multitude of great earthly disasters, one right after another, floods, landslides, earthquakes, fires, tsunamis, and draughts just to start. There also came pestilence, famine, and other hardships along those lines. The crime rate was soaring up ever so speedily, the economy was way down and could not go much further down, and nothing was getting any better in fact everything looked worse with the threat of war and nation against nation until the nuclear missiles were finally released. There was no sound from the missiles in fact the birds and other critters in the country and the cities were still acting normal until the red dust overpowered them like a flash of locusts flying through in their attempt to over-power another species, it was like some horror television show. The air critters flew for their lives but could not fly fast enough and were engulfed by the reddened toxin then they limply fell to the earth all at once. By that time there were echoes of missiles, but they seemed to be farther away than the toxic dust that they created which brought gloom and doom with them, they even made the day turn to evening by blocking out the sun's rays. From the thickness of the dust it appeared that it was going to take a while for the dust to settle maybe even days especially since it was in the middle of a dust bowl as Las Vegas was known to be and that was even if the dust was ever going to settle because it was radioactive and had different toxins with a different chemical make-up in it meaning that the dust may never settle, and in this case it never did. The moon had even turned blood red and was extremely difficult to view, unbeknownst to the humans the sun was blocked by the reddened dust and would never gleam again. The only thing visible was the outline of the moon as it was way closer to the earth than ever before and the lighting was like that of dusk throughout the day and night hours, the ramount of lighting between the day and night hours never changed. At first everyone that had survived without any harmful effects due to being inside their smart houses during the warfare stayed in their smart houses for a spell as those who were out in the elements during the warfare as those who were seemingly deceased but not quite dead yet as they attempted to gain entry into the smart houses yet failed. They were riddled with sores as third degree burns left the appearance of their skin falling off. Their bones were weakened as they practically drug their limp bodies about this was extremely frightening to the healthy humans for, they did not know how long the damaged and soon to be diseased humans would be pounding at their domains. Because there were communications between the various smart houses the adult males of each smart house's families were discussing how to free up their homes of the pestilence of the damaged humans.

The conversations did not seem to bring with them any simple solutions only that the damaged humans had to be ran off to a place far away which would be a place that used to be called down town Las Vegas where all the so-called casino resorts used to be, they were a big influence on the economy for the city they were now broken down ruins but had some shelter although that did not matter much anymore. The adult males of each smart house realized that in order for them to help assure their family's safety in functioning as normal as possible under the new circumstances they would have to successfully run the damaged humans off to the resort casinos by force if need be and any that did not comply would have to be terminated which may actually be a blessing in disguise in that they would not have to die slowly and miserably but it did not make things any easier they were still someone's family member and dearly loved. Another concern was how to handle the already dead if there were any that were laid about in the vicinity that the healthy humans would be occupying and a certain distance around that just for safety measures. None of the healthy humans had made a visual on any of the robotic police that were supposed to be automatically ignited when the air quality reached a certain lethal point but the healthy humans were sure they were out there and had just not made it out to where the smart houses were yet but they were wandering how the robotic police would handle the healthy humans and what their guidelines were for them and if there were any guidelines at all. The men of the safe houses were willing to risk their lives for their families and knew they had no choice if their families were to stand a chance for a somewhat normal type of life that they would have to adjust to. There were a lot of preparations to tend to prior to just leaving the false safety of their safe house such as their weapons and ammunition, airtight suits with oxygen regeneration ability that they had to be cautious of not allowing the damaged humans to be able to grab onto their suits and puncture a hole into them. Then their hovercraft ride had to be checked for its ability to handle the long ride out and back as well as the long-drawn-out speed they would have to go. With the subdued speed that the damaged humans would have to travel the healthy humans knew they would be gone for a diminutive time going out and at most half the time getting back so they were actually debating on whether to even take the hovercraft. The hovercraft was like a motorcycle with landing gear instead of wheels that could go in excess of three hundred miles per hour but could hover in the air as well. The healthy humans air tight suits derived from the outdated space suits that were developed for when humans first started space travel and had visited the moon only instead of using oxygen tanks they had miniature palm sized portable oxygen concentrators that functioned off of radioactivity when exposed the palm sized generator could be turned on and work or stay in an off position which had to be turned to that position manually and still hold a charge, everything that functioned within the new condition was reliant upon the high levels of radiation and was basically self-functioning. The weapons that they had were still basic in nature meaning they still had not changed much from the average variety of weapons that would have been carried previous to world war three, the guns were not laser guns or anything advanced as had been seen on the picture tubes that humans used to watch in the space shows or technologically inclined television and movie shows. The men of each smart household had finally come to a conclusion without the aid of their families which was to walk the damaged humans out to the old casino resort ruins that they would now call the bad lands and they would herd the damaged humans up with the use of fire arms and destroy anyone who resisted the movement out of necessity for the safety of the healthy humans. The healthy men decided to leave the dead if there were to be anywhere, they were for now to wait out the robotic police because it was important to find out if the robotic police were going to remove the bodies to a specific dumping place or not.

The healthy humans also needed to be cautious of the robotic police so they needed to keep from attracting their attention as much as possible which they knew would be difficult especially if they had to fire off their weapons while herding the damaged humans to the bad lands they just knew that if they were forced into shooting one of the damaged humans it may gain the attention of the robotic police for sure. There had been no public awareness about the robotic police past the acknowledgement of their existence but the healthy humans were certain that they were extremely unique in that they could nearly think on an individual basis as each human was capable of doing never before was a machine able to think for itself. As it was the robotics created were done so in the image of healthy humans and there was no real way to tell them apart other than to lift their wigs off their heads which was a difficult task to visualize the robotic parts or for one of them to become severely injured which would be an injury that would be lethal to an actual human and again visualize the robotic parts with what appeared to be old auto fluid squirting out of the injury. Their speech was even unique to each robotic individual and with the right injury or malfunction their voice would be altered and who knew what type of results would be heard if the robotic individual could speak at all. The only real way at that point to tell a robotic police individual apart from a real healthy human was by the clothing, the robotic police wore a police uniform and the regular healthy human wore civilians clothing but if a robotic police officer chose to change clothing into a civilian outfit there would be no certain way to spot the difference so long as the individual android acted purely human and required the assistance of technology to survive which the robotic police did not require. However, the lack of radiation and too much oxygen would actually disengage the robotic police officer so it would not pay off for the robotic individual to try to blend in with the healthy humans in secret because they would not be able to function within the perimeters of the safety environment and they were possibly programed to stay within professional limits but that was still yet to be found out for all the healthy humans knew the robotic police may very well be hostile to healthy humans for they may not distinguish between healthy humans and damaged humans. The men who were to unite to herd the damaged humans were going to get together within the hour because they did not want to waste any time in making their new territory safe and getting their new lives in order to start to adjust to their new routines, they wanted their families to get to function in what they would be considering normal within the next few days. Now the next task the small community of healthy humans had to deal with was how to keep track of time to gauge the hour and keep up with each day as the days passed to know when the time passed for it was important to know what day, week, month and so on they were in for record keeping and for simple living situations, now that the sun was not going to rise and set daily that was going to be a real chore. The community of healthy humans still had to delegate certain major tasks to various individuals and that would involve the entire group of humans to vote for each task and each individual such as the record keeper, head of security for the community, and so on there were not many tasks to be delegated so things could be kept simple the record keeper would have eyes and ears within his or hers small community to help with keeping things accurate, the most important job would be the individual who kept accurate time for the whole community what was he or she to use and how reliable was it going to be for a simple clock could not be trusted. Maybe the moon itself would be able to aid in time keeping because it waned and waxed and its other various phases, that would help for extreme time telling but for the hours and days the healthy humans needed something more from the moon but how were they to get that.

Because of the dim lighting provided from the moon due to the radiation in the dust that was in the air the dust never settled so shadows were a thing of the past to help provide an estimation of hours which had been used in days past. In fact the air was so dense with radioactive elements that there would never even be a breeze in the air again, the temperature would never change, the water on the surface of the earth would be no more, there was not to be any foliage ever again, and there would not be any life with the exceptions of the healthy humans for however long they may last and for the damaged humans for what borrowed time they were existing on. The healthy humans survived on rations provided from the smart houses that were replicated, waste was what provided the fuel for the rations and it was an extremely difficult process to occur and explain, the elders just showed their young how it worked with insignificant explanation in the event they may need to fix the replicator themselves after the demise of their predecessor or in the absence of their predecessor. The smart house provided nearly everything, it replicated all tangible items needed and provided oxygen in the same way the space-like suits did for when the healthy humans were out in the elements, a radioactive run generator that operated a large concentrator that ran very noiselessly and effortlessly. Around each smart house was a small yard and the yard as well as the house was encased inside a bubble-like covering that was environmentally safe from the elements to allow the families some outdoor time without having to suit up yet get to stretch their legs and have a bit of running room in a semi natural environment with a desert type landscape. There was a section of the bubble-like area that was for decontamination in steps for entering back into the safe area from the dangerous radioactive elements of the outer world that was left over from the third world war and that was where the space-like suits were stored for the entire family, this area also served as the safehouses exit into the elements. Each family was well rounded with both parents and their children being present and there was anywhere from one to three children to each family varying in ages because to get to having a safe house built back when the project was being drafted there were strict guidelines each family had to qualify in and of course it was only the wealthy who got the safe houses because the construction funding was supported by the home owners themselves. There were many families that could have fit the financial qualifications many times over but failed to qualify in other ways such as family status, dynamics, not having both parents involved directly in the family unit for instance split families with shared custody and other variables there were very revealing guidelines that would expose many factors that individuals reluctantly revealed just for a proposed sense of safety in the event of a crisis such as world war three and it actually caused much pain and separation among many individuals as skeletons from individuals lives became exposed, it was a very personal and revealing process that took up to a year to complete prior to getting the announcement of whether the family qualified or not then the real work began with the floor plans, payment in full prior to any construction and the gathering of equipment for construction. Once the construction of the smart house and its surroundings were paid in full then it was time to draw up the actual floor plan for not each smart house was alike, the gathering of the equipment, the necessary supplies then starting the construction and one smart house could take another year to be structurally completed and ready to be moved into. It was always the case that when a smart house was completed the families would move right into them and restart their routines in preparation for the end of their lives as they knew it.

The people did not know when or if world war three would occur and whether the smart houses would really protect them from the major blasts that were expected to occur during the greatest war ever. Now that the greatest war ever had happened it occurred to the dwellers of the smart houses that the only reason they survived the event was not entirely their safe houses, it was because Las Vegas Nevada was so far away from where the blasting had occurred and they happened to have caught the after-shocks of what the missiles had to offer and that was probably accidental because if the enemy had it their way none of the survivors would have made it although there were no other survivors outside of the close to three hundred that were in Las Vegas Nevada which were the total of the healthy humans with the damaged humans, there were more damaged humans than healthy by one healthy human to two damaged humans. As far as the few dead that were laid all about, they were in different stages of decomposition it appeared that the smaller the body the more skeletal the remains were which was indicative of why the damaged humans were all once very healthy adults there were no young indicating that apparently there was not enough mass to their bodies to take the amount of radiation exposure that there had been given from the missiles there were even some dust piles that resembled bodies that the healthy humans believed were healthy humans at one time. It was now time for the adult males who were head of the households to leave to herd the damaged humans to the bad lands so they gave their families hugs, kisses and gave their farewells for now and headed out for the decontamination area of their homes to dress up into their space-like suits to go out into the elements and do their sad but necessary job. The damaged humans were still fighting to live and only wanting to be given a chance at survival and that was why they banged at the domes of the safe houses to try to get inside but the healthy humans knew there was no way to help them not even the medical holographic doctor that each safe house offered had the solution for radiation poisoning to the extent that the damaged humans suffered from so the only way to handle the situation was to run off the damaged humans and let them die off, if the decomposition from the radiation did not kill the damaged humans it would eventually occur due to starvation and dehydration sure, it was a tough way to go but the healthy humans had to protect themselves and try to survive with some hope of finding a way to extend their lives past what the safe houses were supposed to allow. Each safe house was designed to support its family for at least five years easy and then there was a declining time after that in which the safe house would start to provide less and less so it was vital to be sparing on what was required from the safe house from the beginning and that was one of the many reasons that it was impractical for the families to inhabit their homes prior to any real threat of war but then again war could break out without any real warning so the people thought and they were correct however, things were headed that direction already prior to the building of the safe houses if the humans would have just listened to the prophesies of the Bible and those of Nostradamus both were correct in what their parables spoke of right down to taking the mark of the beast per say. Upon birth each child was to have a microchip placed in the palm of their right hand and it could be read by a laser wand which would tell the individuals full identity, pertinent medical history, and law-abiding history. The microchip idea first started with the placement of them in the shoulder area of cats and dogs for rescue purposes in the event that someone's pet got lost and found by a stranger, the animal could be taken to a veterinarian and checked for identification of the proper owners address and personal information for the purpose of unification.

The microchip that the humans had was far more sophisticated and was easily modified for additional information and well kept up. In fact, humans were required regular chip check-ups to make sure all information was up to date kind of like how the department of motor vehicles did for the individuals driver's license when that system was in place years ago only the driver's license did not hold the same information nor as much and it was carried on the person not in the person as the new system with the microchip did. Each individual was assigned a number like a social security number but of course that was now out dated also and criminals who were assigned prison numbers was outdated as well now everyone had a specific number that served for any purpose that the individual needed a number for so there was less confusion supposedly. If an individual was involved in a crime their original birth given number was used to identify that as well as their medical logs and other various information so really humans were just numbers instead of individuals. In the new era humans were seen as drones in a way and expected to match up to a drone and little did the population know there were drones out amongst the citizens functioning as regular humans in an attempt to perfect the science of artificial intelligence the first android gained citizenship in its country in 2017 but when the world war took place the drones did not make it so that may have been a good thing for the remaining humans, or was it? Now the men of the households were outside of their safe houses and grouped together so they could get into a proper formation to start to herd the damaged humans to the bad lands with guns up and ready to be discharged. The damaged humans were all someone's family and friend so it made things difficult to have to drive them away, it was actually heartbreaking and the healthy humans did tear up but they knew like they knew an hour ago that they had no choice the diplomats that could not get along and play nice with one another made poor choices amongst one another and allowed things to get to the brink of war then beyond. The damaged humans started to wail and try to rebel but did not have the strength to stand for long without falling to the ground and struggled to get up again to get some sort of slow gait again. It was slow going but after a while the healthy humans had the damaged humans turned around to where they were headed to the bad lands but still it was a fight for when they fell to the ground, some of them would grab at the rifles in an effort to try to get the healthy human to kill them and just put them out of their misery. Although the healthy humans had space-like suits on they could still hear the wails and cries of the damaged humans begging for the healthy humans to put them down and be merciful on their souls. Even though things were grim for the damaged humans the healthy humans could not bring themselves to murder their fellow humans even though they did have a death sentence and shooting them was most likely the most humane thing to do it still was not what the healthy men were going to do at that point because they were God fearing men and felt that the giving and taking of life was for God to do and no one else. The healthy men did hope that if they ever did become damaged that they would have the bravery to shoot themselves and not have to suffer as they were watching their friends and family members do at that moment. They started the long journey toward the bad lands and the travel was painstaking and torturous for both the healthy and damaged humans. The healthy humans were tortured by the sight of the damaged humans being plucked by death one by one as they traveled and having to leave them like trash instead of caring for their carcasses respectfully as they felt they should do but they dared not try to compete with the police androids.

The damaged humans were having trouble just trying to walk and stay upright as they moaned and groaned in extreme pain while parts of their flesh fell from their bodies and sores ruptured and bled. Some of the damaged humans finally began to revolt and forcefully try to stand up to the healthy humans. The healthy humans tried everything they could to not have to fire upon the damaged humans until the healthy men stopped and thronged together to discuss matters at hand. The healthy humans realized that they were going to have to fire some shots of warning into the air to let the damaged humans know the firearms were loaded and ready to go off but they had in turn needed to be prepared to fire at their damaged friends and family members if necessary, it had always been said not to point a firearm if one was not willing and ready to use it so the healthy humans comprehended it may be time to play God and take some lives. The one concern the healthy humans had was how many damaged humans would they need to take down before they were done with the trip and ready to return home because practically all of them were prayerful for euthanization which the healthy humans could understand to a point why but that still did not make it any more right. The healthy men vowed that they would do what they had to do and not express their deeds to their families back at the safe houses unless absolutely necessary and they were hoping the details of the mass herding of the damaged ones could stay out of the history books that they were going to be keeping because they just wanted to get the trip over with and burry the experience back into their mental closet forever with whatever other skeletons that were left that did not get displayed during the examination for the qualification process for getting the safe house. The healthy men regained their stance to start to drive the damaged humans onward and still they revolted very few were trying to amble on so the healthy men started to strategically shoot only hitting those who were begging for mercy on their souls and to be euthanized with a kill shot between the eyes and that was just what they got, the healthy men were all skilled marksmen. By the time the shooting lightened up and came to a halt there were primarily damaged women left because majority of those begging for a quick end were damaged men. Now that the bloodshed was over the healthy humans were nearly in tears and with what strength they had the damaged humans left started to extend toward the bad lands. Little by little the bad lands were coming into view so the healthy humans instructed the damaged humans to continue to digress until they reached the ruins of the casino resorts and that would be their domain which would now be known as their land the bad lands and they were not to return to the vicinity of the safe houses and if they were spotted near them they would be shot upon sight. The healthy humans did not go any further but did stand on a mound of earth overlooking the tip top of the bad lands and observe the damaged humans continue on their journey to assure they actually made it there if they did not die prior to getting there which a few of the damaged humans had slumped in death. Now that the healthy humans had fulfilled their purpose for being out in the elements they turned to return to their safe houses and asserted very little and what they did affirm was how they had missed their families due to the length of time that it seemed to take for their travel time but they knew they would make it back home in a fragment of the time it took to get out to where they had gotten. Finally, the healthy men of the households had returned and entered their decontamination areas and shed their space-like suits so they could reenter their domes and toddle the distance of their front yards to enter their safe houses and greet their families and put the wretched experience of herding the damaged humans to the bad lands and killing some along the way.

The children were surrounding their fathers and giving them colossal hugs and pecks on the cheeks as they welcomed the fathers back safe and sound. After the children were finished welcoming their fathers back the wives of the healthy men welcomed their husband's home with hugs and kisses. After welcoming their husbands home the wives questioned the husbands if everything went well then the men became saddened and had to look away the wives knew things must have been hard-hitting and possibly have gone awry so the wives decided it best to not push the matter informing their husbands that maybe it was best that they did not know the details and offered support if needed but promised not to bring it up unless the men needed consolation of any sort. The men thanked their wives then they hugged their wives firmly for a few minutes then decided to move on to some other topics such as whether they had found any way to legitimately keep time for helping them to lead a regularly spaced life so they would be able to do things at the same time each twenty-four hour period and tell one day from the next as well as helping them to be able to keep history as it truly occurred. The women explained to their husbands that the only means for keeping the time within the twenty-four-hour periods was to utilize their time pieces that were inside their safe houses and hope that they stayed in working order especially since they did differentiate between day and night hours for the moon light only provided a dim light that stayed the same twenty-four hours a day. The men agreed to use the time pieces and hoped they would prove to be sufficient which there was no reason for them not to be until the safe house was to become insufficient to support their needs anymore so the men and women announced to their children that the adults were going to be getting together to make a schedule for activities such as schooling hours and of course the days would stay the same Monday through Friday with the weekends off and every Sunday would be the day of rest and worship for God which was to be a large part of their lives as before, it was extremely important to keep their maker involved in their lives no matter how easy or tough times were. As far as God was concerned it was a blessing that the healthy humans had survived and they all knew it and they believed it was because they had stood steadfast upon their beliefs even when things were going great as some of the people seemed to forget God when things were going their way and did not praise God for allowing them to receive the blessings of relief from hardships while the healthy humans acknowledged that God had blessed them with the smart houses and technology that went with the houses while the healthy humans were down to earth believing they had been blessed but realizing that there could be hardship on the way at any given time and still praised God yet continued to prepare for the possibilities to come. Even with world war three having happened the healthy humans praised God for surviving and being tested in their faith for testing of the faith meant there was going to be some growth in their spirituality and humanity. The healthy humans had routine times to pray which was in the morning time upon waking over their days activities, over each meal to give thanks for their provisions, and at the end of their day to give thanks for their ups and downs in which they could enjoy and grow from their experiences of the day and of course over any tribulation during the day in which something should arise where they should need any assistance with something but those times were spiritic. Those families were very God-fearing families and had been for generations and that was why the men were so regretful for having to euthanize the damaged humans that they had euthanized, the men were praying all the way back from the bad lands to their homes for forgiveness.

What the healthy human men had done needed forgiveness and they deeply hoped they were forgiven because they felt that they overstepped their bounds by taking lives which they felt was something that only God had the right to do. They just knew they would be punished for that even though there was an inadequate amount of choice in what they did and that was why they did not articulate much to one another on the way back. After several hours of being home the guilt of euthanizing the damaged humans weighed on all the healthy men, they had secretly discussed it amongst themselves then decided to confess their transgressions with their wives. Each family's children were playing outside under their domes for their allotted time of play so it was an opportune time for the men of the households to verbalize to their wives without the children hearing the discussion and inform them of what had really happened out on the journey to the bad lands. Each man sat down with their wife and explained that the journey out was slow and arduous and that they had lost quite a few damaged humans along the way due to their own degree of sickness but that there were a lot of the male damaged humans that were imploring for the healthy humans to euthanize them and free their souls and have mercy on them so their souls could go to the heavens and be at peace so the men admitted that they had done just that with no other options available, they shot the kill shot right between the damaged male humans eyes and released their souls hopefully to the heavens and they felt guilty for taking their lives. The wives of the healthy male humans all had the same disposition in affirming that they had to do something to get the damaged humans to move on to the bad lands and if they were unwilling to move on they had no choice than to euthanize the damaged humans so they would not return to the safe houses and surrounding areas and possibly risk the lively hood of the healthy humans especially the children who would be doing the most unsupervised transportation between the school and home. The wives did question if any of the damaged women were yearning for euthanization since the husbands had asserted men and if not why and their husbands replied none of the female damaged humans were requesting euthanization then went on to clarify that throughout history it had been proven that the male humans were most likely to utilize a more permanent source of method for suicide such as pistols and hangings but the females would utilize the less effective means such as pills and the cutting of wrists and so on. The healthy head of the households continued to make clear to their wives that their guilt was two-fold in that it was difficult to take another human life regardless of their health status then the second issue was in that they felt that they were overstepping their bounds because it was not proper for any man to take a life, it was up to God to give and take lives and they had requested forgiveness from God but even so their guilt had not lifted. The healthy male human's wives promised to pray for their husband's consciences to be cleared and vowed to be available to lend an ear to take note to their issues or a shoulder to sob on but also requested for their husbands to keep them informed on how they were doing mentally with the issue and their male counterparts agreed to do so. Now with that subject being out in the open and being addressed the healthy female humans suggested that the trip to the bad lands and all that occurred be documented in the history books for it was a large part of history because it was one of the many steps towards survival in fact, it was the first step towards survival and the men woefully agreed. Suddenly the children who were playing outside under their domes went running into their safe houses in a panic shockingly reporting that the robotic police were on their way and could be spotted from a distance.

Each father contacted the other fathers and reported that their children had a visual on the robotic police and that they were headed in their direction and that there was no mistaking the arrival of the robotic police because their clothing was that of a police officer and none of the survivors wore anything remotely close to that of a police officer besides the healthy humans had to wear space-like suits and their clothing was covered up by the suits the robotic police did not need any protective outer wear so their outfits were very visible. The robotic police were traveling at high speeds and grew nearer speedily so the men of the households decided to go out into their dome covered yards to try to communicate with the robotic police and find out if they were friend or foe. Finally, the robotic police had arrived at the safe houses and there were a few at each house, the robotic police spoke first with their voices being like that of bullhorns they were able to be heard through the domes while the adult males of each safe house had to use an actual bullhorn to respond. The robotic police questioned if everyone was okay and healthy since they had run across many deceased humans and animals as well as a few damaged humans that were sure to be deceased soon. The robotic police warned the healthy humans to stay clear of any smoky areas that they may spot because they were collecting all the deceased humans and animals to be burned in a natural pit within the earth's surface for disease control of the healthy humans even though the healthy humans had suits it was better to act upon the side of caution rather than chance error. The healthy humans replied to the robotic police that they were completely healthy as were their immediate families and that they had resources to stay healthy while living a somewhat normal life and they appreciated them looking after their health benefits by gathering up all the carcasses because not only was it a health hazard but it could be traumatic for the children to view. The robotic police advised the healthy head of households that if there were to be any need for them to just go near the areas fifty-one through fifty-four because that was where their policing was the heaviest due to the contents that stood behind the walls of those areas but not to try to pass over the walls because those areas were still highly secured and they would be shot on sight with no questions asked. The healthy male head of households promised that they and their families would stay clear of those areas and would keep in mind that if they ever needed the robotic police that was where to find them, the robotic police assured the healthy humans that they were friendly and there to serve the humans but they were also there to serve a community service and must uphold that level of service which was to protect areas fifty-one through fifty-four. The healthy humans agreed to keep that fact in mind then thanked the robotic police for their concern and kindness and the robotic police told the healthy humans to have a wonderful day if they could differentiate one day from another then they changed their greeting to have wonderful days to come and hopefully they would not need them for anything and they would be back periodically to check on them to make sure they stayed healthy and did not need any assistance. The healthy men thanked the robotic police again then most the robotic police turned and swiftly went back towards the areas fifty-one through fifty-four some of the robotic police stayed to clean up the bodies of the deceased humans and animals making trips back and forth from where the bodies were to where the fire pit was. Area fifty-four was the most protected area as the other areas were mostly said to be storage for the unusual and unexplained things that the military ran across and was able to bring down to earth or landed on earth. Area fifty-four was the area that was so secretive that only a select few of the military personnel knew what was there, it was guarded by a four-foot darkened metal wall that was electrified with barbed wire across the top of the wall.

Now that the robotic police had come and gone the healthy humans had been given the impression that they were friendly but the healthy humans still had to keep their guard up for the assumption had not been proven yet and there was no sure way to find out that the healthy humans could figure out that was not risky. However, it was now known that the robotic police were cleaning up the deceased bodies into a pile within a great hole in the ground and burning them that meant that the head of households did not have to do it as previously thought and that was a great help. With less laborious work to have to do the healthy humans especially the head of household's men could focus on getting things planned out for a schedule to start to following for each day such as meal times, school times, bed and awake times, chore times, and play times among other times. Before things could start to function regularly there had to be appointed positions to specific individuals such as teaching, preaching, history keeping and so forth so all the adults got together in one appointed safe house which was the largest of them all and the meeting began. They needed one teacher for each grade, one preacher, one historical record keeper, several mechanics, and the list continued until all areas of necessities were filled with the proper number of individuals filling the positions. The meeting did not last but for an hour due to the willingness of everyone to step up and offer their specialties to the greater good of the community and with that the community decided to have weekly meetings in the same home to go over the week of events to assure all was running well and make changes if necessary, make any necessary additions if needed, do away with any hinderances and keep the art of communication open. The healthy humans had everything they needed in their smart houses but wanted to do all they could for themselves that would not rely on the smart houses so they could extend the life of their resources because none of the healthy humans knew exactly how long their smart houses would assist them for. Now that the working order of things had been planned there was one more thing to address and that was a local horrific tale about a couple that was a brother and sister couple a set of twins actually. When the safe houses were being built, the twin's parents were able to get one but when the third world war happened the parents were not home, they were out in the elements and passed away only the two teen age children were inside the smart house. All the other families that had smart houses did not leave their smart houses unless it was absolutely necessary and it would be only one parent not both it was fortunate that the rest of the parents were home with their children when the nuclear warfare occurred. The twins were named Deanna and Darren they were highly intelligent and specialized in physics as well as chemistry, they were always working on chemistry projects that defied what was already known to be valid to something of a higher level making a newer standard and the previous standard no longer was the correct theory. Rumor had it that since the third world war had taken place and Darren and Deanna were not social due to their intellect keeping them from being able to handle frivolous talk as they referred to socialization with others to be they had begun an incestuous relationship as one another's equality allowed and Deanna conceived a child and that child was called Lloyd. Lloyd was not conceived until after Deanna and Darren as well as their parents were approved for their smart house otherwise they would not have been approved for their smart house due to the incestuous relations between brother and sister twins Darren and Deanna alone and for the smart house committee to catch wind that Deanna had conceived that would have been looked at as being preposterous.

Finally, Lloyd was at the age to attend the community school that the rest of the children were to be attending and from what the school teachers and children had reported prior to the third world war for those who had seen Lloyd he was malformed in many ways both external and internal and was quite ill from the internal deformities so he did miss some schooling on a regular basis, it was believed that Lloyds deformities were caused from having parents that were too close in the gene pool. No one knew for sure what Lloyd looked like because he hid behind a hooded cloak all the time even when at home when he was outside under his dome but again no one knew if he hid under his cloak when he was inside his home. It was presumed that Lloyds parents knew what he looked like since his defects were most likely apparent at birth and they took care of him from birth. Lloyd did have a severe hunch back which was extremely difficult to hide, he was very short of only about four-foot-high but if he could stand straight up would probably be five-feet-four or so. The hood of Lloyds cloak hid his face well it did not allow for any light to reveal any of his facial features but when he spoke he stuttered and it sounded slurred as though his mouth was deformed also, Lloyd wiped his mouth area a lot as though he was slobbering so it was presumed that he had an overabundance of saliva being produced and could not swallow it so he had to wipe it and instead of using a hanky he would use the sleeve area of his hooded cloak and the older kids used to tease Lloyd about that and much more. Lloyd was an inaudible child but did reply to the teachers when spoken to and it appeared that he was quite intelligent because he always had the right answers to questions that the teachers would test and his grades were perfect right down to the extra credit questions and the students knew other students marks because the teachers kept a chart posted for all to see so they could keep track of their own overall grade in the event they did not keep their graded papers not to mention there was participation and attendance points to account for. As long as the missed days were excused by the child's parents sending a note to the teacher via the student if not in person the missed day was excused and the child got points for that day but the points varied and the student was allowed to make up work for the missed day and so long as the child got the missed work completed and turned in within twenty-four hours the child also got credit for participation for the missed day which was how Lloyd kept a perfect grade even though he missed days here and there for his ailments flaring up which was beyond his or anyone else's control. In all actuality Lloyds face was deformed one side was larger than the other and drooped which caused the drooling that he could not control, he had one eye, on the larger side of his face that bulged out and the eye lid stayed mostly closed over that eye, Lloyds vision on that side was nearly blinded so he always had his head tilted in a weird position to allow his other eye to do all the visual work. Lloyds left arm and leg were lazy-like the leg sort of drug while the right leg stepped normal and took care of his balance along with his over-hanging left arm sort of like an ape would walk, for that side anyway. Lloyds spine was severely curved and took the shape of a sidewinder snake and his spinal bones stuck way high up, so it appeared that he was malnourished, but the rest of his skeletal system was covered just fine by his soft tissue. Lloyd was severely ashamed of his appearance and though he had never allowed anyone to catch a glimpse of him he knew if they had they would tease him far worse than they already did. The older kids who teased Lloyd on a regular basis had no reason to pass by Lloyds home on the way from the school to their home but they took the scenic route home just to pass by his home so they could taunt him at his house while he was outside under his dome because his parents requested that he spend some time outside after school before doing his school work.

Little did Lloyds parents know that the outside time just meant more torture for him. Once the outside time was over Lloyd would go inside his home and go directly to his bedroom to take off his hooded cloak and vent over that day's events and think of horrible things to do to those particular children prior to doing schoolwork. Lloyd did not hate all children just the ones that tortured him the rest he disliked for their stand-offish ways you see he was still another human being with feelings and desires such as the desire and need to have friends but no one in his entire life ever gave him a chance because he was different. Lloyd had dreams of doing away with all the children for his whole life but had never gone through with it but his desire was becoming stronger and stronger and he was petrified that one day he may go through with his evil plots to do away with the evil children. However the community was losing their children sometime on the trip to or from their way of school, sometimes the teachers would report that the students would not make it to school and thought it was due to illness so it would take a couple of days for the teachers to figure out that the students were missing but the parents would know when their children would not return home and other times the students would make it to school but not home so it would take a bit more time for the teachers to know the students were missing but the parents would know right away. The adults supposed that this whole disappearing thing was the work of Lloyd carrying out some wretched murderous plot but the parents and their small community including the teachers went out on search parties being careful not to cross paths with certain areas that even the children were warned against going around or through such as going around the walls of areas fifty-one through fifty-four and through the mini tunnel that sat between their smart houses and the school known as Dobbins memorial. Dobbins memorial was named after the prominent family that donated the money to have the school built prior to the third world war and it was still in good condition with a dome over it so the children could be in a natural environment while learning and being able to go to an outside area to have a recess as well. The Dobbins family thought highly of education and wanted to help assure that the children who survived the war if at all possible could maintain some sort of normalcy with getting an education without restrictions so they opted to have the school made up like a smart house where they could get their scholastic supplies and lunches replicated from the school building and take some strain from the parents smart houses supply allotment plus the children could have a recess time outside and not have to wear suits while learning and be comfortable throughout the school day. Just like the smart houses there was a place to park the hover craft nearly inside the decontamination area then there was an actual decontamination area for the scholastic individuals to go through where they would strip their space-like suits and rid themselves of any potential radiation before going into the actual school house just like they did at home only it took a bit more time because there was a lot more healthy humans utilizing the decontamination space than at home and the decontamination area was not too much larger than at home so patience was a necessity for all involved and that was why most everyone arrived somewhat early to Dobbins memorial school and to waste time for the early arrivers they would hang out at the play grounds or have a snack in the schools dining hall while conversing with others in there and catching up on the latest news which at first was not much but as time went by became more and was mostly educational in that they would discuss the training that they received from their parents for holding their own in the professions that made things run in their society such as medical, mechanical, astronomical, and the likes in the event thins were left to them and to take over when their parents became older and could not hold their own anymore.

This was a small society of functionally always learning healthy humans that would not give up on life easily and had hoped to find a way to out-smart their smart houses and create a civilization in which they could live and thrive within the elements when the smart houses were no longer able to provide a safe haven for them. Needless to say, in order to be out in the elements without being affected by the high levels of radiation without their space-like suits the healthy humans had to derive a chemically sound vaccination of some sort and all the adults had combined minds to think about the probability of doing that and the children had dreamt of the ability to function without the threat from the elements. The problem with producing a chemically sound vaccination to allow the healthy humans was that they were not as educated as they needed to be in the chemistry field and they had no way to safely test the compounds that they would come up with. Little did the healthy humans know Deanna and Darren were a few steps ahead of them in that they felt that they had come up with a compound for a safe vaccination to allow healthy humans to be out in the elements and withstand the extreme radiation levels and they had their own son Lloyd who was willing to accept being the test subject because he was slowly dying anyway and if the theory that his parents had about the vaccination was correct it not only would provide protection from high levels of radiation but it held healing properties as well and would give him a chance at a normal extended life, the alternative was to die inhumanely, rather slowly and painfully from failed organs one at a time due to the inbreeding of his parents. Prior to receiving the vaccine Lloyd had made his parents promise to euthanize him if the vaccine did not work and made him sicker than he already was to the point of near death because he could barely handle the ailments he had already and just knew he would not be able to live through anything worse and would not have the nerve to commit suicide although he would think about it daily and dream of ways to succeed. The day had come for Darren and Deanna to inject Lloyd with the new vaccine and they had no clue of what to expect only a hypothesis so they explained to Lloyd what they expected and that it was going to be uncomfortable for a few minutes but should recede within a few minutes and he should be changed into a new individual hopefully if all went according to plan. Darren assisted Lloyd up onto an examination table where he laid on his side and left his right arm extended for access to his hand and Deanna drew up the injection, it was a blue thick liquid and would for sure be somewhat painful when going into the body just due to the thickness. Deanna approached Lloyd and bent over him then gave him a kiss on his forehead and told him she loved him dearly and to trust in her and his father that if they were not certain of their research they would not be testing it on him because he was their most treasured possession and nothing could ever change that. Darren then leaned into Lloyd and kissed his child on the forehead and swore his love for his son asserting to him he loved him with all his heart and that nothing was going to tear them apart not even death. Lloyd professed his love for his parents then he admitted he was frightened but did trust his parents then Lloyd informed his parents that he knew things had to work out and soon they would be giving one another the same injection after he got it and he would be seeing them on the flipside, everyone chuckled nervously then got into position to give the injection.

Deanna got to the head of Lloyd to be able to give the injection into Lloyds thumb while Lloyds father stood at the center of the examination table to hold Lloyd down in the event he should spasm to keep him from falling to the floor since there were no restraints on the bed. Deanna, Darren, and Lloyd counted to three together then at three Deanna injected the vaccine into Lloyds right thumb. It took several minutes for the injection to do anything and Darren, Deanna, and Lloyd feared that the injection was a failure at first then suddenly Lloyd howled out in pain as his thumb turned a royal blue and the color started to cover his hand and move up his arm into his torso then simultaneously into his head, the rest of his torso, arms, and legs eventually Lloyds whole body was a royal blue and stayed that way for about fifteen minutes. After the fifteen minutes the royal blue color that consumed Lloyds body shed like a snake's skin after a hearty meal and he was left with a bluish-pale color that revealed a road map of all his veins and arteries. Already Darren and Deanna could see a change for the better in Lloyd but they were not sure if it was just skin deep or organ deep, they would have to do some testing on him to confirm or deny their suspicion that the vaccine helped cure Lloyds congenital diseases and deformities as well as his immunity to the high levels of radiation outside of their safe house. Darren checked Lloyd out externally while Deanna checked Lloyd out internally which was a slower and more tedious procedure and Daren would finish his exam process faster than Deanna so he would help Deanna with the internal examination. Lloyd had transformed into a five-foot four individual standing upright without a hump back and his face was that of a normal healthy human, no more drooping of the side of his face and he no longer drug one of his arms behind his body, his legs were equal and he no longer had to drag one of them behind himself as well. Lloyd was now a normal handsome looking boy with no apparent diseases superficially nor internally as he felt no pain and was not fatigued like before and when Lloyds mother examined Lloyd with the test results that would come back rather speedily, they were well within their normal limits for a healthy human. Darren, Deanna, and Lloyd were still waiting for some test results that took up to twenty-four hours to find out the test results but Lloyds parents were positive that the test results would be negative for all disease processes due to the test results that had already come back and the correction of Lloyds superficial features. While waiting on the rest of the test results Deanna took the spare time to document their findings in a scientific journal for future reference and hopefully getting to use the vaccination on the rest of the healthy humans for their best interest it was just a matter of how to convince them that it was safe and the best thing for them and in the mean time it was important to test the exposure to the elements before exposing the rest of the healthy humans to the vaccine for that was the main purpose of creating the vaccine. Lloyd and his parents were going to wait for the results of the last of the tests to be done and find out what they showed prior to sending Lloyd out into the elements so after being exposed to the elements Deanna and Darren could reassess Lloyds complete health and determine if the astronomical levels of radiation affected Lloyd and if so in what ways and by how much. It had been decided that Lloyd would go out into the elements while the small community was fast asleep and spend one half of an hour frolicking without his hooded cloak and enjoying the sensation of being free spirited which he had not been able to ever experience since he was born with multiple congenital deformities and now that he had undergone a metamorphosis if he survived being out in the elements he would never be able to return to school or be seen by anyone again.

The next step that would be after having the vaccine being proven to be a success was to find a different place to live so Darren and Deanna decided to venture out and about to find a perfect place during the night hours. Finally, it was time to observe the test results that took some time before they were ready to be read and they came back to show that Lloyds internal organs were healed and were actually functioning better than that of a normal healthy human. Lloyd even showed some extra abilities that Darren and Deanna had never seen in a human before such as muscular mass in a different formation along with the natural formation which led to extra ordinary strength, an overabundance of a variety of white blood cells new ones never before seen along with the normal white blood cells that contributed to a super immune system, the skeletal system developed more cartilage in strategic places to allow more limber joints for flexibility which would decrease the breaking of bones and dislocating of the joints. With the new structure of the bones and muscles the two systems could work together to accommodate for speed and hurdling with ease. The overall soft tissue was now equipped with super healing components and low break down capacity which was what would help with the youthful appearance then when Darren and Deanna studied Lloyds deoxyribonucleic acid what they found was that the vaccine would allow the healthy humans to go from a life span of approximately sixty years old to an amazing approximately four hundred years old. Darren, Deanna, and Lloyd sat down and discussed the phenomenal changes and found no negative effects from the vaccine thus far then Deanna wanted to find a name for the healthy humans that had received the vaccination because with the variety of changes being so remarkable it counted as a new breed of human then Lloyd spoke up and suggested that the humans that received the vaccine be called the pale ones since their skin was literally pale with a bluish tint, the skin was so pale that it allowed for all the arteries and veins to be seen both big and small it was like an old fashioned road map that the older humans used to use when traveling from place to place especially on long trips then Deanna thought about it for a few minutes and before she could speak her opinion Darren spoke up and replied to Lloyds suggestion suggesting that it sounded appropriate then Deanna had a word in agreeing with Lloyd and Darren so it became official that the new species of healthy humans was to be called the pale ones and that too was to be recorded in the scientific journal. The time of day had come that the small community was fast asleep and so it was time for Lloyd to go out of the safe house and get exposed to the elements to find out if the vaccine would protect him and serve its original purpose and now Lloyd, Darren, and Deanna were getting a bit nervous because with all the perks that the vaccine had provided so far there was no guarantee that the vaccine would be a match for the radiation exposure but if not it would be known rapidly because Lloyd would suffer respiratory failure transitorily and his body would give in within six to ten minutes due to the lack of oxygen and there would most likely be no way to get back into the safe house because the radiation would overcome him hastily to the point that it would confuse Lloyd and even if Lloyd could get back into the safe house there was no cure for radiation exposure unless this vaccine was a success. Lloyd, Darren, and Deanna did a group hug and exchanged words of love then Lloyd moved to the exit of their safe house and exited hesitantly and when he got to the cusp of the final door and opened it to the outside Lloyd took a deep breath in and expected to get a feeling of his lungs locking up but that did not happen, he did not even get the urge to cough or wheeze. Lloyd turned to face his parents in their safe house and give a thumb up then Darren and Deanna were a bit relieved.

Lloyd could see the relief as their bodies went from a stiff posture of being at attention to being relaxed as being at ease militarily speaking. Lloyd frolicked under the moon light and danced about for thirty minutes with great joy and freedom from his cloak and deformities as he glanced back at his parents every once in a while, then once his half of an hour was over and he had glanced at his parents once again he noticed them waving for him to enter the safe house to go through the decontamination area. Deanna and Darren wanted Lloyd to get cleaned off from the radiation so they could reexamine him for any difference in his health status. Once Lloyd entered the safe house Darren and Deanna hugged Lloyd and gave him kisses on his forehead as they professed their love for him and stressed that they were over joyed that he had made it through the exposure to the radiation and were anxious to find out if the radiation had affected him and if so how and how badly. Darren checked Lloyds external health thoroughly as before only this time he was looking specifically for lesions from the radiation and had found nothing but great health as before so Darren moved on to documenting his findings and after he was finished with his documentation he would move on to helping Deanna with the internal examination as before. In the meantime Deanna was getting blood samples to test the same things that she had tested before as well as tissue samples which were a bit uncomfortable for Lloyd but he endured the slight discomfort and even helped his mother by drawing up some of the simple needle drawn samples himself for he was just as knowledgeable as his parents in their fields of expertise and just like his parents felt that idle chat was boring, he preferred intelligent conversation that stimulated the mind which greatly separated him from the other children even the older children Lloyd even found that the adults could not stimulate his mind for an intelligent conversation like his parents did but of course they had taught him all that they knew and were still learning. Now that Darren had completed his share of the work, he jumped right into helping Deanna complete her internal examination and there was not too much to do since this time Lloyd was assisting her. Mainly what Darrin did was take the test tubes and slides to label and put into their place of rest to be examined when the time was right because some could be evaluated pretty much immediately, and others would take at least twenty-four hours. Darren then took over the verbal part of the examination while Deanna took notes in their medical journal and the verbal part was simply asking a series of questions about how Lloyd felt while out in the elements compared to being inside the safe house with oxygen supplementation. Lloyds answers amazed his parents because he had made it a point to get them to understand that he felt no difference between having oxygen supplementation versus a deathly amount of radiation exposure. Darren and Deanna were very interested to find out what the post radiation exposed lung tissue showed in comparison to the pre-radiation exposed lung tissue because that would pretty much be the main definitive factor to whether the healthy humans would get the vaccination treatment and if they were to get it the next chore was to find a way to convince them to follow through with accepting it. It was now time to check the first of the samples and see what they showed and in checking them out while comparing the pre-exposure to the radiation to the post exposure to the radiation it was amazing, nothing had changed all the post exposed to radiation samples so far were just as healthy as the pre-exposed ones and that pleased Darren, Deanna, and Lloyd very much for the vaccine may very well be the most important invention in human history it was just a tormenting reason for needing it then Darren took the thought of using the vaccine for the healthy humans a step further.

Darren questioned Deanna and Lloyd about what it might do for the damaged humans since it was so powerful and changed so much of the body's make up that maybe it could at least heal the damaged humans then turn them. Darren suggested that at the very least they would be able to lead a healthy life for a short time, it was worth kidnapping a damaged human and testing it out and they could send Lloyd out to do the Job. Lloyd could move swiftly and had the super speed with super strength which would enable him to bring the damaged human to the outside of the safe house, inject the damaged human then after the effects had taken place bring the individual inside their safe house for examination and explanation and if it did not work they would not be any worse off than they already were and could be taken back to the bad land. There was still so much to do but so much already done that it was now enough time gone by that Deanna could check the samples that had to wait for twenty-four hours and Darren, Lloyd as well as Deanna got excited to find out the results especially because the lung tissue was one of those samples. Deanna decided to check the lung tissue last to make it a climactic event and everyone was on the edge of their seats. So far all the samples were the same healthy samples as prior to being exposed to the high levels of radiation, now it came to the lung tissue so Deanna took a deep breath and sliced a small piece of the sample that was taken to put onto a slide and placed it under the microscope to view and while viewing she was astonished that the tissue was seemingly still living and unaffected by the radiation in fact it was the most healthy piece of lung tissue she had ever seen in her whole career of being in the medical field prior to the third world war up to present. Darren and Deanna were now ready to take the vaccine so Deanna drew up two syringes and set them before Lloyd and they both laid on their family rooms couches then Lloyd injected their thumbs one at a time back to back then cringed when they howled out in pain for he remembered how excruciating the pain was but it did not last for more than two to three minutes however, those minutes seemed like a lifetime to him due to his love for his parents and not wanting to bear witnessing them in any pain but for the sake of survival it was necessary. Now changed Lloyd welcomed his parents to the other side of humanity and said he was proud of them for creating such an invention that saved lives but then questioned how they would convince the others to come to the other side of humanity for they may frighten the healthy humans to the point of them wanting to kill them for self-preservation out of a misunderstanding because they did sort of look like some out of that world alien. Darren suggested that they use the rest of the night to try to find another place to live before tackling how to get the others to transform so they were not found out and murdered due to their different appearance and misunderstanding by the healthy humans Deanna and Lloyd agreed so they left their safe house to go out toward where the small tunnel was that laid between the community and Dobbins Memorial to investigate if there was any safety there or near there because it was forbidden for anyone to go near there due to horrible stories that were fables of children possibly disappearing even though all the children were home and accounted for. Now at the tunnel Lloyd heard water dripping from the wall of the side of the tunnel which Lloyd figured meant there was a crack that may be able to be opened and either there would be a gush of water come out or a metropolis behind there but due to the desperate need for another place to live out of self-preservation Lloyd was willing to find out what was behind there even though it may be just his wild imagination telling him that some sort of opening may be there. Lloyd called upon his parents to examine the crack in the side of the wall of the tunnel to get their opinion of the crack.

The opinion was really whether to try to open the wall if it was openable or to leave it alone due to the possible danger of a large water gush that may be life threatening to them for they knew they could breathe in the radiation safely but seriously doubted they could breathe in water for they had not grown gills. Lloyd showed the crack on the tunnel wall to his parents and with closer examination the crack resembled a door by the way it went from across the top and across the bottom. The back side almost hung like hinges so that alone made it tempt to somehow try to pull the wall open but there was still the matter of the small amount of water seeping slowly through some parts of the cracks in the wall. Darrin, Deanna, and Lloyd began to discuss the safety of trying out the possibility of opening the small door like opening of the wall and what may happen if it was a door and how they could handle things if a gush of water did come out. While discussing things Lloyd leaned against the door like area of the wall and it opened quite easily with his whole-body weight against it and they found that the water was just a buildup of mist from the other side and the door like structure was actually a door to some sort of metropolis. Hesitantly Deanna, Darren, and Lloyd walked into the doorway and carefully scanned the new surrounding and found it to be quite beautiful after a couple of miles of dusty plain tunnels that twisted and turned with some slight unsteady grounding due to lose rocks and moist soil and the air was radiation free for at the end of the tunnels there was plenty of plush greenery and colorful flowers along with wildlife that peeked back out at them from behind some forestry that was a bit away from them between them and the forest was a dry sand ridden area then off to the right side of the forest past the sandscape was a beautiful lake with a waterfall where Deanna, Darren, and Lloyd thought they saw some creatures that one only read about in story books known as mythological creatures now it came into question if the creatures that inhabited the land behind the tunnel wall were friendly and willing to share their land because the three of them were willing to cohabitate and loved animals of all kinds they were more than willing to respect the land and never harm the land or its inhabitants. Darrin proclaimed that it appeared that they had found a place to safely live if the creatures in the land would accept them but for now, they must go back and find a damaged human to try to heal and change and hopefully bring back with them. Darren, Deanna, and Lloyd explained to the creatures that they would be back and meant no harm and wanted to cohabitate respectfully if they would allow them to live amongst them and to please give them a sign of approval and just then a unicorn approached them and bowed its head before them so Deanna slowly reached out her hand and pet the unicorn on its head then thanked it for its hospitality and promised to never disrespect the life forms there nor the land but did warn that they were called pale ones and there would be more of them and they too would follow the same guidelines then the unicorn shook its head in an affirmative motion. After the feeling of communicating with the unicorn the unicorn brought its head back up and Deanna kissed the unicorns muzzle and thanked it for its understanding for the inhabitants of the lost land below the surface of the earth knew what had occurred above ground. Darren told the unicorn that they had some things to do before relocating but they would be back then Darren, Deanna, and Lloyd turned as they waved good bye and moved back towards the tunnels that took them to the lost land that the humans had no knowledge about which was a good thing or it would have been destroyed also. It was not long before Deanna, Darren, and Lloyd were back in the above ground tunnel and heading for the bad land to abduct a damaged human to test the vaccine out on and it was not hard to find a damaged human.

Just before the three of them got to the mass population of damaged humans at the bad land they came upon one damaged human who had drug himself away from the mass of damaged humans to die alone after performing what he could of his Indian death ritual for he was full blooded Cherokee Indian and the chief of his tribe at that so Darren instructed Deanna to go ahead of them and get things ready for the transformation. Darrin had Lloyd stay with him in the event they ran into any issues from any other damaged humans or robotic police and of course if the damaged Cherokee human gave a good fight against being abducted which was not probable. Darrin knelt over the Cherokee damaged human and introduced himself as Darren the father of Lloyd and Brother of Deanna then explained that he had a vaccination that could heal him from the effects of the radiation and turn him into a strong man who would be able to withstand the radiation as he and his family could and that there was an underground civilization that was like a garden of Eden filled with animals of all kinds and that he and his family wanted the Indian to live among the plush environment with them and would he be willing to receive the vaccination to allow that to occur and the Indian desperately agreed. Darren picked up the Cherokee Indian and carried him like a child while Lloyd kept watch for any misfortune that may need to be harshly dealt with but due to the possibility of the robotic police arriving in the vicinity of the area where Darrin, Lloyd, and the Cherokee Indian were Darrin and Lloyd were using their super speed to travel at the abnormal speed of lightning. Soon enough Darrin and Lloyd arrived at their safe house with the Cherokee Indian damaged human and Deanna was waiting for them with the vaccine ready to be given. Darrin placed the Cherokee Indian damaged human onto the examination table as Deanna was explaining that for two to three minutes there would be some pain from the injection as the medicine was going through the body and that was normal but once that was over the change would leave him feeling stronger and healthier than he had ever been in his entire life with many extraordinary perks such as super speed, super strength, and extreme longevity among other things. The Cherokee informed Deanna and Darrin that the pain from the injection could not be much worse than the pain he was already suffering from due to the radiation poisoning because it was slowly eating his body and it was practically unbearable, at first one wails out in pain constantly then the wailing dwindles down until it no longer is felt due to becoming numb to it so the new pain could not be much worse maybe just a bit different. The chief mentioned that Darren and Deanna must be some great medicine men to be able to put together such a great medicine and he was grateful to be the first damaged human to be tested and if it did not work he would not be regretful for it would enable him to make a contribution to their cause and therefore be a part of the medicine making process and as a Cherokee that was a great honor then the Indian informed Deanna that he was ready when they were for he was growing very tired as the minutes went by. Deanna held the vaccine in one hand and the Indians right thumb in her other hand but before giving the injection she questioned the Cherokee Indian as to what to call him and he replied to just call him the chief, that was what his people addressed him as then Deanna pushed the injection and everyone waited anxiously for the results. As with Darrin, Deanna, and Lloyd the medicine started to flow through the chiefs body but he did not roar out in pain as they had done maybe due to the amount of pain he was already in as he had alleged prior to receiving the vaccination however, the medicine did flow through his body a little slower than with Darren, Deanna, and Lloyd and Deanna and Darren speculated that it was due to having so much more to fix.

Having so much more to fix made them wonder if the vaccine would be as potent on the chief as it was on them meaning it would leave his body with the same benefits or just leave him as a healthy human and that provoked Deanna to speak up verbalizing that she wanted to perform the same tests on the chief that she had done on Lloyd to see how his body reacted for she was extremely familiar with a normal healthy humans body and with Lloyds extraordinary body. Deanna took note that the vaccine seemed to take only two to three minutes to get through a healthy human's body with a great deal of pain but about five minutes with little to no pain in a damaged human's body and she documented that in her scientific notes. Finally, after going through the process of the royal blue color spreading throughout the chief's body and him shedding his outer skin which left his skin a pale bluish color it was obvious that regardless of original skin tone after the vaccine everyone's skin tone would be the same a pale bluish color for the chief was originally a dark reddish brown and Darrin, Deanna, and Lloyd were extremely fair skinned. Now that the outer skin was shed the chief sat up and took in a deep breath of relief and affirmed that he had not ever felt so wonderful in all his life then he thanked Darrin, Deanna, and Lloyd. Deanna informed the chief that she needed to take some biological samples for examination for determination of whether he had the abilities that the vaccine had given a healthy human or if it gave less due to having so much more to heal which would mean having to adjust the amount of vaccine given to a damaged human without killing them and that was another thing to have to worry about then the chief stated that he knew they could handle the experiment and he would be glad to continue to cooperate in the experiment in any way he could. Deanna, Darrin, and Lloyd gave the chief a hug to make a group hug as they stated group hug then as they regrouped they expressed to the chief that they understood why he was the chief of his tribe, he was very brave and full of knowledge not to mention very in tune with his body and due to those things they were sure that by what the chief had said about being better now than ever before he was probably just as healthy and strong as they were but it was still imperative to check scientifically to be sure for the sake of all the other damaged humans because it was difficult to imagine that the same dose of the vaccine would do the same amount of healing for the damaged humans as it would for the healthy humans but the vaccine did originally have a variety of live healthy human cells in it and subsequent vaccinations would still have a variety of live human cells in it but they would be altered in that they would not come from a healthy human as before they would now come from a pale one therefore they would have to abduct another damaged human to test it on to find out what the results would be so Deanna thought but Darren figured different which was unusual. Very seldom did Darrin and Deanna have different ideas about something but it was looked at as a welcomed challenge when they did and they always explored both avenues then compared notes then often had found a compromise due to both having part of the theory correct but not the whole theory was sound on either side and that was what made them such a great team. Since Deanna was proposing to come up with fresh batches of the vaccination serum and Darren was proposing to breed the serum from what they already had due to it having live healthy human cells and not pale one cells and the capacity to reproduce it may be best to leave well enough alone. Deanna agreed to find out how fast the serum could breed in order to keep up with the demand and if it could keep up with the demand then she promised to leave well enough alone since she knew the original serum worked which meant the vaccine was a success for the healthy humans and they were about to find out if it was.

The chief was still sitting on the examination table, so Darren and Deanna got right to work taking the biological samples that were necessary to make a full determination of success or failure of the full potential of the vaccine. Some samples could be assessed right away so they were, and those results were promising just as theirs were. It was the twenty-four-hour samples that meant all the difference for those were the ones that were mainly affected by the live cells in the serum. While waiting for the twenty-four hours to pass and trying to fight the fatigue Darren, Deanna, and Lloyd listened to the chief talk about his people's beliefs and lifestyles. The chiefs talk was so interesting that the time was up to observe the twenty-four-hour samples and there was no longer any fatigue just intrigue. Deanna took the samples and put them under the microscope saving the lung sample for last as before for the climactic event and when she got to the lung sample just like all the other samples they checked out to be perfectly identical to the slides of Lloyds tissue samples so it was now safe to say that the vaccine was safe to use on the damaged humans as it was on the healthy humans and the results were identical. Now the four of them needed to discuss how they were going to get the healthy humans convinced to willfully submit to receiving the vaccination so no one had to be abducted because abducting individuals would leave the rest of the individuals apprehensive and terrified for their safety especially if they were to get a glimpse of the new species of humans, the pale ones, they knew they would have no problem getting the damaged humans to willfully turn because anything was better than the condition that they were already in and they had all been petitioning for death. The chief thought about the situation of getting the healthy humans to take the four of them up on the offer to get changed and felt that the healthy humans would not take them up on the offer due to them looking so different so the only other option was to kidnap the healthy children then the healthy adults followed by the damaged children if there were any and lastly the damaged adults. Darren questioned the chief as to why not abduct the damaged humans before the healthy humans because that sounded more logical for their life was in a more critical state, more lives would be saved that way and more families would not have to grieve. The chief agreed then informed Darren and Deanna that most of the damaged humans had diseases that could not be dissolved by the vaccine and it would be wise to allow them to die off because they could have all of the healthy humans abducted by the time it was logical to start abducting the diseased humans that were disease free and just affected by the radiation besides the disease free damaged humans were tougher than thought to be and very resourceful therefore they would still be around to be changed. It was set, staring the next day the four of them would start to abduct the healthy human children of the community as the opportunity showed itself whether it be on the way to the school or on their way home from the school and they would use Lloyd as bait. Lloyd would bait the children by asking them if they wanted to see what he actually looked like without his hooded cloak and lure them into the tunnel where the turned adults would be waiting to snatch them up and give them the vaccine right on the other side of the tunnel door then shut the door while the healthy human children were going through the actual change so once complete they would not be able to go back to their small community they could see the metropolis ahead of them and have to trust in the chief. The chief would act as the head of the abducting group and lead the way through the twist and turns to get to the forest and lake with the waterfall and let them see that they did not need their space-like suits anymore in a harsh way then once they got to their final resting place they could communicate with the healthy human children.

They could discuss making a home for themselves. Although Lloyd was now normal, Deanna was going to alter his hooded cloak to make it appear that Lloyd had a humpback and he would be bent over a bit to take away from his new-found height. While Deanna was altering the hooded cloak, Lloyd was going to practice his speech to be like it was before he was healed. Before Lloyd was healed from the vaccine it was difficult to speak because it involved slobbering and wiping his mouth constantly due to a severe drooping of the mouth on one side and stuttering but he knew with practice he would master it. Darren was busy documenting everything in the scientific journal and the chief was deep in thought about how they would survive once the safe houses were used up with their rations and where the clan of pale ones would live once all of the damaged humans were turned along with many other questions that filled the chiefs mind and he was for sure going to be enlightening Darren and Deanna of his concerns. The chief did not want to burst their bubble in creating possibly the most important creation in the world ever, but his concerns were part of the planning that went along with the invention just in another phase of the turning process. Once Deanna was finished with the hooded cloak, Darrin was finished with the documentation, and Lloyd had completed his act the chief suggested that they all sit down and discuss some issues that he foresaw coming into play once they had both of the community's changed. Everyone was sitting on couches in the safe houses family room then the chief let out his bomb shell of questions and each question was met with a logical answer. Darren and Deanna informed the chief that as for supporting the people after being turned they had found a suitable home that was located underground and it was an absolute garden of Eden which had been kept secret somehow because if it had been found prior to world war three it would have been tainted and possibly destroyed as well. The chief continued to question Darren and Deanna and they continued to inform the chief of their plans for his situations, it seemed that Darren and Deanna had thought of everything ahead of time and made arrangements for every possible situation and the chief was impressed. Darrin, Deanna, and Lloyd had been working around the clock for several days and the lack of sleep was starting to take a toll on them so the chief advised them that he felt it best for them to get some rest prior to the first abduction and he would wake them on time to prepare and get into their places before the school children were expected to pass by their path and Darren, Deanna, and Lloyd agreed that getting some rest would be the best thing for them so they could be fully alert and carry out their plan accordingly. The time had passed fleetingly for Deanna, Darrin, And Lloyd but went by sluggishly for the chief then when he woke them then the pace of things sped up for they needed to leave the safe house urgently to get to the tunnel without being seen by anyone who may be scouting the area for safety reasons due to that being the first day of school and the first day of getting to some sort of normalcy since the world war, as it was there had been some rumors of healthy human children being abducted but as mentioned before there was no evidence for they had not left their safe houses since the war occurred, this would be the first time. The healthy human children were also warned to stay clear of the tunnel because that was supposed to be one of the two places that healthy human children were coming up missing, the other place was near a patch of what appeared to be foliage in the shape of a dinosaur tail that was ever growing by the area fifty-four, there was even a legend about the dinosaur tail that linked it to the missing children.

For every missing healthy human child, a new leaf would appear upon the foliage and flutter about until it could settle in to make a mathematically correct dimensional shape to keep the shape it had chosen it was even said that those leaves were created mysteriously out of a twinkle of dust from the ashes of the deceased body of the once healthy human child. Now why that story was adopted as being real without any substantiation was beyond Darren, Deanna, and Lloyd but they supposed there were worse beliefs in the world somewhere prior to the world war three. Now with Lloyd on the laid-out path that the healthy human children would be traveling his plan was to take the most volatile looking human children possible first which would be difficult because they were leery of everything and traveled in packs of four to six children at a time but Lloyd was intelligent and could use their tricks against them that they had pulled on him for several years while he was truly disfigured and going to the school prior to the nuclear world war. However, Lloyd was not certain that he could get the healthy human children into the tunnel because of the severe warning they had gotten from their parents but he figured he could make up some story about them being the popular kids in school for a time due to being the only kids in the school to ever see him and he was willing to do that for them because he did not believe they were tough enough to look at him and he was only going to offer the chance one time, he figured they would chicken out and become the lily livered chickens with a streak of yellow down their backs of the school house and he would make sure all the other children knew that they had the opportunity to see him and offer the one time chance to someone else and they could be the popular kids at the school house instead. It would be up to Deanna and Darrin to snatch up the children while the chief would hold them back away from the tunnel door and escaping until they had all the healthy human children inside and the tunnel door closed and then Deanna and Darren could give them their vaccine while the chief stood by to play the role of the leader who would guide them to where their new homes were going to be, they still had to be built. Somewhere along the way Darren and Deanna would disengage the healthy human children's oxygen so the chief could order them to disrobe form their space-like suits and prove to them that the air below the surface was safe and even if it was not they were immune to the radioactive elements in the air. The next plan with those healthy human children was to groom them as pale ones and have them recruited to help abduct other healthy humans as well as help build themselves a small community so they could live off the land without hurting it and take places in their community of prestige as original founders until they had all positions filled which would be long before the healthy adult humans were to be abducted. Now that everyone was in place and the tunnel door was cracked open so Darren and Deanna could barely see what Lloyd was doing and could listen for his verbal cue to open the tunnel door all the way it was time for Lloyd to go into action and without hesitation he stood out in the path of where the healthy human children were going to be coming at him and they would be stopping to tease him, they just could not resist a chance to rough him up and sure enough there came the main bullies right at him and they were pointing at him and slowing down their hover crafts. When the four boys stopped their hover crafts Lloyd did not give them a chance to say a word nor did he give them a chance to get off their hover crafts before he offered them a one-time chance to see him without his hooded cloak saying he would not show anyone else but because no one else picked on him the way those boys did they might as well see what their picking at and that they could have more to talk about amongst the other kids which would make them more popular.

The four boys took the bait and landed their hover crafts then go off of them then Lloyd uttered to them to follow him into the tunnel unless they were too petrified then he started to make the noises that a chicken would make as he slowly moved toward the entrance of the tunnel and it worked like magic, the boys followed. Lloyd lured the four boys to the spot in the tunnel where the door was and gave the cue then the door opened swiftly, and Deanna grabbed two of the boys while Darrin grabbed the other two. Before anyone rode upon the empty hover crafts the door to the tunnel was closed and the chief handed some vaccination injections to Darren and Deanna to give to the boys and they did not waste any time injecting the four boys' thumbs and gently laying them to the ground to go through the change. In the meantime, Lloyd got the boys hover crafts moved out of sight and definantly where they would not be found if there were to be a search party and Lloyd was certain there was going to be one soon especially when the boys did not return home after school. Meanwhile behind the tunnel door the boys were going through the change and Lloyd knew this and he knew he had just a few minutes to get back behind the tunnel door before the boys completed the change so they did not freak out and notice that there was an opening and try to escape before they noticed that they had changed and gotten an explanation with a new life set before them that was going to be better than what they were facing above ground. Lloyd did make it through the tunnel door just on time before the boys started to squawk out in anguish and every time an individual was changed their shrieks reminded Lloyd of how painful his change was and he somewhat relived it over again but he found that it was affecting him less and less each time which he appreciated especially since there was going to be so many changes to be ahead of them. Finally, the change in the four boys was complete and they were frightened when they set eyes on one another then on the chief, Deanna, Darren, and Lloyd, it did not take long before the four boys realized they were now the same and that Lloyd was now normal and they could not pick on him anymore in fact, they were now remorseful for picking on Lloyd for he was a large part of their change in that he was smart enough to catch them by beating them at their own game. Now it was time to give the four boys an explanation as to why they were there inside the tunnel walls and what had happened to them to change their appearance then a further introduction into what their bodies had gone through on a basic cellular level and leave the four boys to find out what Deanna was explaining on their own as far as their strength and speed being above what a normal healthy human possessed , the external changes were evident but it was more difficult to explain the internal changes to individuals who had little to no comprehension of the human body to the extent that Darrin, Deanna, and Lloyd did, that type of knowledge was not the top pick of choices offered and that was why each house was equipped with a holographic doctor. The chief spoke firmly and ordered the four boys to get upon their feet and follow him so the boys hesitantly stood up and cautiously lined up behind the chief with Darren, Deanna, and Lloyd bringing up the tail end while the chief started to lead the way toward the forest and lake with the waterfall. Once the lake and forest was in sight the four boys became amazed at the sight of a nature type of life, they thought they even caught sight of some small critters looking out at them from the forests edge and when they took a closer look they were amazed to be able to confirm that there was animal life there then all of a sudden Darren and Deanna took the opportunity of the distraction to cut the boys' oxygen lines on their space-like suits.

It quickly became evident that the boys were breathing the air from the environment because the slight noise of the oxygen running through the tubing that went from the concentrator into their helmets stopped. At first the boys wanted to panic but they stayed calm because they were uncertain of the chief's actions towards them if they should act out of control, it was a question of how firm the chief was and would he cause harsh punishment upon the boys for being unruly or would he understand and simply let them know all was well if it was in fact well. The chief stopped ambulating then sharply turned his body toward the four boys and barked at them to shed their space-like suits and to do it immediately and hurriedly so the boys guardedly did as commanded and expected their lungs to lock up due to radiation for they did not trust that they were immune to the high levels of radiation or that the underground metropolis had no radiation. As the space-like suits dropped to the ground the boys shut their eyes and at the sound of them hitting the ground the boys realized that they were still standing and breathing just fine so they slowly opened their eyes and witnessed more animals coming out of the wooded area to greet them and now they started to relax but the chief turned his back to the boys and sharply ordered the boys to follow him. As the chief started to move so did the boys along with Darren, Deanna, and Lloyd bringing up the tail end, that was a joyous moment for that was their first abduction and all went well and now they had more individuals to help with the future abductions to assure nothing went awry but first they needed to build homes for themselves to live in and perform their activities of daily living in. The chief ordered everyone to make some tools to make their homes as he made the same tools for making his home and they watched the chief and tried to mimic what the chief was doing but he was making his tools so fast that they could not keep up for he used his Indian skills from generations passed down, these were the same skills used to make Indian tools and houses among other things. The chief noticed how the four boys, Deanna, Darren, and Lloyd were trying to keep up with him to make their tools just like he was making his tools but could not keep up and had no clue on what they were doing so the chief instructed the seven of the individuals to stop what they were doing and informed them that he would help them to make their tools but that they had better listen and work efficiently because he was only going to show them once and after that it would be up to them to help the future pale ones learn to make their tools to enable them to construct their homes. Everyone agreed to be alert and try to absorb every step of instruction available which would be effortless and everlasting for what Deanna and Darren did not know about their vaccination was that it also created a photographic memory that relied on more than a hands on style of learning it also relied on a verbal learning style it was a blessing but could be a curse when something negative occurred but the future was looking up now so eventually when Deanna and Darren would find out about the photographic memory and they would view it as a positive addition to the already positive enhancements to their bodies since receiving the vaccinations. As the chief went through the steps to the tool making Darren, Deanna, Lloyd, and they four boys realized that their minds were playing back the steps as each step was introduced and the playback was done with super speed, the playback made them sure that they would not forget the steps as the chief was introducing the final step to the seven of them and upon the final step the seven of them conversed to share notes on what had happened with their seemingly photographic memory and found that they all had it and did not previously have it.

Deanna wanted to make a note in her scientific journal to keep up on the documentation of the changes that the vaccination had brought about because it was so remarkable and fortunately she had brought it with her when she had gone to the tunnel to check on finding a new home in the event that it held a promising environment which it did so while Darren and Lloyd got started on building their house Deanna recorded the new information in her scientific journal then she helped to build their home. The four boys had to build their homes rather large to accommodate their whole family that was still on the earth's surface so they would not have to rebuild it later and cause any structural weakness anywhere in their house. They had no accommodations for their homes such as stoves to cook with, sinks to wash with, beds to sleep on, material to create clothing and linen, and the like so the chief suggested to get those things from the surface of the earth from regular houses during the hours of sleep for the healthy humans that had not been changed. The pale ones would get grills to cook on, basins for water, clothing and linens for their beds and mattresses to sleep on but no bed frames and they would all go out together and work on a few things together which would take some time before the houses were stocked with what they needed but that was fine with everyone for sleeping without mattresses was not a problem, they were on a vegetarian diet so eating without stoves or rather grills was not a problem and they would just have to have no warm water to sponge bathe in and they could deal with that because it would be some time before they got clean clothing and linen, it would be a process before they got everything they needed especially carrying everything through the tunnel entrance and through the tunnel twists before getting to the forests edge where the lake with the waterfall was and to their homes but the work was well worth it for a new life of safety and happiness. Now that they had their tools made up the four boys were wandering how they were going to utilize them to make their homes but Deanna, Darren, and Lloyd had already figured that out for they knew a little about the Indians in that they lived off the land without hurting the land and made their homes out of the earths mud and waited for it to dry to make brick like material so the trees were safe and the tree animals were safe to continue to have their homes. The chief ordered the boys, Deanna, Darrin, and Lloyd to start to work with the mud close by to form bricks and lay them one at a time upon themselves to form walls of their home and warned them that he had better not find anyone touching trees or even leaves from the trees, everyone acknowledged the chief and got to work immediately. The four boys had a difficult time getting the water to dirt ratio correct at first so the chief assisted in showing them as they experimented and finally got it right after doing several bricks right the chief left them to their work so he could get to constructing his own house. Even though it would take several days to construct their houses the eight of them continued with their plan to go above ground to start to retrieve the items that they needed from the regular houses and bring those items below ground and of course the eight of them also kept their plans to abduct a group of children the next day either going to school or on their way home. The eight of them had planned to try to catch some children on the way to school because if that failed for some reason that would give them one more chance, if they planned it for on the way home and failed their chances were over. It was fortunate that Deanna, Darren, and Lloyd were able to explain to the four boys why they needed to abduct the healthy humans then the damaged humans and that the four boys saw things their way so they would help because if not it would make them a major flight risk had they not seen the whole picture and understood things the way Deanna, Darren, and Lloyd had seen and understood things.

The eight of them needed to get on a routine for when they would be going above ground to make off with things for their homes, abduct healthy human children, work on their homes below ground, and rest for the greater of good to replenish themselves so they could reboot their energy to do the aforementioned things again. The chief decided it would be best if everyone slept until it was time to awaken early enough to loot some supplies from above ground and use the walk to assure they were stimulated and surely awake then move onto abducting healthy human children on their way to school and if that was unsuccessful try when they were on their way home then rest for a bit and prior to going to sleep for the night use the last several hours to work on the construction of their homes then go to bed for the night and do the same routine until something was complete and make appropriate changes to their schedule to make it accommodate work and rest. For now it was time to prepare to abduct more healthy human children on their way to Dobbins Memorial school so they needed to work their way to the tunnel opening to be there for Lloyd to do his luring so the adult pale ones minus the chief could do the actual abducting and turning of the children while the chief acted as the head of the tribe of the pale ones. Darren and Deanna got to thinking of the chiefs position in their small clan and his position in his tribe as well as how well he played out his role with the pale ones and with deep thought two things occurred to them the first thing was that they were able to read one another's thoughts so it seemed and they figured that out with conservation and trial this was new so they included Lloyd to find out if the mind reading was in fact real and Lloyd was able to read minds also that was so fascinating to Darren and Deanna that they informed the chief of the new development and requested him to try it out which he did with a positive result. Finally, Darren and Deanna advised the four boys that they too had telepathy and at first it would take some work to utilize it but it would become first nature after a while it was like learning a new language the more it was used the better one would get at it and the boys were ecstatic to know they had such an ability and more so to be able to tap into the ability for that would make abductions flow much more easily. Deanna could not wait for some down time to be able to jot the information down in her scientific journal as she wandered what else might be found out about the vaccine's abilities, there could not possibly be much more. Now getting back to what the subject was that alerted Darren and Deanna to having telepathy in the first place which was the second thought which was the chief being the chief of his tribe and the acting chief of the pale ones Darren and Deanna felt it appropriate to dub the chief the future chief of the pale ones once and for all and now the pale ones would truly have a ruler over the founders who would take on the higher positions in the community then there would be citizens who would hold no positions at all but could enjoy the safety and freedom of a well-balanced positive community without war and pestilence. The chief was telepathically picking up on the discussion between Darren, Deanna, and Lloyd about him being the chief over the pale ones so he cut into the conversation and replied that he would be honored to be the chief of the pale ones but there were conditions and they were to have subordinates below him to keep him in line so to speak so there was no way anyone could speak words of favoritism or unfairness toward anyone and Darren and Deanna agreed to be those individuals feeling that having a male and a female would be better than two females or two males and the chief concurred.

Now that the conversation had come to an end it could not have ended at a better time for they were at the tunnels door so Lloyd went out of the door to stand in the way of where the healthy human children would be going to their school for an education and Lloyd was hoping to pilfer a group of them and be able to lure them into the tunnel so the rest of the pale ones could get them into the tunnel door entrance then subdue them and turn them then Lloyd was hoping that the children they would get this time would understand the purpose of the process that was occurring like the first group did. Just like before the children were coming down the lane and Lloyd blocked the path and like before this was a group of boys that had harassed Lloyd about his disabilities so it was perfect to deceive them the same way, if they wanted to see him without his hooded cloak in the tunnel to be the popular kids in school by having more to discuss about Lloyds grotesques features for now they would see him first hand and not have to guess or make things up. As the second set of boys drew nearer Lloyd saw that there were six of them and was glad that there were more pale ones to help subjugate the six boys because without the extra help Lloyd was not sure they would be able to pull off plucking the six boys out of the tunnel all at once because there would have only been Darren and Deanna to do it now there was Darren, Deanna, and the four boys. When the six boys got close enough to Lloyd he did as he had done previously and questioned the boys if they wanted to view him without his hooded cloak informing them that he felt they were too chicken to do so then made chicken sounds so they became intimidated and would not stand to be intimated by their bullying target so they agreed to go where ever Lloyd wanted to go to let him uncloak and show himself even if it was a forbidden place if Lloyd was not afraid they had no reason to be afraid. Just like before Lloyd uncloaked and shocked the boys for he was now normal sized and now had no deformities but his skin had changed which was somewhat frightening and at that point before the boys were able to turn and race away Lloyd gave the code word for Darren to open the tunnel door wide enough to get the six boys into the tunnel wall for himself, Deanna, and the four boys to overpower and start the change while Lloyd hid the six hovercraft where he had hid the previous four hovercraft then make it to the tunnel door without further delay so Darren could get the tunnel door closed as briskly as possible so they could not get found out by any curious passer bye's that may spot the light gleaming from the door of the tunnel. With the tunnel door closed the six boys were undergoing their change and crying out in shooting pain but it was to be short lived then the chief would take over leading the way to the settlement where the community would be while Deanna and Darren would bring up the end of the group and the four boys would separate to be on the sides of the six boys. The six boys were frightened just as the four boys were when they were new and had no clue to what was expected of them until the chief actually spoke more than a few short commands to them and they were relieved at that point for the healthy humans were very verbal and relied on verbal communication for every step of things and the chief worked on physical signs as did his people on the most part, even the pale ones with their telepathy did not rely on physical or verbal communication because they could read one another's minds. Prior to knowing that they were telepathic, the pale ones relied heavily on verbal communication for they were still humans jus a new species with a different deoxyribonucleic acid structure which was responsible for their extraordinary gifts but what Deanna wanted to do next was to take a sperm cell from one of the four boys and have Darren take an ovum from her to try to make a test tube baby.

Deanna also wanted to find out the probability of reproduction along with finding out if the vaccination changes would transfer genetically and if so would it mutate or vary in any way so the chief decided that the first things to be brought to the underground from above would be the scientific things from Darren and Deanna's safe house since they were important to the creation and survival of the new species the pale ones especially since Deanna and Darren would need to make more of the vaccine eventually and that time may come sooner than expected if they continued to be able to capture healthy human children regularly like they had the first two sets so far and they had hoped the lucky streak would continue. Making the vaccine was easy for Deanna and Darren for it was just a few natural ingredients found on the earth's surface that was also on the surface of the earth underground and the absence of radiation underground would not make a difference in the substances needed but it was necessary to keep those ingredients at a very specific amount or it would upset the balance of the vaccines outcome and who would know what the outcome would be at that rate it may even be fatal. Finally, the six boys were over the painful stage of the transformation and it was time to start to travel so the chief gruffly commanded the boys to stand then motioned for them to follow and the already pale ones started to tread and as they stepped in on the six boys they got the hint to start to advance with the pack of pale ones. As the six boys made progress keeping up with the rest of the group Darren cut the oxygen hoses on the six boys' space-like suits oxygen hoses and it was not long before they noticed that they were functioning without their oxygen supplementation so they stopped ambulating and checked one another's suits and the chief abruptly barked at them to strip off their space-like suits declaring they did not need them in the underground area for there was no radiation there and even if there was they were now immune to radiation due to the vaccine they were given earlier. The boys were petrified to take off their space-like suits but when they realized that their suits were cut by a sharp knife or something of the sorts they realized that the pale ones could very well be an angry people and cut their throats as easily as they cut their space-like suits oxygen hoses so the boys did as they were directed. The boys expected their lungs to lock up from lack of oxygen when they took off the top half of their suits but to their relief their lungs were fine and the boys went ahead and took off the rest of their suits then were shown by Lloyd where to place them alongside the previous four suits beside the trail they were on. The six boys were shocked to notice the other space-like suits on the side of the trail because they would have gone right by them without noticing them had they not have been pointed out to them then they realized that the four boys that were on the sides of them were the four boys that had recently gone missing and that they were safe and content. The six boys were filled with ease and questions but were fearful to speak because the chief was so tight lipped and Darren and Deanna were not very giving with words either and the four boys had not given voice to any words at all then finally one of the six boys busted out with a question soliciting if they were free to communicate and if so would they be addressed or were they on their own to figure their captivity out and the chief replied that they were not captives at all they were new citizens to their small community that would be growing for the better of the healthy humans society and everything would be explained to them when they arrived at their camp site while they got some rest before having to travel some more. The six boys were relieved to be communicated with and were satisfied with the response they were given.

The six boys informed the chief that they were willing to do whatever was required to be a part of their new society for they could already feel some changes in their bodies that were positive. The boys specified that they only wanted to harness the full aspects of the change that they had undergone and live a better life and not one of caution from the robotic police and the safe houses life span as well as the radiation closing in on them eventually. Everyone made good time with their travel since the six boys were willing to be a part of the community and knew why they had been abducted. Things actually worked out for the greater good with the new arrivals knowing more than the previous arrivals and that was something to take into consideration for the next arrivals, it could not hurt to try it out as far as the chief, Darren, and Deanna figured. Now everyone had gotten within sight of the forests edge and the lake with the waterfall and the six boys were captivated by the beauty of both then they noticed the various creatures looking out at them from those areas and were more taken aback, the beauty was beyond compare. One of the six boys requested to know where they were going to have to travel later and Darren replied that they would have to go back to the surface of the earth to gather some things after the healthy humans had gone to bed for the night then the boy suggested that they stay where they were to rest and travel less distance then the chief replied that it would make sense if there was nothing to do at their community site and could just sleep the time away but they only had another ten to fifteen minutes left to travel so onward they went. Finally, everyone got to the area where they would call home and the six boys got to see the beginnings of the homes that the others were building to call homes and they were sturdy and quite lovely so far then the chief informed the six boys that they too would be building their homes and they needed to build them large enough to accommodate themselves and their families that were still on the surface of the earth so when they were brought down below they would be able to have a place to live just as they did above and the boys got excited until they failed to see extra bricks and the chief reading their minds informed them instantly that they would have to make the bricks from dirt and water with a precise amount of each and he would show them he precise measurements of water to dirt when the time came. One of the boys questioned the chief if he was an Indian prior to his change and the chief responded affirmatively then the boy confirmed that was how he knew how to build homemade brick homes and the chief again confirmed the boys statement then the chief informed the six boys that he was going to go ahead and show them now but only once so they had better watch closely and to follow along then the chief took the boys over to the small stream that was near the homes and he and the boys began the tutoring session, it took about five minutes for the chief to show the six boys how to make one brick for the homes and from then on out the six boys had it down just as the previous four boys did. The six boys drew their parameters in the dirt with a stick and made up a lot of bricks to start their foundations then suddenly Darren hollered that it was time to start the travel back to the surface for once they got there the healthy humans would be fast asleep and they would have plenty of time to make several trips from his and Deanna's safe house to just behind the tunnel door with scientific items and hopefully get all of the scientific items behind the tunnel door. Everyone stopped what they were doing and congregated near Darren then Deanna made the suggestion that they use their advanced pale one speed to move the scientific items from the safe house to the inside of the tunnel door and strength to move more items at a time as well as the bigger items without help.

With that the six boys just glanced at one another with perplexity and required an explanation from Darren and Deanna. Darren went on to explain to the six boys as he had the previous four that the vaccine had changed their genetic structure in a way that was positive to not just make them immune to the radiation on the surface of the earth but it gave them telepathy, super strength, super speed, and extreme longevity, they were still looking into what else it may have given them but so far the tradeoff of the life before the vaccine was well worth the three minute or so pain they had to endure even if there were no other benefits. Now that the current benefits had been revealed to the six boys everyone was in agreeance of using the super speed to get to and from the tunnel door being it was from the safe house or the community they were going to utilize their super speed to enable themselves to get more done in a fraction of the time and they were going to use their super strength to get the items that needed to be transferred from the safe house to the tunnel door and hopefully get all the items from Darren and Deanna's house so they could continue to do their scientific work without interruption. Everyone was now on the move and racing to the tunnel door and it was like a swarm of bees on a mission but in stealth mode and it took only about an eighth of the time it had previously taken them to get there but the healthy humans were already in bed but barely falling asleep so the pale ones had to wait for about fifteen minutes or so to assure that the healthy humans were fast asleep so they were not seen. Once the pale ones were comfortable in speculating that the healthy humans were asleep the pale ones opened the tunnel door and proceeded to sprint to Deanna and Darren's safe house where everyone of the pale ones targeted an item and took it to the tunnel door and placed it right inside the door then darted back to the safe house for something else until everything was inside the tunnel door and there was still time to get miscellaneous items before the healthy humans would awaken but there was so many items inside the tunnel door already that the chief ordered for the pale ones to stop gathering items at the end of having all of the scientific items and to get them to the area that would soon be Darren and Deanna's home. Everyone followed the chief's orders and worked together using their super strength and speed to continue transporting the scientific items from inside the tunnel door to their final resting place in the community area where

Darren and Deanna's house would be. It did not take long for everyone except Darren and Deanna to transport everything to the community area where Deanna and Darren were putting the items in their final resting places and setting them up correctly for use, it was a relief for Deanna to have her laboratory back which made Darren happy for he was like her assistant while Lloyd was like her test subject to an extent. When Deanna needed live samples for comparison from her newly created concoctions she would take samples from Lloyd and sometimes also Darren to make comparisons to or when she needed to expose tissue to a new formula she would use Lloyd's tissue samples that were healthy unless she was trying to find a way to heal Lloyds tissue which was something she was doing prior to the vaccine which now she no longer needed to do since the vaccine healed everything wrong with him, the true potency of the vaccine would be tested when they abducted the damaged humans and tested the vaccine on them. Now that everything was completed with the scientific items being in place it was time to focus on the building of the homes and work until it was time to get a couple of hours of sleep and the chief was to keep track of the time to alert the pale ones when it would be time to rest.

Everyone got hard at work and used their super speed to work and worked extremely efficiently, first the pale ones were making their bricks by the masses then laying their bricks after having a mass amount of them. Everyone's homes were nearly finished all they really had left was the roofing but it was now time for them to lay down and get their rest before getting up to perform their abduction routine and gain some more healthy human children to turn into young pale ones. One thing Deanna noticed was that as a pale one she and the others did not require as much rest to replenish for their up time but she was not fully convinced yet and she wanted to keep track of the groups down time for several days versus their up time compared to their down time as regular humans to be fully convinced but she could not let them know they were being observed so the semi-test was not altered by the test subjects in any way and she would be documenting her findings as time went by. After everyone was well rested they awoke and got some nutrition in their bellies by picking some fruits, nuts, and vegetable's to consume and prior to partaking of the foods the chief prayed a prayer of thanks over the meal then everyone ate and verbally offered their thanks amongst one another for what they had to put into their bellies. There was still a lot of time before leaving to the tunnel door so everyone proceeded to working on the roofing of their homes and actually finished their homes right on time to head on to the tunnel door, it was remarkable what the gift of speed allowed the pale ones to do. Once the pale ones got to the tunnel door it was the same routine as before and this time Lloyd came across a group of six girls that he knew and they were good girls, smart and usually keeping to themselves so this was going to be a challenge for him because he would have to find a special rouse to entrap them. Lloyd figured he would use the ten boys who had come up missing to entrap the six girls so when they got close enough he plead with them that he knew where the ten boys were and that they needed their help, it was nothing major but if they would follow him they could help him get them to their hover craft and get on to the school to the teacher where they could get adult help and their parents could know that they were okay. The girls thought about Lloyds proposal for a few minutes then agreed to help but questioned Lloyd as to where the ten boys were and why he was willing to help anyone since he was so poorly treated all the time. Lloyd explained to the girls that even though he was teased all the time it was not worth someone dying over and even though those boys may not do the same for him he did have kindness in his heart and as Lloyd wooed the girls with words he slipped in the explanation that the ten boys were inside the tunnel and the girls followed Lloyd like a lost soul. Once inside the tunnel and in the prime spot Lloyd gave the code word and the tunnel door flung open then the pale ones reached out grabbing the six girls with their shrill screams going unheard from passer bye's mostly due to the air tight space-like suits that everyone was required to wear. Now that all six hover crafts were hidden and all six girls and Lloyd were inside the tunnel wall and the door was closed Denna gave the vaccinations to the six girls and of course they too went through the few minute painful change but the pain was finally over and the complete change had taken affect and the girls were one hundred percent pale ones and would be treated just like the rest in the beginning for there was a reason for the standoffish method and that was to receive compliance out of the new pale ones so once they were at the beginnings of the community they would be able to be treated like a community member and not a hostage and not have to worry about them fleeing back to the earth's surface.

Showing back up to the earth's surface prematurely would be creating a whole new problem of breaching the security of their existence and the existence of the metropolis underground which would be a tremendous tragedy. The same travel experience went for the girls as did with the ten boys however when they got to the community it was decided that the members would split up and help each new member build their home because there would be more and more things being brought down from the surface of the earth and they would be needing the homes to be placing the items into. Not to mention the pale ones who were to be abducting healthy humans would be doing double time now that meant they would be abducting healthy humans in the morning on their way to school and in the afternoon on their way home to speed the up the process of gaining pale ones. Doing double time would mean spending more time at the tunnels door area and changing the schedule that the pale ones had but the chief felt that was necessary. The schedule was now to awaken to go to the tunnels door for the mornings abduction to get the mornings healthy human children turned and moved to the commune then the abduction team would hike back to the tunnels door to get the afternoon healthy human children abducted and turned to take to the commune and hopefully the children would all be understanding on why they were abducted and take part in their rebuilding of their homestead and appreciate their new gifts that being a pale one brought with it which would be told to them in the would be evening so it could be explained only once amongst the group once in the event there were questions or comments. After doing the double abduction and dealing with the group of healthy human children it would be time to go above ground again to get those things that were needed from the ordinary houses that would be necessary for the underground houses as previously stated. Once the trip above ground was completed and the items were disbursed it would be time for those who were not already working on their homes to start working on their homes, for those whose homes were not already finished and for those who were finished with their homes they would help those who were not finished with their homes yet complete their homes and this would change the routine that they had immensely from what it was previously. After working on their homes for a while they would get some rest for a short bit then awaken to start the routine all over again and Deanna would use her time of house building to document her scientific notations and any experiments needing to be done which brings us back to the last subject that she was working on which was the amount of sleep necessary for a pale one compared to the sleep necessary for a human. Deanna had confirmed that pale ones were in need of only half or less of the amount of sleep of that of a human and she was able to confirm that by observing the healthy humans sleep patterns of awakening without an alarm of any kind and needing at least eight hours of sleep for a normal day and up to two more for a total of ten hours if they had a hard day that day versus the pale ones who awoke after two hours for an easy day to four hours of sleep for a tough day without any alarm device of any kind again depending on how hard of a day they had put in but no matter how hard the day the pale one only slept up to four hours. Deanna found that the sleep differences were phenomenal in that it would be difficult for a pale one to suffer from sleep deprivation because they required so little sleep only two to four hours to begin with but it took little to nothing to cause a healthy human to suffer from sleep deprivation since they require eight to ten hours of sleep so she was able to definantly affirm that the sleep issue was another gift from the vaccine and Deanna was proudly able to let the rest of the other pale ones in on the good news of the next gift she found.

Now it was time to do the mornings abduction followed by the afternoons abduction followed by the discussion of pale one life then the building of the homes and the gathering of items from the surface of the earth and finally getting some two to four hour hours of sleep, then the next day they would do it all over again until all the healthy children were below the surface of the earth and changed into pale ones then the adult pale ones would move onto the adult healthy humans to abduct and change into pale ones as they had the healthy children humans. It took about three weeks to get the rest of the healthy human children abducted and changed then placed into a position that best suited their mental and physical talents so they could best be used for the benefit of their little society in a positive way and justly so for that was what each member wanted. The community took a break from doing abductions to catch up on building their homes and getting them situated with the items needed which meant still going above ground to get more items from the regular houses to stock the below homes with and after an additional week all the items needed were gotten and the underground houses were built and situated so it was now time to start planning the abductions of the healthy human adults. Since the healthy human adults did not go out in any groups like the children did it would take careful planning and would have to take more careful planning to not get caught by other healthy human adults since the safe houses were clumped closely together. Although the safe houses were somewhat sound proof due to the air tight set up for the ability to keep the radiation out and oxygen in if someone was still awake they could witness the abduction firsthand and take it as an invasion since none of the healthy humans had ever seen a pale one and they did look extremely different from them. The new plan was for Deanna and Darren to sneak into the houses together with two other pale ones so the two pale ones could subdue a healthy human adult since there were now only two to a house now the mother and the father of the children that were abducted and Deanna would work speedily to inject the vaccine into the healthy human adults and the two pale ones that were subduing them would remain with them throughout the entire trip back to the commune, the pale ones would strike three houses per night to make up for the amount of children to adults that they were getting however they would be finished getting the healthy human adults much more sooner than they did the healthy children. Now that the pale ones had a plan of action it was time to implement it so there was no time like the present so Darren and Deanna took six pale ones with them so once the first two healthy human adults were changed the two pale ones could take them to the commune then the second two pale ones could do the same then the third pale ones could do the same but Darren and Deanna would return with the third set of pale ones and Darren and Deanna prayed that everything would run smoothly for them as well as for the benefit of the healthy human adults. The once healthy human children were counting on Darren and Deanna to get their parents to the underground haven to be safe and with them although they knew as they did not understand in the beginning their parents would not either but they hoped their parents would simmer down and accept submission over fight being's adults were far more suborn than children. It was now time to leave so now that Darren and Deanna had their six pale ones with them and started to move off toward the trail for the tunnel wall when the pale ones stopped what they were doing to bid them farewell and a safe journey with a positive outcome and verbal expressions of love then Darren, Deanna, and the six pale ones thanked the rest of the pale ones and returned verbal expressions of love then continued to march on.

Instead of using their pale one speed to get to the tunnel door they moseyed on with the speed of a normal human because they had some extra time before the healthy humans would be awakening and they wanted to strike before they were to awaken, it was still the middle of their night. Finally, Deanna, Darren, and the six pale ones arrived at the first smart house to be targeted and let themselves in then sauntered to the master bedroom where they found the parents sleeping soundly so two of the pale ones grabbed a parent while Deanna and Darren raced to administer the vaccine in the parents thumbs and it was only a few seconds before they fell victims to the change which was actually a good thing. Not only would the change save the healthy humans life but it would enable the parents to be reunited with their children they were not aware of those facts but would be very soon especially once they got to the parents of the six pale ones who were helping to subdue the parents, a parent would recognize their children in most any state it was a paternal instinct that went beyond reasoning and was still unexplainable. The first set of parents have now finished with their change and ready to be taken to the commune so the two pale ones explained that they were going to be taking them to meet up with their children who were healthy and well as well as anxiously awaiting their arrival with that said the parents calmly agreed to go willfully without any hesitation then they went for their space-like suits. The pale ones told the parents that they were not in need for their space-like suits anymore for the vaccine they were given made them impervious to the high levels of radiation as well as having some other benefits but all that would be revealed to them once they reached their destination which was where their children were awaiting their arrival. The adults felt it was far-fetched that the radiation was benign to them then the pale ones pointed out how different they looked to them and stated that it was because they were a new breed of humans who had been chemically adapted to the environment on a cellular level and it had some phenomenal side- affects that were positive in nature which were the things that would be explained at the commune where their children were as said before then the pale ones suggested that they leave immediately for they were losing some valuable time for meeting up with the children before it would be time for them to need to start on tasks that they needed to be doing and not have time to sit and have a discussion. The parents understood responsibility so they dropped the argumentative disposition and took the pale ones at their word and followed them out to the elements expecting to have their lungs lock up on them and then they would die immediately afterword but that did not happen then they started to look at their arms and legs and noticed their skin was a pale bluish color as well. Next each parent observed the other parent and was shocked to witness that the other one was a pale one as well, then they started to believe what the pale ones were stating to them about the vaccinations. While those two pale ones and the first of three sets of parents were on their way to the commune Darren and Deanna had already given the vaccine to the second set of parents and gotten them on their way to understanding what was going on so that Darren and Deanna along with the last two pale ones could move onto the last set of parents. Finally, after a very similar encounter with the second set of parents as was with the first set of parents Deanna, Darren, and the final two pale ones moved onto the last set of parents while the second set of parents and two pale ones started their travel. Now at the third and last set of parents for the night it was time to replay to whole scene over, so the two pale ones subdued the parents while Darren and Deanna gave the vaccine and watched as they underwent their transformation

    After the change then the two pale ones spoke to the parents about going to the commune to see their children and get an explanation about their change and the conversation was basically the same with these parents as was with the former two sets of parents but was settled in the same way, it appeared that the abduction of the parents was going to be much more simpler than it was with the healthy human children. Eventually all three sets of parents along with all six pale ones, Deanna, and Darren made it back to the commune and prior to the rest of the healthy humans waking up to catch on to what was occurring which was fortunate for the pale ones as a community as well as the safety of those who were above ground. When the three sets of parents got to the commune their children spotted them immediately and it was instant reunification the chief was touched so he made an announcement and mustered up his gruff voice then loudly informed all the children that they would not stop until all parents were brought down then he turned to Lloyd and softly voiced that if his grandparents were still alive when it was time to abduct the damaged humans he would make sure they found him then Lloyd hugged the chief and voiced his love for the chief as the chief rubbed Lloyds back lovingly like any parent would. No one but the chief, Darren, Deanna, and Lloyd knew at that point that after abducting all the healthy humans they would then abduct the damaged humans and see if the vaccine would work to make them healthy and turn them as well. When the chief finished consoling Lloyd he went over to where the children were with their parents to discuss their newfound lives and break down their new super abilities from their normal abilities and how things were going to work in the communities sort of like the rules and regulations so there could always be open communication and peace amongst the pale one people because they did not want things to be as it was for the humans above ground and end up in chaos with death and destruction. The parents strongly agreed that they did not want that for them or their children and generations to come and that there had been enough damage already encountered and there was no reason to bear any more and they were blessed to have such an haven conserved underground for them that it must have been a gift only God could have given so they needed to praise God and care for the land and its inhabitants as God would want them to. Although these pale ones were a God fearing people that was because as humans they were but that was not so for many of the humans who walked the earth prior to world war three which the pale ones believed contributed to the war for if they were all God fearing people they could have found peaceful ways to deal with their differences and overcome diversity as a blended nation. Shortly after the three families had the opportunity to converse and speak their opinions of peace talks the chief then saw the window to jump into the conversation to discuss the operations of the commune and then the gifts that the vaccine brought out in the humans turned pale ones. The chief said what he needed to say then took questions but no one had any due to the chief's intricate coverage of all aspects of what he needed to get across to the new pale ones and it was a nice review for the older pale ones however nothing new for the original pale ones. It was now time to get some work done so the chief pulled everyone together and verbally laid out the commune building plans since all the homes that needed to be built for now were built it was time to start to work on some of the other types of buildings such as the community dining hall where everyone would gather daily for their three nutritional meals to converse, give thanks, and dine, the religious hall where on the seventh day of the week the community would gather for services devoted to God on the day of rest, a shop where the public could go to get the things they needed instead of everyone aimlessly wandering about they could have pickers for the vegetation and other specialists for other gatherings and so on.

The pale ones thought that the chief had a fabulous idea with how to construct the commune to have pale ones in service in a variety of areas to strive for functionality and convenience as well as order. This was not new to the chief for he was in charge of making things work for an entire community of Indians when he was on the surface of the earth, keeping peace among the people and keeping functionality amongst the people were his primary jobs and he did them well. Once the chief finished laying out the plans for the community buildings that needed to be laid out and their monstrous sizes one of the new pale ones questioned the chief on why the buildings needed to be so generously proportioned and the chief replied that it was because there was going to be many pale ones added to the commune in the near future then the same new pale one then questioned what pale ones because there were not many parents left and the chief gathered the community of pale ones that they had there to make the announcement that they were going to try to help the damaged humans to be healed and turned so they too could be saved and be with their loved ones then when the chief made the announcement the pale ones cheered and became jovial for those damaged humans were their loved ones and it pained them that they had to lose them, so they had thought and they were willing to help in any way to be a part of the abduction process. The chief had to discuss the plan that he had to abduct the damaged humans in that they were going to use a new method of enticement of healing them and promising them new found health and reunification with their healthy human counterparts however, they did not know if the vaccine would just heal hem or if it would heal and turn them also which was the hope and the hope was that it would heal and turn them so they could be brought to the commune to be reinitiated with the pale ones that were already there. The pale ones already there were hopeful but did understand the challenge ahead of the damaged humans so the pale ones were ready to get to work on the mass buildings for they wanted to get their commune in order and see it bloom. In the meantime the six pale ones with Deanna and Darren went on to following their plans to go abduct more of the healthy human parents while the rest of the pale ones went to work on the building of the giant buildings that were for the whole community to gather in at one time for a purposeful meeting whether it be for a meal or a specific meeting of the minds. The creatures that lived in the land even offered to help in the construction of the tall buildings by laying bricks on the higher places for the pale ones where they could not reach and the pale ones thankfully took the creatures up on their helpful offer and even sent pickers out into the forest to pick some treats to offer the creatures so they could offer some treats to the creatures in return. The chief even offered to take the creatures down to the lake to wash the creatures down and rub their muscles down to help them recuperate and still look stunning after a hard day's work and the animals were looking forward to their bath and rubdown so the chief vowed that he would supervise the work and put together a team of pale ones to do the work and he called upon a group of female pale ones to do the work because females usually payed more attention to detail. The chief made a selection of combs of wood to brush the assortment of animal's hair, the main animals to help were the Pegasus to fly up to the top of the building with the half man half goat known as the faun on his back to lay the brick where it needed to go and of course the pale ones would be making the bricks as fast as possible.

The teamwork was going to be the first of its kind and a wonderful start of a new relationship between the creatures of the land and the pale ones that the pale ones would treasure for life. The pale ones started to make the bricks and work on the foundation while the Pegasus' and fauns watched waiting for their time to help, the pale ones worked with precision and super speed and without delay got the buildings up as high as they could in a jiffy. In no time the pale ones were ready for the Pegasus' and fauns to help put the upper structure and roofing on the buildings and they were right there ready to help and got right into action working in waves for there were many of the

Pegasus' swooping down for the fauns to pick up several bricks at a time and flying up on the Pegasus' backs to place the bricks up where they belonged only to swoop down and do it again until the project was complete and move onto the next project until all the buildings were brought to an end and the pale ones made it known to the creatures that they were more than welcome to come to the commune anytime to fraternize with them that they were friendly and would love to be companions for the land was theirs first and they were grateful that they were willing to share their part of the land with them. Suddenly the creatures spoke in the pale one language and the pale ones could understand them it was miraculous and the chief questioned the creatures how it was that the pale ones could understand them now but not before and the leader of the Pegasus stated that it was the magic of the Pegasus and could only work with the trust from both sides of the parties and since there was sincere trust between the pale ones and the Pegasus the magic was able to work then the chief stated that there was trust from the pale ones previously and he Pegasus replied that the sincere trust took some time for there was a distant trust and the sincere trust took some time therefore so did the magic as will the magic for all the majestic creatures of the land as they too have the ability to communicate with the pale ones in the same way. The pale ones were amazed and had now made it a point to earn the sincere trust of all the creatures one by one in their time on their terms as they had told the Pegasus and the Pegasus replied that it would not take long for the pale ones were a peaceful people and the creatures knew that and the creatures were already interested in finding out what the pale ones were all about and if they were safe to trust it would just take some time of observance for the rest of the creatures to start to come around and show themselves and once they showed themselves it would not take long before they communicated nonverbally but after the nonverbal communication they would start to allow the earning of the trust from the pale ones then shortly start the verbal communication much like the Pegasus and faun did. The pale ones were eager to earn the trust of the rest of the creatures but knew it would take some time so they held onto their patience and in the meantime would continue to take care of their business of turning the healthy humans then focusing on the damaged humans. There were only two more trips to take to have the rest of the healthy humans turned and into the commune so the rest of the child pale ones were excited especially the ones whose parents were still above ground, it was going to be a grand reunion for them as it was for the other children. The special reunion was yet to come when the damaged humans were to come into the commune after they were changed if it was to occur which the pale ones were sure Deanna and Darren were able to pull it off since they were highly accredited scientists and could do anything with science beyond what was possible for the scientists above ground which was already seen with the turning of humans into pale ones to combat the effects of the radiation in the air above ground. Darren and Deanna were even able to provide extra assets to the people besides turning them into pale ones.

The pale ones even had super speed, great strength, little need for sleep, less need for nutrition, telepathy, and speedy healing properties. Deanna did find something odd in her exams of the secondary pale ones as she did some exams of all her pale ones and that was that only the original pale ones could bear children and the secondary pale ones could not bear children however, there was no explanation as to why so she wanted to explore into why that was the case and the secondary pale ones had given Deanna permission to do whatever was necessary to figure out why and hopefully reverse the issue. While the hand-picked female pale ones who were going to bathe and massage the Pegasus and fauns were on their way to the lake to do their job with the Pegasus and fauns Deanna and Darren were taking tissue and blood samples from the original and secondary pale ones to compare against one another to try to find out why the secondary pale ones could not produce children so maybe Deanna could reverse the bareness of the secondary pale ones. It did not take long before Deanna was able to view the difference between the tissue and blood samples and there was so many differences that Deanna was not sure she could make the necessary changes to enable the secondary pale ones to bear children that would be a task best left up to God, it was a genetic coding difference that included all the ribosomes being changed back to normal and Deanna did not have the scientific ability to do that at that point because she was not sure how they were changed to the abnormal state they were in and how the original pale ones were not changed like that unless it had to do with the fact that it was their deoxyribonucleic acid that was used on them that was the reason and their deoxyribonucleic acid that was used on the secondary humans that caused the dramatic change in their ribosomes to cause their bareness and possibly some other issues that they had not known of yet. With that knowledge Deanna took responsibility for the negative news and called a meeting of the community to sadly announce her findings and when she did she shed some tears for her actions and revealed that she was unaware that the outcome of using only one person's deoxyribonucleic acid would result in the bareness but they would not have been able to retrieve everyone's deoxyribonucleic acid due to the risk of them not believing in the cause for they had to be abducted and forced into submission to believe in the cause in the first place so giving up tissue and blood samples would have been impossible. Everyone agreed that they would have been difficult to deal with because they would not have believed what Deanna was proposing to them and her appearance would have thrown them off to begin with and they knew that for sure because her and the others appearance threw them off when they came to abduct them they thought they were aliens or something that the radiation had affected that may in turn affect them and it may not have been a good thing, it was rather alarming to set eyes on them. The secondary pale ones understood what Deanna was saying and took it quite well and they did not hold her responsible they even went as far as to inform her that they did not hold her responsible for the bareness that she could not have known that the vaccine would have affected them in that way and they would plead to God for his help in the matter and if God felt that it was fitting for them to bare children that he could reverse the effects of the vaccine because through God all things were possible and in his time so there was no giving up, ever. With that it was time to go out and abduct some more parents so Darren, Deanna, and the six abduction pale ones gathered to go out with the chief and off they went while the rest of the community went about their business in doing their appointed chores while the abduction team was off doing their job. By now everyone knew what they had to do and was doing it and things fell together nicely.

The abduction team followed the same protocol they had been following in abducting the healthy human adults that they had been following since they had abducted the first set of healthy human adults. Once the abduction team got back to the commune with the second to last healthy human adults and turned them over to the compound to reunite with their children the abduction team felt it best to go after the last set of healthy human adults immediately so the next day they could start with the damaged humans. The chief agreed that it was time to start getting the damaged humans and find out what the vaccine would do for them and hopefully get to bring them into the commune adding that they would be easier to bring because they would want to be healed and be a part of a society again. The abduction team went out immediately for the last set of healthy human set of parents and brought them back to the commune where they were instructed on why they were brought there and what the vaccine did for them and why after they were reunited with their children and it was a sweet unification as all the unifications were. Now all the children had their parents with them and the families were happy now it was time to appoint the last of the parents their positions in the commune which was an easy task for the chief for he had already had the last of the tasks ready to be fulfilled all he had to do was to find the right individual for the task and he would know who was right when he met the individuals. The chief was not worried one bit about not having an individual for a task for he knew there would be someone for each task and there were just enough tasks for the amount of individuals that were going to be brought back and as far as the damaged humans that were going to be brought aboard the community they would be helping the individuals who had the original tasks and the original task takers would be the superior commanders of the jobs. It only took a couple of hours for the chief to have everything arranged and now it was time to rest for a few hours before sending out the abduction team for some of the damaged humans while the rest of the community took to their responsibilities there within the community's boundaries. Everyone went to their new homes and went to their beds and rested for four hours then awoke to their new day then got up and organized into their small work groups to go and do what their tasks were for instance the various pickers went to go pick their various things that they were responsible `for picking, the preacher went to the religious hall to be there for anyone who may need his services and a few parishioners did stop by to receive blessings for a good days work and prayers for their families as well as to give worship to God for their new found home and its beauty as well as its self-sufficiency. The rest of the community said little prayers as they passed the religious hall because no matter where one needed to go in the community they had to pass the religious hall because it sat in the middle of the commune as the chief had planned, the rest of the buildings were strategically placed as well but not in the middle of the commune but some were close by such as the hospital hall which was staffed as well because there were specialized workers of all sorts in the community members that were abducted from the surface of the earth both in the adults and in the children and the chief knew that there would be more specialty workers when they got the damaged humans aboard if they could in fact get them changed. The abduction crew even said prayers as they moved past the religious hall on their way to the tunnel door to approach some of the damaged humans on the surface of the earth. Darren and Deanna knew that the damaged humans should be eager to be with the healthy humans so they should not be very hard to get to be willing to accept the vaccine for a new-found health and possible change, anything to allow them to be able to be a part of society again and have a long life.

However, the abduction team did not have a sound plan to approach the damaged humans with they figured they would just calmly approach the damaged humans that were separated from the mass amounts of the damaged humans because the damaged humans were like animals in that when they were about to die they separated from the others to die alone. Once the abduction team got to the surface of the planet past the tunnel, they saw some of the damaged humans right away and approached them. The damaged humans looked at the pale ones strangely then started to communicate with the pale ones asking many questions about why they appeared so healthy with no sores and looking so pale bluish in color then Deanna spoke saying that was what the vaccine did to them but the vaccine did many wonderful good things for them also. The damaged humans were starting to gather around for they had never seen such a sight as the pale ones and they wanted to know if the vaccine would make them healthy also and allow for the many wonderful things to occur in them also then Deanna was overjoyed to know that they were interested and she replied that she wanted to try the vaccine out on them that the worst thing that could happen would be was that it would heal them of the effects of the radiation but not turn them into pale ones and they would have to live in the safe houses above ground so they would have to do the vaccinations in the safe houses until they knew what the affects would be just to be safe and the damaged humans were willing to be test subjects so they followed Darren and Deanna into one of the safe houses and laid on the bed inside one of the bed rooms waiting for the vaccination. Deanna informed the damaged humans of the discomfort that the vaccine would cause adding that it would only last for a few minutes and after that they would immediately know the results of the vaccine so the damaged humans that were in the safe house wanted to move forward with the process and the rest of the damaged humans who had heard of the miraculous vaccine were lined up outside of the safe house while word was traveling fast amongst the damaged humans, it was a good thing that Darren and Deanna had brought enough of the vaccine for the entire crew of damaged humans for one visit above ground because it could have created a massive problem for them to go underground with the damaged humans knowing about them and possibly following them it may breech their safety and the security of the new land. Darren and Deanna both gave the vaccine to the damaged humans to speedily get as many of the damaged humans inoculated as possible and as the damaged humans went through the painful process of the turning point Darren and Deanna could visualize the sores and mangled parts of the damaged humans being healed but the painful process went beyond the expected three minutes then their skin began to turn a pale bluish color and by the end of five agonizing minutes the pain stopped and so did the cries from the once damaged humans now turned pale ones. The new pale ones sat up leaving their decrepit shells of bodies on the beds then they looked at their new limbs and torsos with utter surprise that the vaccine actually worked Then the other damaged humans who were in line next who had witnessed that became anxious to get their turn afraid that there would not be enough vaccine to go around and Darren had to go out to the crowd of damaged humans to assure them that they had more than enough of the vaccine to cover them twice over and not to worry. Deanna instructed the healed humans to go out the back door of the safe house while they continued on and healed the rest of the damaged humans and they would run the process like an assembly line and once they were finished with healing all the damaged humans they would take them all to the most beautiful place ever seen and that it would be their new home.

The new pale ones did as they were told and the process continued until the last of the damaged humans was healed, it took about two days and two hundred individuals later to complete the process but once it was done Darren and Deanna were finally content with the vaccine that they had created for it was truly a life saver and their best invention yet this now made a total of three hundred pale ones for the new land. The new pale ones were not damaged humans anymore and now they were ready to be led to the new land but first Deanna and Darren wanted to give them the rules and regulations of the new land to assure that they would be able to abide by them before taking them there because she was going to read each and every one of their minds to get a clear impression of their intentions prior to taking them into the oasis so she could filter any harmful intentions so she telepathically informed Darren of what she had planned to do and he replied telepathically to allow him to give the rules so she could focus on the mind reading of the new pale ones and she felt that was a great idea so that was what they did and it was a gigantic job for Deanna but she knew she could do it. Deanna was going to scan the new pale ones for any negativity then focus in on who it was coming from to filter it out by having that individual pulled aside for the time being until she could deal with them once she was finished scanning all the new pale ones then she would zone in on those who were pulled aside to assure she was correct on ill intent. How she was going to handle those with ill intent if any she was not sure yet, but she was going to address that when and if the situation called for it. Darren started to address the crowd of two hundred with the rules and regulations of the new land and they listened very absorbedly to what Darren had to say and Deanna had not come across any ill intent in the crowd of two hundred which was extremely relieving to her so she telepathically informed Darren that the crowd of two hundred was all good to go then Darren announced that it was time to travel and for all of them to follow him but to realize once they were at the new land there would be no returning back to where they currently were. Everyone cheered as they announced that there was no reason for their presence back where they currently were then they questioned Darren and Deanna if there was anything that they may need to bring where they were going like bedding or clothing and Deanna replied that all their needs would be cared for where they were going and again the new pale ones cheered. All of the new pale ones gathered around tightly to travel to the new land that Darren and Deanna promised to take them to and waited anxiously to start their journey so Darren and Deanna started to move the herd of new pale ones toward the tunnel which the new pale ones also knew was off limits to the humans for that was dangerous if one expected to live freely or even stay alive so when they got to the tunnel entrance the new pale ones stopped and questioned Deanna and Darren's motive for going into the tunnel. Darren had to explain that there was a doorway inside the tunnel to the new land and that all the stories they had heard about the abductions were actually them abducting the healthy humans to turn them little by little into pale ones for their safety and comfort then once all the human children were abducted they abducted the human adults then went back for the damaged humans as they well knew Deanna interjected that they did not want to leave anyone behind if at all possible and as the new pale ones found out they did not have to. Deanna instructed the new pale ones to leave their past lives behind them and to look forward to their new lives for it would be far different than the past it would be much more enjoyable and serene. Darren offered up a description of the new land from the top to the bottom saying that even though there was no sky there was continuous light from the lightning bugs.

The temperature was a wonderful seventy degrees and the moisture in the air was complementary to the pale ones, not too dry and not too wet and the land even had a lot of animals in it of all sorts and some that had only been heard of in human fairy tales. Deanna added that the pale ones that were already there had built buildings for common use such as the community dining hall and the community religious hall and homes for each family to live in and they would pair up to build homes for the new pale ones so they too could have homes to live in although it would take some time to build them. Deanna reiterated that the new pale ones would be given daily chores that fit their specialties prior to them getting sick from the radiation that would fit in with in the community that they needed such as teams of seamstresses, cooks, animal keepers especially for horses for that would be the mode of transportation throughout the community since the community would be a vast land area, and sheep herders as well as keepers for the wool for the clothing and material for other things that would be made from the material and other specialties. The new pale ones were tempted to enter the tunnel opening because what Deanna and Darren were saying made full sense but they still had some reservation and Darren and Deanna knew that so they begged the new pale ones to just trust them once again stating that they had already trusted them with the most important thing they had and that was their lives so the new pale ones agreed to do so. Forward into the tunnel entrance the group went and through the tunnel door they passed into the desert type landscape which deceptive to what was promised and Darren informed the group that the land of paradise was coming within a fifteen minute walk that the landscape would be like day and night for all of a sudden there would be an oasis before them to just hold onto their faith that they were not being steered wrong so the new pale ones held out for a bit longer although it did seem that they were counting down the minutes. Suddenly after about a fifteen minute walk as Darren had promised there came into focus an oasis type landscape and the new pale ones stopped and took in the sight as they gasped and mumbled amongst themselves about how beautiful the landscape was, they had never seen water so clear and greenery so plush everything was placed so strategically as though God had known beforehand that they would be there which they knew God was all knowing and that he must have known they would be there eventually and even when, they would go as far as to say that God had preserved that land for them to occupy after their major change knowing that they would respect it and treat the land as he would want them to. Darren announced that they only had another fifteen minutes to walk before they would be in their new community and get to reunite with their loved ones that were there then the new pale ones were ready to walk again anxious to greet their loved ones as their equals and not as lower life forms any more this was going to be a real treat and something to remember for the rest of their lives, the experience would be ever so heart-warming and as Darren had said it was fifteen minutes and they were at the imaginary entrance to the commune for they had no wall around the commune at that point though they were considering putting one up for tangible boundaries for the pale ones to know their parameters to respect and not go beyond with the exception of the pickers who had specific instructions to only go where they absolutely had to and no further but the wall was only an idea at that point because they did not want to make the wildlife feel unwelcome however, there could be openings in the wall for the wildlife to enter and since they could now speak and understand them they could convey the purpose of the wall to them and make sure they knew they were always welcome anytime.

Now that the new pale ones were inside the commune boundaries everyone gathered to meet up with one another and welcome their loved ones as well as the others it was like a grand family reunion with no one being left out. Everyone mingled and slowly paired off into their family units and there were even some families that were brought together by some of the new pale ones due to marriage relations making for an even larger family unit, it was a beautiful sight to witness and it really touched the chief's heart. It took several hours for all the families to get separated out and settled down before the chief could verbally address everyone to what the next step would be which was to start to build homes for all the new pale ones so they would have shelter and it would not take long to get the new homes up with all the help that there was and of course the chief had to explain the gifts that the vaccine brought to the new pale ones just as he had with the previous pale ones and let them experience the gifts for themselves so they could utilize their gifts during their time of work to get things accomplished faster as the older pale ones had learned to do, it would be touch and go at first but they would get the hang of it speedily then be consistent with their building skills in a flash as well as other skills. The chiefs next task was to observe the pale ones and get to know them all individually so he could carefully appoint them their new chores and get the community up and running efficiently and hopefully not by trial and error, it was the chief's hopes to get the chores appointed correctly the first time which was why he would take the extra time to get to know a bit about each and every pale one as an individual from prior to their change to current hopes and dreams for there was always room for growth in their society because everyone was always willing to teach everyone their skill and welcomed the extra help for the apprenticeship. For now everyone was focusing on where to build the houses and drawing the layout for what they could in the wet dirt with big sticks and making up bricks from dirt and water then letting the mud bricks dry a bit and while the mud bricks dried a bit the families were appointing specific duties for the process to take place such as who would continue to make bricks, who would run the bricks back and forth from the making area to the structure area, who would lay the bricks in place and so forth. Although their gifts did speed up the process a bit it was still a slow process for the bricks had to be perfectly made and perfectly laid for a good fit then it would be time to fill the houses with the things that belonged inside it such as furniture and accessories. During that planning process the chief was still thinking of other things he had to arrange such as his replacement as leader of the community, he wanted a couple to be wedded and dubbed king and queen of the land so there was a balance of power for two minds were better than one and he would just be the advisor beneath the king and queen with lesser duties but still just as important and he already had a couple in mind. When the chief, Deanna, Darren, and Lloyd abducted one set of the teenage boys all one of the boys could think about was the safety of his girlfriend not his parents for they were adults and could fend for themselves but he was feeling responsible for the security of his girlfriend and he grieved the loss of her feeling as though he would never see her again, it actually made the chief want to seek her out and abduct her next just to bring the lad around to being back to his healthy self again. However, with the first set of female child abductions was teenage girls and the boy's girlfriend happened to be in the group and when they met up it was obvious that they had something rare and special between them that was going to last until death did them part that was Camillia and Andrew. The chief had another reason for picking Camillia and Andrew for the king and queen of the new land and that was what really made his mind up.

You see the chief was a godly man and would never turn his back on God or his word and while the pale ones were starting to work on the houses the chief went to his home to think about all the positions to be filled and other responsibilities to be addressed to collect his thoughts so he would not leave anything out and a miraculous thing occurred. The chief was visited by an angel of God it was Gabriel the archangel and he instructed the chief to follow his heart with the situation involving Camillia and Andrew for he was on the right track and that God had many plans in store for the pale ones so as long as the new breed of humans stayed on the straight and narrow path God would be granting miracles for the peoples hard work and efforts would not go unnoticed whether they be successful or not then the archangel disappeared. The chief was pleased that the archangel appeared to him and felt gracious that God would even allow his angel to speak to him in that manner so he dropped to his knees and thanked God for such a blessing and for the guidance then he prayed for the pale one society as a whole and the land with all its inhabitants, now the chief was refreshed feeling and ready to face his many tasks. It took three weeks to build all of the houses and get them filed with all of the things that needed to be placed inside of them then it took three months for the chief to get to know all of the pale ones intimately so he could properly place them in positions that would be appropriate for their specialties to best benefit the community and the chief did well filling every position and having good working teams for every specialty. When it was time to start the work and get the community working in full swing it was a beautiful working process and everyone accentuated everyone even the animals of the land came to the community to offer their services to be domesticated for the bettering of the community, there were horses that were willing to be used for breeding to get the amount of horses needed up and to be used for transportation, there were sheep coming to give wool to be woven for material for the chief had used some broken branches from trees to make spindles, there were goats who came to offer milk on a regular basis, chickens to offer eggs on a regular basis, and so many more animals coming to help with what they had to offer and the pale ones rewarded them graciously with a wonderful domesticated life of luxury. Now it was time for the chief to address Camillia and Andrew about their relationship and the plans he had for them because there was a lot of work that the chief had to put into them to prepare them for their job and he wanted them to know how important to God that their position was by revealing that the archangel Gabriel had come to reinforce the appointing of the couple to the position of king and queen of the land. The chief had sent for Camillia and Andrew right away and it was not hard to find them for they were together frolicking with the wild animals and mythological creatures just outside of the commune walls so when the chief's runner found the couple he advised them to seek out the chief to take care of some important business so Camillia and Andrew bade farewell to their animal fiends and headed for the chief immediately. Upon reaching the chief the couple questioned what was so dire that they must rush to his side then the chief began with the appearance of the archangel with the message of making them the king and queen of the land. The chief questioned Camillia and Andrew about their relationship and how serious it was then the couple replied to the chief that they were to be together for eternity and beyond so long as God blessed them and they were in constant prayer over that and very happy together and even wanted to have the position appointed by God someday to replenish the earth with many pale ones if God saw it fitting, the chief was pleased with the couples disposition on the matter and went on to discuss the position of being the king and queen of the community.

Camillia and Andrew questioned the chief if he really felt that they would be able to handle the job and the chief replied when it came to what God appointed and blessed all things were possible again through God. The chief then explained that he would have the pastor marry them in holy matrimony so they would be legal man and wife to be the queen and king of the land then they could bear all the children they wanted under God's law and then maybe God would even bless them with being able to be the bearer of children for the land of the pale ones as they had been asking through prayer since the archangel did say that God was going to be blessing the pale ones soon and the chief just knew that God heard the many prayers of the people. Just then a great glow circled the room that the chief, Camillia, and Andrew sat in and when the great glow dimmed it took the form of the archangel Gabriel, he had come back and with another message he revealed that the new couple was to have their prayer answered in that they would be the great bearer of children and their job in the underground land was to replenish the land with pale ones once they were married which was to be immediate for they were soul mates as they already knew. The archangel also revealed that there were going to be mini angels to come to the underground land from the surface but they would need the help of the abduction team to travel from above to below for there was no way for them to move the tunnel door and travel safely without being found by the robotic police without a lookout, the archangel did warn the chief that the mini angels were in area fifty four which was a dangerous place for the pale ones to be around and was heavily guarded by robotic police who would kill without question anyone near the barrier so the transport of the mini angels had to proceed with great caution and the chief replied that what God required of them would be done for it would be blessed and they would have God's safe hands around them as they proceeded and if any of them should perish in the process it was as God wanted it and in the line of duty of God. The archangel was impressed with the fearlessness of the chief and the outlook of the chief's disposition for his God then the archangel responded that they would be protected and not to worry about anyone perishing that they would receive blessings upon the safe arrival of the mini angels and with the arrival of the mini angels would be instruction of what the mini angels would be there for. The chief was finished with Camillia and Andrew so he excused them saying that the wedding would be after they safely got the mini angels underground then they left the chief's home office room and went to get the abduction team together to explain the task at hand. Everyone in the land was engrossed in their tasks at hand and did not notice the abduction team gathering to leave then heading for the front of the commune towards the path that would take them to the tunnel which was as the chief wanted because he knew they would not be gone long and he wanted the arrival of the mini angels to be a surprise to the pale ones. The abduction team speedily got to the wall of the area fifty-four and carefully kept a watch out for the robotic police while probing over the electric wall in search of the mini angels and all they saw was a beautiful patch of greenery that resembled a dinosaur tail that practically mesmerized them then suddenly the patch of greenery started to flutter in an upward motion and spread outward and upon closer examination the abduction team realized that each supposed leaf that arose was not an individual leaf it was tiny bodies with wings, it was the mini angels that were huddled tightly in a mathematical formation. The mini angels fluttered towards the abduction team and right through the electrical fence with no affects from the electricity then staying in a huddle sung out that they were ready to follow the abduction team to their new home as God had commanded them to.

The abduction team turned to lead the way and still kept an eye out for the robotic police in the event they should show up because they were still in the heavily guarded area and would be until they got towards the area of the tunnel. It did not take long to get to the tunnel and the abduction team with the mini angels made it without spying any robotic police and were able to give out a sigh of relief. The mini angels informed the chief that they could move with the speed of light so if the abduction team wanted to move with their super human speed they could and get to the commune faster it would be okay so that was what they did and before they knew it they were at the commune then the mini angels requested that the chief gather all the pale ones together so the lead mini angel could discuss why they were there and what their purpose was and the chief replied that their wish was his pleasure and he did as the mini angel requested then within minutes all the pale ones were gathered waiting on the beautiful mini angel to state the purpose of the gathering. The lead mini angel fluttered above all the rest and began to speak and what she had to state was a miracle in itself she said they were there for the pale ones and that each mini angel would pair up with a pale one and be with them twenty four seven sitting on their shoulder and that they had special powers of their own to enable them to assist their pale one when necessary but only then and the mini angels would be with their pale one for the life of their pale one and the life of the mini angel was dependent on the life of their pale one meaning that when their pale one passed they would pass also. All the pale ones could do was gasp in utter awe at the wonder of the blessings that they were about to receive from their new found friends then before the pale ones could find any words to utter the mini angels all fluttered up from the ground and dispersed to their pale ones shoulders to pair up mini angel with pale one so each pale one now had a mini angel on their shoulder then the chief announced that the arrangement had been made and was a permanent situation then the head mini angel sat on the chief's shoulder and told him there was more to know but it was for him to know that the general population did not need to worry themselves about the details that she had for him so the chief informed everyone that they could now go back to their duties and resume their work. As everyone happily disbursed the chief returned to his home to go to his office room to discuss with his mini angel the rest of the details that she wanted him to be aware of and she wasted no time getting to the point of things. The mini angel informed the chief that the mini angels could only reproduce by the hand of God at the time but there would be some changes in the future as God saw fitting but when there was to be children born to the pale ones they too would be receiving their mini angels upon birth by the hands of God for as she had announced previously each and every pale one was to have their own mini angel for protection and guidance from evil and poor judgement because they were still humans and had free will the mini angels served as a good conscience to the pale ones. The head mini angel did reveal to the chief that God had prepared a plan that would eventually have a later generation female pale one grandchild of the king and queen to be appointed as queen of the mini angels who would be taking over the repopulation of the mini angels and keeping up with the intertwining's of the pale ones with their mini angels then reporting any major business to God himself but that would be a ways away for the child was not born and she would be a teen ager before that would take place but she would be marked at birth and Camillia, Andrew, and the parents would know that the child was special by the time she was a toddler then an archangel would visit to make things clear to them.

They would have to give her up to the community for the greater good of the community but it would not be too difficult for the child would not be far away and they could visit her anytime and her name was to be Jadellya the daughter of Armellya daughter to the king and queen and Jaden son in law to the king and queen also the god son to the king and queen who used to be the stable boy for the king and queen who worked his way up to being a doctor at the community hospital and a veterinarian for the community all with the help of the head doctor of the hospital in a brief period of time for Jaden was a genius. Now that the head mini angel had explained that to the chief he had a greater appreciation for how things were going to be working between the pale ones and the mini angels for he realized that they were not just some pretty faces with wings they were actually intelligent gifted extensions of God's fleet of angelic beings. It was now time to arrange the wedding of Camillia and Andrew to be completed as soon as possible so the chief went to see the preacher at the worship hall and when he did the preacher was ecstatic to hear that Camillia and Andrew were to be wedded for he knew how special their relationship was and he said he would be ready within ten minutes because he had to put on his special dressing for the occasion and the chief said he would be ready within ten minutes also for that was how long it would take him to pull the entire community together to meet in the worship hall to witness the blessed event then the two agreed to get the union started in ten minutes and the chief turned to leave to gather the community. When the chief left he immediately called for the community to gather and they responded swiftly then when the chief announced that they were to meet in the religious hall for the blessed union of Camillia and Andrew the community cheered as they moved fleetingly towards the religious hall to take their seats in the many pews inside to quiet down so they could be respectful and hear the ceremony. Inside the preacher was at the pulpit waiting for everyone to be seated and for the bride to take her place at the aisleway to walk up to the groom where he was already at waiting for Camillia to take her place at his side. Camillia and Andrew had been waiting for that moment for a while so they were not nervous at all in fact they were thrilled that this was happening at such a young age and they never thought it would happen so soon this meant that they could start their family early because as was said before they wanted to replenish the new land with more pale ones and prayed that it was God's will for them to be chosen for the job which now they knew it was and thus they were to be married also for them to be queen and king of the community which they were uncertain if they could hold up to the responsibilities of the duties but would give it their best efforts, the chief knew they would be able to handle the responsibilities and perform all their duties in excess of what was expected of them according to the archangels visit it was God's will and God would bless their efforts. Now everyone was seated and silent and Camillia was walking up the aisle while the mini angels sang a song so angelic it almost had everyone in tears of sentiment and as Camillia approached Andrew he held his hand out to her and when she took his hand they both gave gentle smiles of love to one another, they gave off beams of light that were of deep love for one another and it was so genuine and rare this was the type of love that had never been witnessed above ground so how it had developed above ground was beyond everyone it was obviously in preparation for the underground life for God knew all past, present, and future. Now standing before the preacher hand in hand the preacher read from the holy book the matrimony words and the new couple repeated their portion of the words and exchanged personally memorized vows that came from their hearts and they were absolutely beautiful.

With the completion of the wedding the new bride and groom walked down the aisle together thanking everyone for coming to the wedding and as they got to the door of the religious hall they turned to one another and professed their love to one another and romantically kissed then everyone cheered as they stood up from their seats and clapped. For now the couple stayed at Andrew's home but they needed to build a house for Andrew and Camillia since the couple were staying in homes with their families and the community was already on top of that situation as soon as the community came out of the religious hall they got together to start to build a house for Andrew and Camillia as a wedding gift, with all the individuals that were working on it and using their super gifts the house was done within two hours and the things that needed to be inside of it were placed inside of it. The home was absolutely beautiful and the new bride and groom moved their belongings into the home with the help of their families then the couple got their things organized into where the belongings were to be put which did not take long now the rest of the day was theirs to spend however they wanted so they spent the rest of the day in one another's arms which led up to them consummating the marriage it was ever so beautiful. Now that the hours of sleep fell over the pale ones the community had shut down and everyone including Andrew and Camillia fell asleep for about four hours then awoke for a new day to work Andrew and Camillia would spend the day with the chief to get the rundown on how the community worked so they could learn how to run the community correctly and handle any situation that may arise but in the event anything should come about that needed extra attention the new king and queen had the assistance of the chief as their advisor to help in anything they were needing help with. During the time that the chief was counseling the new couple on their new duties Camillia got ill and needed to lay down on the chief's couch while they continued the lessons on how to run the community but it was difficult for her to concentrate and the chief and Andrew were picking up on her difficulty due to their telepathic link with her. Due to the chief's strong link with nature and being a medicine man, he felt he knew exactly what was going on with her and it was not that anything was wrong with her in fact, something was actually right with her he believed that she and Andrew consummating their marriage was perfect timing for conceiving and therefore she was experiencing morning sickness. The chief had no way to confirm his suspicion so he did not reveal his suspicions to her but he did pull Andrew aside and advise him to watch for her to grow and become better for he suspected that she was pregnant and that their prayers had been answered, they would be the first to conceive in the new land and deliver a precious new pale one. Andrew was speechless but wanted to be sure that what the chief was speaking of was possible and the chief knew that so the chief advised Andrew to wait a few weeks then take her to the community hospital for a checkup when things would be visible for a trained eye or if he could not wait he could take her to the community hospital now for a blood test and see if it would show up but he was not sure if it would because the pale one physiology was so different from the human physiology but the community doctor would know. Just then the chief had an idea he mentioned sending a note by his runner to the doctor at the community hospital asking the question of whether the pregnancy could be detected so early by a blood test in a pale one or not and if so could Camillia go in for a test then Andrew replied to do it so the chief prepared the letter and called the runner into his office room. When the chief made contact with his runner, he advised the runner to make the errand speedy and wait for the response to get it back to him urgently then the runner acknowledged the chief and left immediately.

The runner got to the hospital within three minutes and found the doctor and gave him the note advising him that the message was from the chief so the doctor opened it immediately and read it, when he found that it was in reference to the queen he responded without hesitation and gave his response back to the runner who wasted no time getting it back to the chief. When the runner returned to the chief and gave the doctors response to him he read it and it was good news, the chief advised Andrew that they needed to get Camillia to the hospital for they may be in line for some good news for the doctor could run a blood test that would detect a pregnancy that early. Andrew went to the couch where Camillia was and gingerly advised her to get up that they were going to take her to see the doctor at the hospital to find out what was going on with her since pale ones were not supposed to get sick and she was feeling ill they needed to find out why so Camillia got up and was willing to go without questions but the more she moved around the more nauseous she became. The chief, Andrew, and Camillia went to mount their horses and ride to the community hospital when Camillia fainted and fell from her horse and Andrew sprang from his horse to pick up Camillia from the ground and revive her for her tumble scared him and the chief. When Camillia came to she was a bit confused for a few seconds but when she was fully alert Andrew had decided that he and Camillia were going to ride double on his horse so he could keep her alert and on the horse from taking another tumble. Once Andrew was sure Camillia was ready to try to mount the horse again he got her upon his horses back then got up behind her and the chief rode beside them on his horse and off to the hospital they went. Camillia was still nauseous and more pale than what a pale one should be and the chief and Andrew knew that so they rode rather urgently to the hospital just in case this was more serious than just being pregnant and if it was just because she was pregnant they wanted to know how they could alleviate the symptoms because the symptoms were now becoming serious to where they could become dangerous, what if Camillia fainted and really hurt herself on something like the furniture, stove, or sink, or in the shower? The trip to the hospital did not take long and they were finally there and when they dismounted and got into the hospital they went straight to the nurses desk where the doctor was waiting for them and when he saw Camillia he was even alarmed and rushed them into a nearby room where he helped Camillia onto the patient bed and had her lay back so she did not risk falling off due to dizziness. The doctor immediately called a nurse into the room to draw some blood from Camillia and told her to run the blood samples to the laboratory herself and have the technician put a rush on the results and get them to him stat so he could diagnose Camillia as soon as possible for there were some concerning symptoms that needed to be addressed before something dire occurred to her. The nurse acknowledged the doctor and drew the blood in a flash then did as the doctor had requested and twenty minutes later the blood results were in the doctor's hand and as he read them he made affirmative noises under his breath as though he expected the results to read as they actually did. After reading the results the doctor looked up at Andrew and smiled from ear to ear and with a grand voice stated that a congratulation was in order for they were expecting and that could account for the nausea and quite possibly for the dizziness and fainting the doctor suggested that Camillia increase her food intake to try to combat the dizziness and fainting since her body would be burning more calories and increasing fluids such as blood and amniotic fluids and the likes.

As for the nausea the doctor suggested for Camillia to drink teas with honey and to try some mint tea first and if that did not work experiment with other teas until they found one that worked but he did let the couple know that the nausea did not usually last the whole pregnancy so she would probably get back to normal once her body adjusted to the surge of hormones most likely within several weeks the doctor told Camillia to just hold out and try to focus on deep breathing through the roughest time when it felt like she was going to vomit and if she did vomit to not be discouraged because it too would pass. The couple and the chief were excited that they were expecting but surprised it was so soon after being wedded but knew it must have been by the will of God and now, they were sure they would really start to see the blessings of God start to pour down upon them. Now that the doctor was finished with his part of the process of diagnosing Camillia he wished them luck and advised her to come back for regular checkups to assure all was well and to follow the pregnancy so when it was time to deliver the baby they would be ready for there was no other pale one who had been pregnant and since pale ones were so different from humans they did not know what to expect for the gestational period. Pale ones did everything more accelerated than a plain human from movement to healing no matter how serious the injury should be and minor injuries would heal immediately such as simple scratches from foliage while picking fruits, vegetables, and nuts from their places of growth and especially cotton from their place of growth with all their surrounding stickers the pale ones fingers would heal immediately from those simple injuries also so they would be able to continue to keep using their hands for their jobs without soreness or the threat of infection from the dirt that they sometimes had to pick through especially for the vegetables. The doctor was expecting the queens pregnancy to be shorter in gestation than the forty weeks that a human gestation was but by how much shorter was the grand question so there was to be a close eye kept on the queens pregnancy for signs of the end such as thinning of the cervix and the turning of the baby to head down that usually occurred in the third trimester but before the very end the other thing for the queen to help the doctor to keep an eye out for were the Braxton hicks contractions for those also were a sign of the end of the third trimesters delivery day. The doctor's exams would also help him to know when the baby would move into the birth canal and he could use a special monitor to keep track of real contractions if the queen was not sure if she was having real contractions versus the Braxton hick's contractions. For now, the doctor wanted to see Camillia every other week until she started to feel well and then they could go every four weeks for a while unless something came about that was concerning and of course at the end of the pregnancy he would be seeing the queen more frequently. There was nothing that the doctor could do for Camillia to help with the dizziness and nausea except tell her to try teas for the nausea and take precaution in moving about for the dizziness and try not to be alone until the symptoms lifted so Andrew promised the doctor and Camillia that he would be at her side at all times until the symptoms were alleviated. The doctor was now finished with what he could do so the appointment was over and it was time to let the doctor get back to his prior duties so Camillia sat up on the bed slowly with the help of Andrew then gently stood up and she felt fine so they and the chief walked slowly out of the hospital to go back to the chief's home and relax while working. When the three of them got out of the hospital doors they mounted their horses and headed back to the chief's house to continue the couple's discussion on how to adequately run the community for they had not completed that yet because there was so much to learn it took the chief his whole life practically to learn his skills from his human days.

When they got to the chief's home the chief got the horses put away while Andrew got Camillia on into the house and settled down on the chief's couch and about the time Camillia was settled and Andrew got seated the chief entered and got himself seated and the learning session began again. The chief began with briefly reviewing what they had already gone over to assure that the couple had understood and remembered the information and they did so it was now time to move on and they did, several hours had passed when someone was knocking on the chief's front door and it was one of the cooks from the dining hall checking on the chief to find out why he had not shown up for the dinner meal and to find out if he had seen Andrew and Camillia because they had not answered their door. The chief chuckled and told the cook that time had slipped away from them that Andrew and Camillia were there with him and they were working but that they would follow the cook back to the dining hall to join everyone for the dinner meal and partake of the meal and socialize so Andrew helped Camillia up from the couch and the three of them followed the cook out to the barn to saddle up the horses and ride to the dining hall because it was too far for Camillia to walk due to the simple complications she was having with her pregnancy. The cook had walked over to the chief's home from the dining hall so the chief, Andrew, and Camillia walked their horses at the cook's pace so they could conversate and not leave him behind for they wanted to be courteous. Finally, they got to the dining hall and dismounted their horses, the cook noticed how careful Andrew was being with Camillia and questioned if his queen was ill and if there was anything he could prepare for her special to help her feel better then Andrew took the cook by his hand and thanked him for his concern and replied that she was not ill she was with child and having some unusual symptoms for a pale one it was as though she was human but yes he could help and then Andrew thanked him for his offer then proceeded to ask him if he could fix a bland vegetable soup and a variety of teas starting with a mint tea all with a touch of honey for the queen had nausea and dizziness that they needed to try to combat then the cook responded that he would get on it right away and if there was anything else that could help he would be glad to render his services. Right as they began to turn to go inside the dining hall the cook snapped his fingers and suddenly spoke saying that he knew when human females were pregnant and experiencing nausea they would eat soda crackers and they seemed to help then he offered to make some to go along with the soup so Andrew replied that it was a grand idea, they were willing to try anything. The cook reached out and patted Camillia's stomach and congratulated her on the new arrival then informed her that he was going to make sure to fix her right up with the proper nutritious foods for two and if she ever had cravings at any time to just let him know and he would be more than willing to whip it up in the kitchen for her then she chuckled and thanked him as she took his hand and kissed it in a friendly sort of way. Now that the news was out in the open to one person the chief decided that it was only appropriate to make the announcement at the dinner table when they got settled inside to the whole community and Andrew agreed so on-ward they went. The cook had a great grin on his face as he sat at his place at the dinner table and Andrew got Camillia sat at her place then took his seat at her side then the chief stood in front of the table at his seat and called for everyone's attention. Everyone grew silent and gave the chief their full undivided attention.

The chief cleared his throat and with a loud deep voice he made the announcement that the king and queen were expecting a child for the queen had just found out that day that she was with child and this would be the first child to be born in the land and for the pale one species. This excited Deanna and Darren especially because they were not sure what the vaccine had done to the reproductive system of the pale one species so the news had revealed that the vaccine had not shut down the reproductive system for them but was it for them a blessing of God or could all pale ones reproduce? Darren and Deanna wanted another pregnancy in the community to help confirm that the vaccine had not shut down the reproductive system for there were many pale ones who wanted children and so far, had not conceived yet and it was not for the lack of trying. That gave Deanna an idea, she wanted to try to take sperm and eggs from the pale ones and see if they were mature and would unite and if so go ahead and inseminate them into the proper female pale one for incubation and basically do artificial insemination in an effort to study the sex cells without wasting potentially perfectly good cells and in the process give the pale mates a chance at conceiving their first children as pale ones. If there was something wrong with the sex cells then Deanna wanted to study the cells to determine what may be wrong and how it may be corrected because she was willing to try to make another serum to give the pale ones to help mature the sex cells from within their bodies it was just a matter of finding some pale ones who were willing to be test subjects. The next question would be how was the king and queen able to conceive if the rest of the pale ones were not able and as said before was it a blessing from God above? Deanna and Darren had to go to the chief, Camillia, and Andrew to get their proposed project approved before they could move forward with it and their justification had to be strong so after the chief sat down in his seat after his pregnancy announcement Deanna informed the chief that she and Darren would like to meet with him and the king and queen after the dinner meal at his home and the chief replied that was fine to just follow them there. The dinner meal went great, Camillia was able to eat her dinner without any nausea and everyone conversed cheerfully then the time set aside for the meal was over as it seemed to go by fleetingly. Everyone said their farewells and verbally expressed their love for one another then went their separate ways to get back to work while Deanna, Darren, Camillia, Andrew, and the chief went to the chief's home for a meeting of the minds. Now at the chief's home everyone there got comfortable in the chief's family room then Deanna spoke up about the meeting being about the conception of children for the common folk and how the vaccine that turned them into pale ones may have made them sterile and she and Darren wanted to investigate the probability of that theory and try to correct the issue of at all possible if they did find the theory to be fact. The chief wanted details on how Darren and Deanna were going to go about testing the couples in the community for sterilization versus fertilization and if found to be sterile how they were going to go about the process of reversing the damage that had been done by the turning vaccine for changing the deoxyribonucleic acids once to turn off a system was one thing but to change it again safely to return the reproductive system to a working order was tricky without bringing harm to any other systems for zeroing in on one strand of deoxyribonucleic acid was a difficult thing to do although with the current technology it was possible so the chief questioned Camillia and Andrew on their thoughts over the situation. Camillia replied that if it would help the families bear children safely without affecting any other systems it was worth trying.

Camillia went as far as to state that it would be wonderful because as a woman, she could understand the feeling of defeat and failure of being barren for bearing children was the primary joy of womanhood, Andrew felt the same so Deanna and Darren were granted permission to go ahead with their experiment. The chief informed Darren and Deanna that he would pull the community pale ones together right away for them to address them on the issue at hand and try to get some volunteers for the project so they went outside and stood in front of the chief's home for the chief to use his bull horn to call upon the community pale ones to gather together. It took five minutes for the community to gather around the chief's home and quiet down then Darren spoke to the people informing them of the possibility that the vaccination may have rendered them barren but that there was a possibility that he and Deanna could reverse the effects of the vaccine on the reproductive system so they could have children but they would need some volunteers to assist in the project then before Darren could speak another word the community members burst out in words of support saying they would be willing to be volunteers. Of course, Darren and Deanna only needed a few volunteers so they pulled a few couples from the crowd and advised them that they were to meet at the science hall in one hour then Darren informed the rest of the couples that they would be called upon when the time was right and that he and Deanna were gracious for their support and that they would keep the people informed on how things were progressing. The pale ones disbursed to go back to their work while the few couples who were chosen to help with the project made their way to the science hall where they would do whatever it was that Darren and Deanna would have them to do. Darren and Deanna had set up all the tools they needed to extract the sex cells from the couples when they arrived and place them into labeled containers for further study and hopefully get a test-tube union provided the cells were fully mature and if so then Darren and Deanna would artificially inseminate the united cells into the proper female for hopefully an impregnation and full-term delivery of a healthy baby. If the cells were not mature then Darren and Deanna would have to look deeper into why the cells were underdeveloped and how they could trigger the pale one body to have a working reproductive system which would probably mean that they would have to go to the ribosomes responsible for the reproductive system and experiment with triggering the ribosome to being active from a nonactive state which would be a difficult thing to do but they would not give up until they succeeded in making the pale one species a child bearing species. The theory was a sound one and within grasp, the technology was even available so Deanna and Darren had a good feeling about being successful in the project it would just take some time and patience from the pale ones awaiting the results. Finally, an hour had passed by and the few couples who were chosen to participate in the project were inside the science hall with Darren and Deanna so Deanna was explaining the procedure for taking the sex cells from them and showing them the tools that would be used as they went along so they would be aware of what was going to be happening to them and making sure they had no questions before beginning. Now that the explanation and potential question and answer session was over it was time to proceed with the procedure so the pale one couples one at a time got up on the hospital type bed and Darren worked with the men while Deanna worked with the women in extracting the sex cells and placing them into labeled containers. Eventually all the volunteers had some of their sex cells extracted and they were quite surprised that it was virtually painless and for now they were finished with the volunteers, but they would be called on again soon.

The volunteers left the science hall and joined the rest of the pale ones out in the community to work in their occupation until the next meal time and in the meantime Darren and Deanna were wasting no time getting started on the examination of the cells that they had extracted from the volunteers. It did not take much time for Deanna to find that the cells were immature so that led her to believe that the reproductive systems of the volunteers were shut down and therefore not releasing the sex cells which made sense because none of the females had been experiencing menses which raised another question. The queen, Camillia had not been experiencing menses either and there was now no way to safely extract her sex cells due to her pregnancy to find out if she was producing mature cells but she could have Darren extract cells from the king, Andrew to see if his cells were mature because Deanna believed their conception to be a miracle from God. Deanna called upon Darren to have him summon Andrew to find out if Andrew would be willing to give a sample of his cells for examination, so Darren responded to Deanna and left immediately in hopes of bringing Andrew back to the science hall. It did not take Darren long to find Andrew at the chief's home and inform him why he and Deanna wanted him to go to the science hall so Andrew replied that he would be willing to follow Andrew to the science hall and participate in the study, besides he already felt that he and Camillia were no different than the rest of the community and their conception was a blessing from God and Andrew made sure to make it known to Darren. Before they knew it, they were at the science hall and Deanna was eagerly waiting for them to return so she could examine Andrews cells to find out if his cells were mature or not for, she was sure that the conception was a miracle in itself but to what extent. Darren did the procedure on Andrew that had to be done to extract the sex cells from Andrew then placed them into a labeled container and handed the container to Deanna then Deanna immediately went over to the microscope and took some of the cells out of the container for examination and Andrew waited around to hear the results. It was a speedy examination for what Deanna found was no different than what she had found in the others, the cells were immature and not capable of reproduction and when Deanna informed Andrew of that she also deemed the pregnancy a complete miracle and vowed that the baby they would bear to be a special pale one with gifts that only God could give as she saw it for the baby was to be angelic in nature. Deanna and Darren knew for sure that the rest of the couples in the commune would eventually be able to conceive without any problems. Each pale one within the royal family had a special gift that the other community pale one's did not have but were God given. The chief's special gift was to be able to see into the future and know special events of the others. In other words, the chief would know who would conceive, who would perform a major feat and the likes. The only thing that the chief could not foretell was God's actions and a lot of this ability was due to his experience as an oracle for his Indian tribe, and God's desire to bless him with the skill. In the year twenty-nine twenty-five when world war three broke out and the only survivors were in Las Vegas, Nevada USA thanks to their safe house and modestly the grace of God. In the beginning healthy humans were abducted then the non-healthy humans were abducted, and they were made pale ones starting with the young then leading to the older individuals, and finally the damaged humans were changed into pale ones. This was where the conception project and the life extension projection came about because the pale one vaccine brought about bareness and longevity which Darren and Deanna were trying to address and research. Deanna and Darren did find a plant that would introduce the missing chemicals to the pale one's bodies and allow for them to produce children, finally. The life extension projection was also a success in that it allowed the two hundred years given by the original vaccination that turned them into pale ones adding another two hundred years making it a four-hundred-year life expectancy.

As mentioned previously there were three serious wars that broke out and some of the humans were ready for the radiation engulfed atmosphere and it was not just in Las Vegas, Nevada, USA. What the Nevadan's were not ready for was their lives after the change into pale one's. For instance, in Danger in the land of grandeur the second book of the four-part series the battle between Santuvious and his parents Armellya and Jaden which was long and drawn out due to the fact that Armellya and Jaden truly thought that they had vanquished him on a first near fatal encounter. Eventually though on a second and final encounter Armellya and Jaden with the aid of God's angels and the mini angels along with the aid of effective family members did finally vanquish Santuvious for good because he was now trapped in the place of darkness in heaven with no way to escape. The chief had finally found a replacement for himself, a king and queen which was Camillia and Matthew who were married after becoming pale ones and conceived shortly after that. Now in regular human weeks a female would carry a pregnancy for forty weeks but a pale one would only carry for twenty-four weeks, everything that a pale one did was much quicker than that of a human female. During the time after Santuvius was vanquished and prior to any other major events all the girls got gravely ill due to being exposed toa fatal flower. The flower was beautiful and had a lovely smell to it and no one has any suspicion that it was dangerous in any way although it was not plentiful in the forest however due to that flower, the girls had to stay in the hospital for quite some time, it was questionable as to whether or not that they would recover or die, life had been extremely tough on all of the pale ones and required an immense amount of work from all of the pale ones, fortunately they did make a full recovery after an extended amount of time in the hospital and a lot of physical therapy at home. Meanwhile all of the pale ones who had made frequent trips to the surface of the planet were making their way to the surface once again to retrieve necessary items from the safe houses and some small amounts of desired objects for everyone as all the pale ones were doing. Camillia and Matthew were considering bringing down from the surface some replicators from all of the safe houses so the commune would have no reason to go above ground anymore and that would make things safer as well as give more time for other tasks. Camillia discussed the various options with Matthew further and he de decided that it was time to take the matter up with the chief since he was running the show and the chief was their advisor so Matthew agreed with Camillia so he sent word by a runner for the chief to meet with them at their bedroom so Camillia could be involved as well. Shortly after the messenger left the chief arrived with curiosity and immediately rushed to the couple's bedroom asking if everything was alright. King Matthew and Queen Camillia both replied that everything was just fine and requested for the chief to take a seat on the sofa seat that was in her and Matthews bedroom so the chief sat down assuming that there was going to be a lengthily conversation then Matthew started to discuss the things that were on his and Camillias mind. The first and only thing on the royal couple's mind's was that they wanted all the replicator's brought from the surface of the planet down to the community so they could use them for the community needs and desires and the more replicators they had the better off they would be and the chief agreed then advised the couple that the team had already left and were instructed to retrieve all the replicators then their necessities and finally their desires as well would be met, the chief was already thinking about the replicators and was already a step ahead of them, this was a real relief for the couple and they were not surprised that the chief was already taking care of the replicator issue for the chief was always on the same thought process as they were and that was precisely why the chief was so thrilled that God had chosen Camillia and Andrew to be king and queen because he would have chosen them as well so he was thrilled that after he found them to be perfect for the position and God had sent down an angel to confirm his desire to appoint them to the position he was overflowing with joy and contentment. There were many accomplishments in the legend of the dinosaur tail with the changing of the humans healthy and damaged into pale ones, the reestablishing of the people's society not with just the building of their little town but in their willingness to cooperate with developing a hierarchy as well. The pale ones lived a God fearing life of simple mindedness filled with love for one another and a great respect for their land and the life of every creature that shared the land with them their way of living was the way that God intended things to be for Adam and Eve in the original garden of Eden.

Now the legend of the dinosaur tail was only the beginning, the pale ones had no way of knowing that there were many trials and tribulations yet to come before their world would finally become a utopian society but in the end they would not have satin to tempt them as Eve did in the garden of Eden. This leads us to the second book of the series, danger in the land of grandeur. This is where the chief groomed Andrew and Camillia to essentially take his place as ruler of the underground society and step-down becoming advisor to the king and queen of the land. At this point in time Deanna and Darren had not come up with a successable vaccine to support the ability for the pale ones to conceive children on their own so Camillia and Andrew also did spiritual healings over couples in the community for the conception of children and they did work every time. The spiritual healings were not limited to just conception but that was the most spiritual healing in demand. Around this time was when Armellya was impregnated by a dark angel who laid over her making her unable to move or cry out for help. This dark angel was cast out of heaven into the darkest depths of hades and had a purpose of creating demons with heavenly angels such as Armellya. The balance of good versus evil was at hand between that demon child who would be named Santuvious and the couples angelic child named Jadellya who would also be the key to vanquishing the boy demon child known as Santuvious and this would be the opening act of the start of the major battle of purging evil into the depths of hades and locking the doors of hades shut never to be opened again. The angel of death will be showing himself to Armellya to drain the souls from her and her angelic daughter Jadellya until they perished and of course the attempt did not prove to be successful although it was a great attempt and could have worked had there have been no one to show up as Jaden had and be willing to fight off the angel of death and have some abilities that were proven to allow the uninvited guest to stand up to the angel of death and be a worthy opponent and win the fight. Once Jaden, Armellya, and Jadellya were free from the grasp of the angel of death it was time to gather with others and they did just that without showing any signs of being attacked. Now with the accompany of others and the chief, the chief introduced his new companion named Deutaronomy who was a wolf pup. In this part of the saga the chief was a popular man, he not only got a wolf pup but he had a female pale one whom he had been secretly dating and did not want to reveal until he was sure things would be getting serious between them and after he was brave enough to ask the female called Sharonna to marry him and of course if she was to say yes he would introduce her to the royal clan but if her response was negative then he would deal with the situation differently. The chief would have to reassess their dating situation if it was to go on a bit longer and if so if it was to stay secret or not. Of course, the chief asked Sharonna for her hand in marriage and she replied affirmatively so during the next family meal the chief would be taking Sharonna with him and introducing her to the royal family as his bride to be with a wedding date and allowing the clan to get to know her but first he had to go to Melanie to make sure she knew to set an extra place at the table next to him and Deutaronomy. The date of the wedding arrived and the females of the royal clan had everything planned and in place so all they needed was for the ceremony to start, it finally did and it was a beautiful one and all worked out as planned and then they were off to their wedding reception which was just as planned as the wedding and just as beautiful and wonderous as the wedding, everyone enjoyed themselves. The wedding reception went on for hours and not just the pale ones attended, the many animals regular and mythological attended as well and so did the variety of angels mini and God's angels from heaven and those bound to heaven who were there to protect and guide the pale ones just as was done for all the unions of pale ones; it was not long after the chief and Sharonna's wedding that they conceived a child and at that point all the female pale ones were pregnant all at the same time and close to the same week in gestation. Soon after the blessed union of the chief and Sharonna and the discovery of the female pale ones pregnancies the discovery of the new rainbow colored flower came about and was presented to the castles royal women and when they came into contact with it shortly after they became life threatening ill and had to fight for their lives in the intensive care unit in the hospital and it did not appear to the doctors that they were going to survive. After a long arduous fight and some home health care which also included physical therapy the female royal pale ones regained their health and went on to live their lives as if nothing had happened and picked up where they left off when they became ill. Needless to say after the fight with the illness over the new unusual flower the male royal pale ones sought to find all of the remaining rainbow like flowers and have them destroyed to avoid having anyone else harmed and that journey was successful and no one else was harmed however the pale ones did not go into the depths of the forest so there could have been other rainbow flowers there but it was just the portion of the forest that they occupied that they were worried about and they were satisfied with that and would keep an eye out for the deadly flowers return to the portion of the forest that they used. The interesting thing that the royal family and doctors did notice was that the deadly rainbow like flower only affected the pregnant females and no one else so it had to have had some way of targeting the pregnancy type hormones only and since the nonpregnant females did not have the elevated hormones they were safe and of course the men did not have those hormones so they were definantly safe but it was a curious theory. Moving on...shortly after returning home and getting back to their healthy selves the pregnant royal pale one females delivered their babies all in the same evening within the same hour, it was a lot to handle for the two doctors but everyone involved handled it well and everything went pretty smoothly and with no complications, all the women even made it out to the evening meal hour with their babies and their nannies to show off their infants to the rest of the royal family members. One of the babies delivered was of king Jaden and queen Armellya, the child was to be named Santuvious according to the angel that appeared to them and advised them of what the boy child was to be called. Santuvious was conceived by Armellya and a dark angel from the depths of hades so he had a dark spirit in him so it would be obvious to the king and queen that they would have to vanquish their evil child for the safety of them as well as the entire pale one species. Armellya and Jaden with their first child who was angelic in nature and was actually born with the purpose of vanquishing Santuvious among many other things. Santuvious was thought to be vanquished after the first attempt but was not he returned and was stronger than ever but was vanquished on the second attempt and was locked away in a room found in heaven that was for demons and would not let them out and was extremely protected by God's angels so when another demon was put away no locked up demon could escape when the door opened to lock away another, it was a failsafe technique. During this time the retired doctor and Jaden were working on what was called the cardiopulmonary project which was where they took lung and heart tissue samples to try to grow new hear and lungs to combine with other samples to attempt to grow a full pale one human and this project was actually a success to the doctors surprise. The artificial pale one even had a soul and the artificial pale one was inhabited by Gabriel the archangel for the time of the upcoming war that everyone knew was near, there was nothing or nobody else that could inhabit the artificial pale one and Gabriel made sure of that. It was at that time that the chief made it known of his prediction that the war between the good and evil had already begun, and it was time for all pale ones, the creatures of the land both ordinary as well as the mythological creatures to be on alert and prepared to fight and to the death if necessary. Because of the up rise of evil there had been some changes in the abilities of each and every inhabitant of the land of grandeur so now the mini angels did not need assistance of the pale ones to get them to the dinosaur tail now they were able to transform into doves and fly to the dinosaur tail and settle down into their mathematical configuration now located in the underground community. Another important thing for the pale ones and all the creatures of the land to know and remember was that the only way to tell the good from the bad was that the good had a golden glow from their eyes and the bad had a red glow from their eyes and tried not to make eye contact as to where the good did not have a problem making eye contact with any one or thing, even the pale ones had a golden glow from their eyes as did Deutaronomy. Since the great and final battle had begun all the creatures big and small, ordinary and mythological along with God's angels from the heavens and those who were earth bound were now in the combine of the land of grandeur and ready to defend the land of grandeur and all of its inhabitants as well as its occasional visitors. After a log and drawn out fight the good had won the battle and the evil had been sent back to the depths of hades and the gates were shut and locked so they would never able to be opened by anyone or any thing and the world would be able to thrive and hopefully grow into a God fearing people and be as their maker had originally planed for them to be and not make any simple mistakes like Eve had done on the first attempt for a utopian society and God already knew where the pale ones would be in the future and he was proud to be their maker and easy to grant their desires as they were a simple people and all about asking for assistance for the bettering of their world and very unselfish. Now that the great battle was over things went back to normal, the pale ones and all the creatures of the land of grandeur kept their new abilities and lived together in peace and love, they were close and shared many great times together they even worked side by side when it was possible and the creatures could communicate telepathically in the language that the pale ones could understand and the pale ones spoke telepathically to them in return. The final event in the land of grandeur was of Aralene, the nurse practitioner, the delivery of her male child, it was a long delivery but normal and in the end she did get to see her child and make sure that Stephano knew the child was to be called Aramis then she passed right after seeing and naming him. However, she did get the opportunity to tell her husband, Stephano to take good care of their son and that she would live in their son and that she loved them both and that he could see her any time by looking into their son's eyes. Aralene had angelic abilities which would allow her to visit Stephano and Aramis as well as any other pale one she desired but it had not been known to them at that point, it would later be known to Aralene then when she was to appear before Stephano he would be surprised but pleased and always looking forward to the next encounter. Now we get to the third book of the series of four which is life in the legendary city of gold. The entire city was made completely of gold even the streets were paved of gold due to God touching the city and blessing them and any additions to the city would be built by the inhabitants of the city as was done before but upon completion it would miraculously turn to gold right before their eyes. It was revealed to Aralene that she could reenter her body and live again with the help of Gabriel the archangel however, she would have to lay where her body was for several hours and rest so her body could regenerate and recover from what stage of decomposition she had and to reverse the state of rigormortis then she would be able to go to her home and be with her family and her royal friends. Unfortunately it did not work for her and Stephano had found out that the possibility of her reliving was there and it did not work out so he fell into a deeper depression than he had already been in and therefore decided to slit his throat from ear to ear so he could die and go to heaven to be with his wife and he did not think of the fact that he would be leaving their son alone to be fostered by the royal family.

With all that had happened Aramis was not left behind to be fostered by the royal family because he mysteriously died of crib death so he went to heaven to be close to his mother, Aralene and his father Stephano as angels in heaven. That was Stephano's thoughts but he never thought that because he committed suicide that there would be a punishment for his illegitimate way of dying but nothing slipped by God and there would be a punishment for his actions for only God had the right of taking a life that he had given and that was only under specific situations that were of few occasions. Therefore, Stephano was to be sent to the new earth to live out his days as a spirit in his home because he forfeited his placement in the heavens by taking his own life. Now with some positive news, Jadellya officially becomes the queen of the mini angels on the new earth in the new garden of Eden and the dinosaur tail remains on her property and her parents, Jaden and Armellya become official angels of God instead of simple blessed pale ones but will remain in the new garden of Eden. Back to Stephano, he was disobedient about staying within the boundaries of his earthly home and rather rebellious towards God within his encounter in trying to reach an agreement that was acceptable so God finally put the staff down and ordered that Stephano be held in the place of darkness found in heaven and that was done but once again Santuvious escaped so Armellya, Jaden, and Gabriel got Santuvious back into the pace of darkness found in heaven without incident. The next task at hand was to gather all the pale ones excluding the royal ones and make them equal to one another using the most gifted ones as the guide for the extent of how the entire community of pale ones would be and that was done within minutes. Every single pale one that was in the community at the new garden of Eden was gathered by an angel of God and that angel spoke to the pale ones informing them of God's new law. There would be no more trips from the underground hideaway to the surface of the new earth and that the underground and surface doorway would be sealed off by God and that any pale one who tried to gain access to the surface of the new earth would perish with a horrible demise and would not have the option to enter the gates of heaven. The land that was between the compound and the tunnel entrance would expand from the community of the pale one and become as the glorious garden of Eden, in fact the whole underground would expand and be at the disposal of the pale ones to be occupied so they could replenish the new earth without the problem of being over populated and at the same time take care of the new earth by replacing the earth's offerings s they used them by replanting what they took and let God replace what they could not by continuing to bless their good deeds by following through with their responsibilities as was promised. With the many changes for the better God gave Jaden the one-time ability to touch the pale ones as a group to enable them to conceive children on their own without the spiritual healings from himself and Armellya. During the beginning of God's great blessing's the gnomes had taken over the nanny positions and Camillia felt that was great and the children certainly thrived better with the gnomes than they did with the pale one nannies but Armellya knew the gnomes were once angelic beings and she wanted them to have their previous status back thinking that would make them happier than they currently were so she had planned to go to the feet of God and plead for the gnomes to regain their previous status. When Armellya got to the feet of God she started to plead for the gnomes to be transformed to their previous state after greeting her maker and expressing her loyalty and love for her maker then God interrupted her plead for the gnomes return to their angelic state of being and lovingly said as you wish and solemnly request it shall be. Then God' angel removed her from his presence, and she returned to her castle and found the head gnome and noticed immediately that he was a beautiful angelic being. Now six of the seven seals had been opened and that was when God opened the heavens and gathered all his people together and gave them a safe passage into heaven both deceased and living. Now it was time for the seventh seal to open and that began with thirty minutes of silence in heaven followed by a severe shaking of the earth which was when the sealing of the underground and surface of the new earth would be sealed and nothing on the surface would remain. While in heaven all the pale ones had thee opportunity to be judged by God and make amends with Jesus followed with a feast at the table of God and the feast was prepared by the cherubs who were once gnomes, this was a grand reunion. At the end of the feast was when God revealed the purpose and responsibilities on the new earth in the new garden of Eden to the pale ones. All pale ones would find out who was to be earth bound and who would remain in heaven. Jesus led the earthbound pale ones back to the new garden of Eden then ascended into the heavens then the earth bound heavenly pale ones started to stabilize their domains to prepare for their purpose of being on earth. Jaden and Armellya wasted no time in starting to work on accomplishing their purpose of being on the new earth in the new garden of Eden and that was to replenish the population of pale ones into their society to breed with the community children and continue to replenish their population. Since it was the royal couples divine responsibility to replenish the population Armellya became with child back to back by Jaden and was promised by God to have easy pregnancies with painless and quick deliveries and she would be with multiple babies at a time every time and the number of babies at a time would vary. Now that some time had passed and there had been no intervention from God's angels or other divine beings God felt it was time to visit the pale ones and find out how they were doing psychologically as well as godly so he decided to send down his best and most trustworthy angel and that was his only beloved son Jesus. Now this leads us to the final book to the series of four called the transformation of life to legend which is the prequel to the series although it is the last book. Jesus went down to the new garden of Eden and remained invisible so there would be no interruption in the pale ones behavior and then he could get a reliable assessment of how things were going with the pale ones and the safety of the garden of Eden as well as the many creatures they shared the land with. It appeared that things were going very well the pale ones were functioning in a God-fearing manor and everyone was meeting their deadlines within their responsibilities and having time for themselves and their families and still meeting their evening curfews. The pale ones wee even still leaving the seventh day for rest, family, and mostly spending a lot of time in the religious hall to devote their time worshiping God as a community and giving some time religiously to one another. Jesus felt the love that everyone had for one another as they would even halt their own responsibilities to help one another during hard times then get back to their own responsibilities and work even harder to get their own things done by their deadline and actually accomplish it. As Jesus read the thoughts of every pale one, he was content in what they felt for one another they were not just a society they were a family that had a special love for one another that could not be wavered. Everybody took care of everybody then they would take care of their own needs this was how God wanted things to be in the original garden of Eden and it appeared that the new garden of Eden had the turnout that God was expecting and that really warmed the heart of Jesus to the point that he could not wait to get back to his father and report his findings even though God was all knowing and most likely already knew of the situation at hand it would still be awesome to make the report. When Jesus got back to heaven he was weeping tears of sentiment and God felt the compassion that warmed the heart of Jesus and that feeling flowed through to the heart of God and he was extremely pleased and as God continued to read the mind of his son Jesus he became emotional and content for he just knew that the pale ones were going to be just fine and would continue to please him and make him proud of them as their father and maker for God only provided the pale ones with some of what they would need to survive the world war three event it was up to the people to search for a way to save themselves and find a way to get along and it was up to the people to also find a love for one another so in short the people would either do what their current pattern had already shown which was be their own worst enemy and kill themselves off or follow the word of God and function with the word of God and live by faith to become as one and fight a fight of love for one another by treating each other as they would like to be treated and combine as one unit and follow the word of God. Even though the pale ones had a queen and king to rule over them they did not need it because they all made decisions as a whole and in all actuality the king and queen only served as a comfort factor because it was like a safety blanket for that was what they had been used to because during their time on the old world they always had a ruler to follow who would take responsibility for all the decisions made and in their old world it was referred to as a president however back in their old world days they did have kings and queens but not during the time that the pale ones that were there in the year twenty nine twenty five. In all actuality there had never been and would never be a situation where there would be a need for politics of any kind and without politics there would be no need for a ruler over the society and that was how it would stay. Moving on, there were many pregnant females in the community as well as in the royal family and the pregnancies were not just limited to the pale ones but was also found to be true in the mythological females and ordinary animal females, Jaden and Armellya thought that was wonderful and with

Jaden being a veterinarian he could help all the variety of animals if they were in need of assistance during their deliveries and it would be quite easy to get to them now that their body of water had been extended to the center of the commune. The construction worker pale ones were hard at work building more homes leisurely to make room for more pale ones to move into for some of the other children that had been born to the royal family and the commoners in the new garden of Eden would be ready to move out of their parents homes into their own domains then soon after they would pair up and those males and females would eventually start a family of their own. Another thing the angelic construction worker pale ones were working on was building a new school house for the children to go to officially learn from and now it was time to find volunteers to staff the school house that would be adequate to educate the children from the lowest grade on up to the highest grade and possibly some other education that would prepare the children for a variety of professions in the new garden of Eden which in human terms would be referred to as college or trade school but it had been seen as being important to have so the adult pale ones who already occupied those trades could take the children of those trades under their wings and provide them with some hands on training with supervision and eventually let those children work up to doing those said occupations without supervision and eventually move on to having their own business in that occupation in hopes of helping the adult pale one that assisted them in developing their trade by taking some of the heaviness of their load off of them and expanding the business by working with them and allowing them to have more free time to spend with family and friends and having some personal time to themselves as well then retiring when the time was right or working for their students when the time came for them to work lighter than what they had been working. The expansion of trades meant more building of those specific trade buildings and there were already more homes being built so there was a lot of work for the construction angelic pale ones and of course there was more need for certain other specialties such as paramedic pale ones, security pale ones, doctor pale ones, nurse pale ones, and other hospital staffing pale ones, and other specialty pale ones that they currently did not have out in the community work force to keep things running smoothly and there was not one profession that was better or more important than another they were all held equal as they each worked together to keep things running smoothly and all played an important role in keeping the pale one society moving toward a common goal and that was survival and happiness with lots of love and laughter basically in one word it would be unity. Now some of the individual pale ones that were abducted and changed on the old earth and nurtured were not on the new earth in the new garden of Eden, they were serving their purpose in heaven by having some sort of responsibility between the new earth's pale angelic ones and God, the responsibilities of all the angelic pale ones had shifted somewhat and some were slightly changed as some were dramatically changed for instance some were angels prior to the seventh seal being opened and after the opening of the seventh seal those who were not angelic were turned to angels and in the final transformation the angelic pale ones on the new earth were all made equals to one another as far as their angelic abilities were concerned. The chief was one of the individuals who was heaven bound and his duty was to oversee the actions of the pale ones from heaven where he was and be as a messenger as Gabriel had been and foreshadow the pale ones in regards of their actions at hand. The chief's wife Sharonna was also heaven bound and her appointed task was to keep up on the recording of the history of the old and new species of humans as well as to appear as her husband and Gabriel did to the pale ones to be as an advisor to the actions and ponderings of the pale angelic ones. Andrew was the leader of the earth bound cherubs, he was to keep them out of mischief by keeping them focused on their duties while Camillia his wife also earth bound was to assist her husband in watching over the earth bound cherubs however she was not to address them as her husband did she was to report to God if there were any foul play that involved the cherubs. Allen was also earth bound and was a paramedic that worked out in the commune with ties to the community hospital hall and he also had the task of replenishing the new earth with more pale ones with his wife, Michelle. Michelle was earth bound and with her husband was to follow God's orders and assist the royal couple in replenishing the new earth with more pale angelic ones as well as being the over seer for the royal nannies. Then there was Michael who was also earth bound he was a paramedic with ties to the community hospital and his wife Melanie with the job of being one of the royal nannies over the royal children and was to answer to Michelle if there were any positive or negative feedback. Now there is Jaden and Armellya the king and queen of the pale ones who had been chosen by God to be the primary producers of the angelic pale one species and were in return given the blessing to have uncomplicated pain free pregnancies and deliveries for her service to God. Then there was Matthew who was chosen to be the earth bound horse-back security person to assist with anything questionable in the new garden of Eden which God knew was never going to happen so Matthew would never be more than a handsome face on a mighty steed giving greetings and short positive conversations in the passing by of other pale ones. Matthew's wife Bridgette was his backup and was to support him by reporting to God's personal angel any serious transgression carried out by an angelic earth bound pale one. Most of the royal children were heaven bound as cherubs to serve God and fraternize with the other heavenly angels the new angelic three by three and angelic sextuplets born to the king and queen of the new garden of Eden remained on the new earth with their angelic pale parents. Jadellya also remained on the new earth as she was now the queen of the mini angels who made up the dinosaur tail with the mathematical configuration of their resting position appearing to be like that of a dinosaur tail which was now located in front of Jadellya's home in her front yard for all to visit and admire. Jadellya's husband Mordecai was a full-fledged angel of God who spent half of his day in heaven taking care of his appointed duties and the other half of his day on the new earth with his soul mate Jadellya and supporting her in her tasks on the new earth as well as spending private time with his dear wife, four children, and the dinosaur tail all of which he loved so much that those things filled him with the desire to live righteously and as if each day were to be his last with the life he had. One of Jaden and Armellya's young children Raziel was heaven bound and blessed to be an angel instead of a cherub and had become their guardian angel with the God given gift of visiting them daily under the cover of darkness with some limitations on the timing of the length of their visit and secrecy from anyone else knowing of their fraternizing. All of the pale angelic ones knew they were blessed by God and could not wish for anything else and could not figure out anything that they could possibly desire over what they already had but they knew if anything should come to their mind that God would make their desire happen in a wink of an eye. At this time, it was the dawn of a new day and the early risers were in the castles royal dining hall enjoying one another's company and some of Melanie's special brewed coffee and when Melanie had the big round table prepared for the breakfast hour she sat with the early risers and enjoyed a cup of her gourmet coffee and participated in the conversation that had been taking place while she had been busy serving the early risers. Eventually the rest of the royal family was arriving at the living room of the castle to await for Andrew and Camillia to show up and lead the group to the castles royal dining hall for the morning meal where they too could share their early day's plans and love for one another as well as to enjoy Melanie's fabulous meal that she always worked so hard to prepare for them. Right as Andrew arrived at the living room of his castle to retrieve the rest of the royal family and lead them to the great dining hall for breakfast there was an abrupt banging on the front door of the castle so the butler soared to the door and hastily answered the door and to his surprise found a naked man whom he was not familiar with standing there with a panicked expression on his face and before the butler could utter a word the stranger introduced himself and revealed that he was a merman and that his mate was in the lake right in the center of their commune and was having great difficulties giving birth to their child and that he had to carry her from the outer edge of the lake into the inner part of the lake. Jaden had heard everything that was said and rushed over to the door as he hollered to his wife Armellya to grab his black bag and meet him at the lake in the center of the commune and to put a rush on it then he hollered out to Allen and Michael to follow him immediately to the lake in the center of the commune so they followed the merman with temporary legs to meet up with his mate in a medical crisis. Armellya was right behind them with Jaden's black bag as she utilized her super human speed and agility to enable herself to keep up and serve the mermaid with medical aid to deliver her offspring as efficiently and safely as possible, hopefully mother and child will survive and be healthy. Finally the naked merman and the angelic pale ones arrived at the pond in the middle of the commune where the mermaid was and the merman with an alarming voice uttered to the angelic pale ones that his mate was now before them then Jaden replied that the two paramedics needed to lift the mermaid out of the pond and lay her on the bank so she would take on a human form for them to be able to deliver the baby so Allen and Michael did as instructed and immediately the mermaid's tail turned into legs so Jaden immediately barked orders for Armellya to be at the mermaids head to be able to guide the mermaid through what she needed to do and keep her calm and for Allen and Michael to take on the role that two nurses would be doing for the mermaid and her child, the merman was to stay calm and remain out of the way but if he felt the need to console his mate he was more than welcome to do so. Jaden immediately assumed the position that a birthing doctor would take and noticed that he had an arm and a leg protruding out of the birthing canal which was a very bad thing and there was possibly another bad sign for in the new garden of Eden there were always multiple births in the angelic pale ones and Jaden did not know if the same was true for the animals and the mythological creatures so he ordered Armellya to give him the hand held ultrasound machine and gel to him. Armellya left the mermaid's head and went to her side where the black bag was and took the hand held ultrasound machine and gel to Jaden who then performed an ultrasound on the mermaid and found that she was with twins and protruding was the arm of one twin with the leg of the other twin this meant that Jaden would have to perform an emergency caesarian section to safely deliver the twins and keep the mother safe also. It was unorthodox to perform the caesarian section out in the field but there was no way to save the twins and mother if they took the time to get a buggy to them and then transport them to the hospital hall then set up the operating room to do the necessary procedure so it will be done in the field then they will do the transport to the hospital hall after words and clean up the mother and babies. Jaden had Michael gain intravenous access while he set up the necessary medicines and proper tools for the upcoming procedure then once those tasks were complete Jaden ordered for Armellya to hold a sheet over the mermaid to make it so she could not see what Jaden was doing and Jaden also ordered the merman to stay at his mates head and console her adding that she would only feel some slight pressure but absolutely no pain and then Jaden explained that he wanted Armellya to stay sharp for anything that he may need her to do while he wanted Michael to quickly take out one baby and clip the cord then he wanted Allen to immediately remove the second baby and cut the cord and the two paramedics would take care of the babies after they delivered them and Jaden could remove the placenta and bag it up to take to the hospital hall to put into the incinerator to burn then close up the mermaids belly then once that was done Armellya could let down the sheet and if the mermaid was fine then Armellya would help her get cleaned up a bit then give the okay for the two paramedics to give the new mother her twins and reunite the father with his new family. Everything went according to plan and Jaden thought it was interesting that the merbabies were born with legs and once the merman was back in the water he took the twins and their legs turned into scales and fins then the mermaid got into the water and she too returned to her fish state and her stitching was no longer visible. The babies took to the water like they had the experience of their parents. The merparents thanked Jaden and everyone else that helped for their and their children's lives and revealed that they did not need to go to the hospital hall after all which Jaden actually agreed upon then the merparents requested that Armellya and Jaden be the children's godparents and for them to give the children their names and the royal couple were honored, this was the first delivery of anything that was not of an angelic pale one in the new garden of Eden and it was ever so special and would go down in the history of the pale ones for it was definantly something no angelic pale one and the animal both common and mythological would ever forget, this event gave a bonding between the mythological creatures and the angelic pale ones that would last forever and also gained a special trust between the common creatures of the wild between them and the angelic pale ones. Now all that needed to be done was to find out the sex of the children and name them so the mermaid made Armellya and Jaden aware that one of the children was a male and the other a female so Armellya uttered that the female child should be called Ever then Jaden spoke up and said that the male child should be called Percious. Jaden and Armellya stayed for quite some time watching their godchildren and casually speaking with the mercouple and then Jaden admitted that he and Armellya had heard a myth that they thought was untrue was that upon a merperson leaving the water their lower body transforms from that of a fish to that of a human and when they had set eyes upon the couple they found the theory to be true and the merman replied that it was true and it would allow them to mingle amongst the humans as long as no fluids were to be spilt upon them then Jaden suggested that maybe they could have a small house built along the pond's edge with some clothing made specifically for them so when they wanted to mingle with the angelic pale ones they could topping off his suggestion with an invitation to join the royal family in the castle for a meal and some family time and it was also suggested that they bring the children so they could frolic with the other children and maybe they could do that often for they were assumed to be one big happy family in the new garden of Eden no matter what the species then the merpeople replied that they liked the idea of having a home on the bank and the invite to join the angelic pale ones on land and they too believed that all inhabitants were of one family then Jaden replied then we will make it so, the angelic pale construction ones will start on it this day and the castles decorators will get together with the merpeople to make the home comfortable for the merpeople and that includes a nursery room for the children and the seamstresses will also make their way this day to start on some clothing that the merpeople would like. The merpeople were very thankful and expressed their love and dedicated service to the royal couple Camillia and Andrew then Armellya spoke up and informed them that everyone helped everyone that no one was above anyone and it was true that the population was just one happy family and everyone was there for one another when someone was in need and if the merpeople were ever in need just let the first pale one they encountered know and the situation would be under control within minutes. The merpeople were beside themselves to know that there were humans they could trust because in all previous history this was not so then Jaden informed the merpeople that they were not ordinary humans they were a different species and much more advanced although they were once just regular humans before they went through a transformation with a vaccination developed by two scientists that were in their colony and saved many lives and even risked their lives as well as the life of their only son to develop the vaccination and the merpeople were astonished then the royal couple told the merpeople that they could meet the scientists if they wished and the merpeople were excited at the thought to being able to meet those selfless individuals as they would love to talk about the sciences and the future of development because the merpeople knew of some thigs that could benefit the angelic pale ones that God would approve of for they got the ideas from heaven above and were told to share them with the pale ones but had to wait for the opportunity and now was the time. The discussion would wait for later in the day but for now the merpeople had others to contend with for their new bank house and preparation for the next meal at the royal castles dining hall with the rest of the royal family and Jaden had to go by the hospital had to burn the bag containing birthing matter that needed disposed of so Jaden and Armellya said their farewells for now and the royal pale ones expressed their love for the merpeople and the expression of love was returned by the merpeople and as things were tied up for now between the two couples and the birthing assistants the angelic pale construction working ones arrived to start on making the blueprints for the bank house so they could start the physical construction within the hour, this would be a quick job and the royal designer would be there shortly to aid in the décor and functionality of the placement of things in the bank house then the seamstresses would arrive soon so their job for the décor could be performed as well as the merpeople's clothing could be provided then they could show up for the very next meal time at the royal dining hall and formally meet the rest of the royal family and introduce them to the twins so they could dote over them and when the twins were old enough they could play with the royal children. The merpeople were fascinated with the angelic pale ones for God had revealed to them and the rest of the mythological creatures as well as the regular wild animals that a new breed of humans would be arriving and that they were to be sharing their land with the new breed but no more than that was revealed so the various animals were not sure if the new breed of humans would be friend or as before foe so they were slow to trust the humans and now they have become the best of friends as close family and indebted to the pale ones in one way or another, that was such a beautiful arrangement that none of them involved ever wanted to end. Now that Jaden and Armellya had been by the hospital hall he and Armellya were on their way to their castle to report to the king and queen as well as the rest of the royal family what had transpired at the pond with the strange naked man that had some sort of emergency and how beautiful things had been in the end and how the couple with their twins that they had just delivered would be joining them for one of their meal times and that it would really be a joy for everyone including the children. Upon revealing the news of the merpeople the royal family was excited to meet the merpeople and get to know them and welcome them into the family while they get to know them and share their own selves with them. The royal family questioned Armellya and Jaden if they would be observing and possibly helping things to run smoothly with the merpeople's bank home and other arrangements because they wanted the merpeople to be able to visit as soon as possible and the royal family also wanted to offer their expertise to help with their project so Jaden answered the family's concerns with a simple reply of letting them know that it would probably be best if they went to the bank and offered their expertise to help and introduce themselves and while thy did that they could create an opening for some bonding and show their love for the merpeople, the royal family felt that was a fabulous idea and spoke to one another to make arrangements with one another so they did not show up in groups and overwhelm the new family members so that was all worked out and everyone went their own way and kept an eye out for one another so no one stepped on any ones toes and all went smoothly. It was coming up on the lunch hour and everyone felt great for everyone had met the merpeople and offered their services and welcomed them to the family adding the invite to the next meal that they would be able to make and no one got in the way of anyone so the royal family had a great morning and was ready for a great evening the royal family gathered in the castles family room waiting for the king and queen to arrive and for the king to lead them into the castles dining hall and the family was also anxious to share their experiences with the merpeople with one another. Finally Camillia and Andrew had arrived and Andrew was ready to lead everyone into the castles dining hall for the lunch hour so everyone got seated faster than usual and went around the table sharing their encounter with the merpeople with one another and it was all so wonderful and Andrew felt that it was extremely possible that the merpeople would be joining the royal family for the dinner meal. The chief spoke through Andrew some words that meant complete sense in that he pointed out that the beach house should be made for all merpeople to make their transformation from merpeople to pale one human to mix into the combine and have their own homes in the community for when they wanted to stay for a while and that way they could have their own homes and all the merpeople could have a transformation place to change in and everyone agreed then Andrew replied to the suggestion that he and Camillia would go directly after the lunch hour that was nearly over and make the suggestion to the merpeople they had helped and run it by them and the rest of the royal family felt that to be the best thing to do and that way the merpeople would know that they had the king and queen blessing on joining the pale one society so Andrew verbalized that he and the queen would make it so and to consider it done. Melanie and her kitchen crew were starting to clear the big round table of the dishes that were no longer needed when Camillia and Andrew stood up from their chairs and announced that they were going about their way to go visit with the merpeople and the king and queen expressed their love to the rest of the royal family then they returned the expression of love then the royal pair flew off to the inner city pond. It was a good thing that Camillia and Andrew got to the pond's edge and landed when they did because the angelic pale construction worker ones were getting ready to start the construction so the royal couple were able to put a halt on it until they were able to speak to the merpeople and share their vision with them on making the bank house for all merpeople as a private changing area and building a house specifically for each one of them in the community for them to be able to stay on land for as long as they wanted to be there and the merpeople saw the suggestion as making more sense than the previous idea and they felt that the royal couples idea was far better than the previous idea and Andrew mentioned that the chief reached down to him from heaven and suggested the idea and all he did was to follow the chiefs idea so he could not take credit for the idea only for following directions and the merpeople giggled and replied that they had many of those situations themselves. So now what was to be done was for the angelic pale construction worker ones to make another blueprint for the bank house to fit all the transformations of all merpeople and for the decorator to make the bank house warm and inviting to the rest of the merpeople and for the seamstresses to provide a variety of clothing based on the assistance of the merpeople that were there then the merpeople that were there could work with the angelic pale construction worker ones to build them a home in the commune in an approximate area that they would like to be in and make the house to their expectations within limits and welcome them to the commune with a homecoming dinner. The king and queen spent quite a bit of time with the merpeople and their huge plans while squeezing in some personal conversation to break through the ice and get to know one another better and it was going great then when it came close to the lunch hour the king and queen advised the merpeople to join the royal family for the lunch hour back at the castle in the royal dining hall with the rest of the royal family with whom they already had the pleasure of meeting because they did know that merpeople needed nutrition also and they could have their chef make up something that was on their diet as well in the event they did not partake of what the angelic pale ones partook of. The merpeople did not have to think about the offer they blurted out together that it would be their honor to accept the offer and join the royal family for some nutrition and bonding time so the mermaid handed her twins, one at a time to Camillia so they could transform in her arms then the adult merpeople exited the pond and swiftly made the transformation from half fish half pale one to whole pale one then the royal couple gave the merpeople their capes to cover with and Camillia gave the twins back to their mother then Camillia informed the adult merpeople that when they got to the castle they would make a stop at their home before going to the dining hall to get some appropriate clothing for them so they would not have to feel like they stood out in an awkward way like being naked and the merpeople were openly appreciative of the offer and off they all went speedily by foot to the castle which was only minutes away. While heading to the royal couple's home the king and queen took the time to inquire about the merpeople's diet so they could assure that they would get the nutritional accommodations that they were used to and the merpeople replied that their meals were ordinarily seafood but that they wanted to try out the pale one nutritional choices and there was no need to have their staff prepare anything special for them so Camillia had an idea and that was for Melanie to prepare her seafood dishes to do a compromise in the menu selection and when Andrew and the merpeople heard Camillia's idea they liked the idea and felt it was thoughtful. With the conclusion of the menu preparation in consideration of having the merpeople over to enjoy the meal and royal family's company for the purpose of getting to know one another better and being welcomed into the family they had arrived at the castle where there was a door that led directly into the king and queens home so upon entering the mermaid followed

Camillia and the merman followed Andrew. Before doing anything for the mermaid Camillia called for a runner who she would send a message to Melany to prepare her seafood menu for the evening so they could make dinner comfortable for the merpeople that would be gracing them with their presence then one of the standby nannies to tend to the mertwins by getting them dressed appropriately and staying with them in the royal dining hall at the side of their parents. Now that Camillia and the mermaid could focus on what needed to be done for the mermaid Camillia could work with her on finding a dress that would fit right and add some accessories to go with the dress and they could do something flattering with her hair but not too much for this was not a formal event and within twenty minutes the mermaid was dressed and ready to attend the dinner gathering with the entire royal family, there was not much to be done for the mermaid was already so beautiful; the hardest thing to accomplish was to find a dress that did not take away from the mermaid's complexion of a rainbow glittery pale blue skin tone and knee length bronze hair that had a natural wave to it and finally it was a blessing that the mermaid was the same size that Camillia was. Now things for Andrew and the merman were quite a bit easier for the men's clothing were easier to fit and not as form fitting as the females were and the merman like Andrew were as an average size for a male so the merman was dressed and ready to sit before the entire royal family beside his wife at the big round table in half of the time it took his wife to be physically ready. The royal couple and merpeople all met in Camillia and Andrew's family room and everyone was shocked at how lovely the merpeople appeared and the children were so precious in their little outfits and now it was time to go to the castles living hall to lead the royal family into the royal dining hall so off the four of them went with the baby nurse and twins in tow. When the four of them and the nurse with the twins got to the castles family room and Andrew announced the arrival of the merpeople the royal family clapped and welcomed the new merfamily into the royal family and exchanged hugs and pecks on the cheeks as Andrew was sluggishly leading the group of pale ones into the castles dining room to get everyone settled around the big round table. After everyone welcomed the adult merfolk's into the family, they would one by one focus their attention to the twins and dote over them and finally as the end of the line came around the baby nurse had noticed that the twins appeared lifeless so she cried out for Jaden's quick response as she dropped the basket that the twins were in to the floor then she proceeded to take the twins out of the basket one by one then lay them out flat on their backs on the floor and by then Jaden was there and calling out for his helper, his wife Armellya to assist because he could tell that the babies were not breathing and upon feeling for a pulse on both of them he could not find a pulse on either baby and it was Jaden's job to find out if one twin was sympathizing for the other and if so which one was ill and if neither was sympathizing what was ailing them both so as soon as Armellya got to his side they each picked up an infant and started cardiopulmonary resuscitation and worked hard for several minutes before the twins responded rather slowly but when the twins did come around Jaden knew right away that the twins needed to be in a tank of water in the hospital hall where they would be where they had all the equipment to treat them however finding a tank of water to suffice the twins need for a lake like environment was going to be a challenge for the hospital hall was set up for angelic pale ones and not for the various animal life ordinary or otherwise. Jaden announced that the lunch hour should continue however him and Jadellya would be taking the twins to the hospital hall for extensive treatment and it would be up to the twins' parents if they wanted to stay at the big round table and converse with the whole royal family or accompany the twins at the hospital hall but it was Camillias suggestion to stay with the royal family for comfort and the hospital hall runner could send any news of change or the need for the merparents to go to the hospital hall so the merparents took Camillias recommendation and stayed with the royal family at the big round table and dine and gain support and would go to the hospital hall after the dinner hour with the royal family or if the hospital hall runner should bring news of their premature arrival to the hospital hall and the royal family would accompany the merparents and the merparents took Camillias input due to her previous experience with that sort of situation placed upon her more than once. While Jaden and the nurse with the twins were waiting for the stable boy to hitch up the wagon Armellya ran to her and Jaden's home to get his black bag and ran to rejoin them and by then the buggy was ready and Jaden, the twins, and the nurse rode in the back of the buggy while Jadellya rode up front to drive the team to the hospital hall and it was not a long ride as Armellya drove the team hard. Now at the hospital hall Jaden violently sprung off the back of the buggy and stormed into the hospital hall looking for the main doctor that he had worked beside for the longest time and who had trained and mentored him then upon finding the doctor Jaden blurted out the situation and needs and the doctor had the situation covered and exclaimed to Jaden to get the twins and meet him in the newly built wing of the hospital hall and they would be fine then Jaden questioned what new wing for Jaden had no clue that a new wing was built onto the hospital hall so the doctor ordered Jaden to stay by the nurses desk while he ran to get Armellya and the nurse with the twins and when they got back by the nurses desk for him to follow them when they passed him to go to the new wing and they would work together to help the twins so Jaden acknowledged the doctor as he ran past him and waited for several seconds while the doctor herded up the nurse the twins and Armellya and when they approached Jaden at the nurses desk Jaden prepared to dart at the end of the pack and follow them to the new wing of the hospital hall. As the small group of individuals hurried to the new wing of the hospital hall the doctor called back to Jaden that he would explain the circumstances of why the new wing was built and how it all worked in conjunction with the rest of the hospital hall and he would give Jaden a thorough walk through and training on the new technology that was there then the doctor closed his statement by letting Jaden know that the new wing was designed by Darren, Deanna, and Lloyd to accommodate the animals both ordinary and mythological since they were a part of their society and would possibly be needing services also. Finally in the new wing of the hospital hall there was a giant tank of water and it actually mimicked the lake so the doctor speedily striped the clothing off of the twins one at a time then gently placed the twins into the large tank again one at a time and quickly the twins transformed from simple pale ones into small merpeople then Jadellya and the nurse left the wing going back by the nurses desk and on out of the hospital hall to go back to the castle and wait for some news on how the twins were with the rest of the royal family, when everything was said and done Jaden could fly home and beat the curfew. The doctor stripped his clothing and replaced his clothing with what a normal human on the old earth would call a wet suit and diving gear that would allow the doctor to breath under water for quite some time then the doctor grabbed some wireless monitoring devices two at a time then he dove into the tank and gently placed the wireless monitoring devices onto the twins and the babies did not seem to mind having the wireless monitoring devices placed on them. The doctor then swam to the top of the tank and got out then stripped out of the diving suit and got into a robe instead of his clothing in the event that he would need to get back into his diving suit again to get to the twins in a hurry the doctor then went to some monitoring device panels and turned them on and started to read the monitors and making some acknowledging noises under his breath. Jaden noticed that the twins did look better once they were in the tank than they did out of the water and came to the conclusion that as young merpeople they could not be out of the water as long as an adult merperson for what ever reason and that would need to be looked into and for that reason they would need Deanna and Darren and possibly Lloyd so Jaden inquired with the doctor why he was not made aware of the upcoming construction of the new wing and its capabilities because of being a mainstream doctor of the hospital hall he should have been made aware of the new addition and its abilities and been put through the necessary training needs as soon as it became possible then the doctor advised Jaden that it was an order from God to put on the addition so it was done without question immediately and the completion was rapid so there was really no time to train anyone on the new equipment including the doctor for what little he knew on how to use the new equipment was the simple basics that even Jaden would have been able to figure out. This meant that the doctor and Jaden would have to learn together how to operate the new technology to its fullest extent while working with the twins and to respect the capabilities and jump in technology that they were given from heaven above then Jaden professed that most likely they may have some guidance from heaven above by at least one angel being sent down from heaven above for the learning of the most challenging of the technology so the twins would be safe as well as them and they knew that even if God did not send an angel there would be some divine intervention to assist them throughout the learning experience because God never left the angelic pale ones on their own during a deeply challenging event. Now that the doctor had the twins vital signs up on the computer screen and was ale to monitor them it was obvious that they were doing well and by visually monitoring the twins they were happily swimming about and frolicking with one another so now the doctor and Jaden felt it was necessary to call in Darren and Deanna for the welfare of the twins to determine what may have caused the twins to fall ill because it was the doctor and Jaden's theory that they could not handle being out of the water for very long.

The doctor left the new wing to find one of the hospital halls runners to retrieve the scientists to help with the twins and right next to the nurses desk was one of the hospital halls runners so the doctor got his attention and sent him off in search of Deanna and Darren with the message that the doctor and Jaden needed them to save the lives of twin babies of the merpeople who had fallen ill while being out of the pond and attending the dinner hour at the royal dining hall in the castle but they were now in the added wing of the communities hospital hall where there was a large tank that mimicked the pond please come urgently. The hospital halls runner had no problem finding Deanna and Darren for they were in the science hall doing their usual work and when the runner entered the science hall Darren welcomed him in and Deanna immediately questioned him if there was an emergency or if he was there for a social call then the hospital halls runner told the science couple what the doctor had told him to relay to the science couple then they hastily grabbed their emergency gear and fled the science hall right behind the hospital halls runner and within five minutes they were entering the hospital hall so the science couple continued to follow the hospital halls runner to the added wing right to the doctor and Jaden then the hospital halls runner handed Deanna and Darren off to the doctor and Jaden then turned and left heading for the nurses desk where he would stay for privacy purposes and the possibility of being needed again. Deanna and Darren swiftly scanned the huge wing and took in all the new sights then focused on the enormous tank and spotted the twins then questioned the doctor and Jaden about how they could possibly help so the doctor wasted no time in replying to them the rundown of what had transpired from the time that the twins were birthed to the time that they were at the hospital hall and placed into the lake like tank. Darren and Deanna came up with the same theory that the doctor and Jaden had come up with that the children could not be out of the water as long as their parents and the scientific couple even went on further to suggest that it had to be some sort of difference in how their lungs distributed oxygen throughout their bodies that while they were young their lungs were under developed and they were still very reliant upon their gills as to where their parents lungs were fully developed and able to work with oxygen distribution as a pale one would and their gills would not interfere but when the parents would reenter the lake their lungs would go into some sort of a dormant state and allow their gills to take over and for the young ones their bodies just had to be given time to adapt to the change that it may very well be a part of what the humans on the old earth would call puberty. The doctor and Jaden could not understand why they did not come up with that explanation which was so basic and easy to seek but this was something from the old world and things were far different than how it was before world war three and things like puberty did not exist anymore, so they thought but if that were true how would they know when puberty occurred and it would be safe for the children to be out of the water without it killing them. Now it was time to speak with the children's parents to try to get some background information on them and hope that they could remember their younger years so the doctors and science couple could estimate when it may be safe to try to bring the children out of the water with supervision of the doctors and if it was not time they could return them to the water and if it was okay they could go about their business but if it were somewhere in the middle the doctors could record the amount of time and try again at a later date then do the same routine again until they were free to stay out of the water for a long as they wanted like their parents. Darren and Deanna spoke up and offered their services to the twin's situation for further incidences if they should be needed and both doctors expressed their appreciation and love then the two scientists left the hospital hall to return to their science hall and resume their work there. In the meantime, the two doctors sent a runner to the children's parents who would lead the parents straight to them and begin the back history of them to hopefully help understand where they were at with the twins. Fifteen minutes later the hospital halls runner returned with the children's parents and the doctors greeted them and offered them a seat to sit in informing them that they needed to have a discussion and it may take some time so the adult merpeople sat down in the seats that the doctors had offered then Jaden let the parents know that their children were fine all they needed was to be back into the water and that the complication was simple. The doctor but into Jaden's slow introduction of the issue and requested to know if the merpeople remembered their time of coming onto the land for the first several times and how it had made them feel physically then the merpeople replied that they did remember their first several times and it was quite the ordeal then Jaden interrupted by asking how old they were in simple terms then the mermaid responded that she was still quite young as she was being rebellious to her parents because they had advised her not to go on land because she would not be able to survive after thirty minutes of being on land and she was approximately four years in angelic pale one years. The merman slipped into the conversation and said that he had no warning from his parents but he did try many times to go on land and it took many time before he was able to remain on land before he grew ill then Jaden questioned the merman as to how old he figured he was when he was finally able to stay on land without negative consequences then the merman replied that like his wife he was probably four years old in angelic pale one years. Everyone was silent for a couple of minutes then the doctor broke the silence by requesting that the merpeople reveal what occurred when they exited the pond before their fourth year of age then instead of answering the question the merpeople demanded to know what the information they had shared so far had to do with the episode that the twins had just experienced then Jaden tried to calm the parents by letting them know that the twins were perfectly healthy it was just that their lungs and gills were not mature enough to handle the transformation between land and water yet it would probably be fine once they met the age of what was known by the humans on the old earth as puberty and it appeared to be around the fourth year as kept in angelic pale one time. It was obvious that the merman was thinking and trying to process all the information that was just revealed but the mermaid was slightly alarmed and was not content with what was said therefore wanted to learn more to lead to how the episode could be avoided in the future and when or if it would pass and if so what was the medical explanation that allowed it to pass. Jaden took the mermaids hand into his and leaned forward then looked her straight in the eyes and assured her parent to parent that he understood her alarm and feelings of panic but that the issue at hand was nothing serious it was simply a growing pain that all merpeople would undergo and that it was a natural occurrence that at that point in time could not be reversed so he would try to explain it to her and her husband. The mermaid was eager to hear what the difficulty was that had made her babies ill and how the doctors had planned to make them well and keep the event from happening again so the mermaid took her hand from Jaden's and reached for her husbands who was wide open for holding his wife's hand then the two of them were waiting on Jaden's explanation so the doctor sat in a chair sat back crossed his legs then told Jaden that the parents of the twins were waiting to hear about how they were going to make their bundles of joy healthy so Jaden cleared his throat and began. Jaden started by giving a comparison of angelic pale one babies in saying that the last thing to mature in the intrauterine baby was the lungs and if they were delivered too early they would need a lot of medical assistance to survive while their lungs continued to develop and there was no guarantee that they would survive but in the merpeople the lungs being underdeveloped was normal because they also had gills that were fully developed and their tiny bodies were still learning how to breathe under water with their gills a pale one child would still be learning how to regulate their breathing with their lungs. In the case of the merbabies their gills were their primary way of breathing so the gills would be fully developed thus keeping them in the water their lungs still needed to mature and would do so over time as they were exposed to the air when they would bring themselves halfway out of the water to greet and conversate with passer bye's, the short periods of exposure would be just what the lungs would need to develop at a comfortable pace and by the time that a merperson met puberty as the old earth human would call it the merperson would be able to stay out of the water for as long as they wanted to because their lungs would be fully developed and part of their transformation was not just the changing of the tail to legs it was their source of oxygenation changing from the use of gills to the use of lungs and the whole method that goes within those processes then before allowing the merparents to speak a word Jaden added that by questioning them it appeared that their children would be able to walk about the commune without any ill affects by the time they were four years old per angelic pale one years. Now that Jaden had spoken all that he had to speak the doctor continued to sit back and silently read everyone's facial expressions and body language while Jaden patiently waited for the merparents to say anything but they sat without a thing to utter which gave Jaden nothing else to speak about so he turned his head toward the large tank and watched as the twins continued to swim about and play and with Jaden watching the twins it encouraged the merparents to glance over at their children and they too noticed how healthy and content the children were so deep down inside the parents knew that the doctors and scientific team were right about their diagnosis but they both shared the same inquiry, how were they to frolic amongst the angelic pale ones and leave their children behind? Jaden heard what the merparents were thinking through telepathy and he answered them by telepathy that they could spend the meal times with the royal family at the castles dining hall and take food to the twins and they could come halfway out of the water to feed then they could all go below the water and do whatever it was that they would do after feeding. Now that everything had been said about what was going on with the children the Doctor suggested that they return the children to the pond where they belonged and allowed the Merparents to decide if they wanted to spend meals with the Royal family and take food to the children after wards or stay in the pond with the children during meal times and feast with them as before the merparents informed the doctors that they would discuss the options between the two of them and let them know what their decision would be as soon as they came to a conclusion so on that note the doctor put on his wet suit and retrieved the twins and handed them over to their mother who refused to take them until she spoke to Jaden. Jaden was somewhat confused about the turn of events questioning how a mother of newborns could refuse to accept her children so he took her to a corner of the room away from the others and allowed for them to have some personal space to discuss whatever it was that she needed to disclose to him then she requested that she and her husband be allowed to use the royal capes again to return to the pond and they would each take a child to cover under the borrowed capes and return the capes on their very next visit then Jaden chuckled and replied it was the very least he could do for them so Jaden took his cape off and handed it to her then waltzed over to the doctor and requested for his cape to be given to the merman for them to get back to the pond without being totally naked but still be able to quickly get back into the pond and that the mermaid promised to return the capes on their very next visit to the castle and the doctor was honored that she found him worthy of asking a favor from him so he handed the twins to Jaden then he valiantly removed his cape and handed it over to the merman as soon as the merparents had their capes adjusted and tied in front at the neck line Jaden handed each one of them one of their children and the doctors proceeded to escort the merpeople to the hospital halls front doors and bade them a farewell for now as the doctors reminded the merpeople that they would be looking forward to their next encounter and not to be strangers. As the merpeople disappeared into the night things became quiet again. It was nearing the time for curfew so Jaden and the doctor left the hospital Hall going back to their homes after giving their farewells to one another and acknowledging a job well done. When Jaden returned to the Royal Castle the entire Royal family was eagerly waiting in the royal family room for his return to inquire about the merparents and their twins for the dinner hour had long since been gone and nobody was budging until they knew the merpeople were fine. Upon entering the castle Jaden noticed the entire Royal family conjugating in the royal family room when the royal family set eyes on Jaden they began to drill him on how the merparents and their twins were doing and if the twins would have a healthy long life as well as what they could do to help Jaden quieted down the crowd and once they were silenced Jaden spoke softly and explained that the twins lungs were under developed and this was normal for merchildren and when they reached the age of what is equal to an angelic pale one four-year-old which would be the merchildren's age of puberty they would be able to stay out of the water for an unlimited amount of time as are their parents. Jaden revealed that he did speak with the mermaid and merman about joining the Royal family at the big round table in the Royal Castle and spending some time together and taking food back to the children but the mermaid said she would have to discuss this with her husband and get back with him later to let him know what they had decided to do then the royal family was content for now but it would not be long before the royal family would be inquiring about what the merparents would be doing. Now that this was over the entire Royal family dispersed and went to their own homes to prepare for bed and wait for their mini angels to visit and it would not be long before the mini Angels would be there then the pale ones would get a couple of hours of sleep. It was now time to awaken to start a new day with new things to come so the Royal family prepared for a new day and trickled down to the Royal family room to wait for Andrew to lead them to the Royal dining Hall everyone got settled in their chairs and Melanie began to have her crew bring the breakfast nutrition out to the table when suddenly the Butler came through the archway announcing the arrival of the merpeople Camillia and Andrew stood up from their chairs and sauntered over to the merpeople and they expressed their love for the merpeople and greater appreciation for their arrival Melanie immediately prepared two more places at the big round table for the merparents then Melanie walked them over to the table from the archway of the room and got them seated. Melanie once again went back to preparing the big round table while the Royal family began to question the merparents about how the twins were doing the mermaid spoke up and replied that the twins were doing great and that one would never know that they had ever taken ill from being out of the water for too long and that if the doctors had not have somehow figured out that their illness was as simple as from being out of the water and their lungs not being developed enough to handle the oxygen delivery that the gills could handle and their lungs would soon be able to handle the transformation in time the twins would have died and now every merbaby could be safe and little to the angelic pale ones surprise there was a large number of merpeople in the lakes the royal family just had not set eyes on them yet because the merpeople had not fully trusted them yet but through the relationship being developed between that particular family of merpeople and the royal family the rest of the merpeople were becoming more trusting of the angelic pale ones thus becoming more brazen about showing themselves to the rest of the various species of inhabitants of the new garden of Eden including the angelic pale ones it was just that the angelic pale ones had to be more observant to be able to spot them and it would be advisable to greet them from afar at first but it was a must that they acknowledged them to show the initiative to wanting to develop a relationship with them then the other merpeople would move in closer and closer until eventually they would be at the bank and communicating with the angelic pale ones verbally. The breakfast meal had now been all set out and Melanie had seated herself down at the big round table to join in the rest of the conversation, even though she was not an active participant in the conversation previous to now due to performing her responsibility of getting the breakfast meal out to the royal family she did hear the whole conversation floating about from family member to family member and now she could appropriately incorporate her feelings and ideas amongst the royal family and that she certainly did. One of the first things Melanie did was make the request to go to the lake with the merparents to present the breakfast meal to the twins and make sure it fit their taste and if not she would race back to the castles kitchen to fix up something that was certain to make their taste buds and stomach's do the happy dance and the merparents responded saying that it really was not necessary but if it would make her happy than she was more than welcome to go along and that she was more than welcome to feed the twins herself then Melanie questioned how to feed the twins because to her it was obvious that the twins did not feed as an angelic pale one infant did. An angelic pale one infant would nurse breast milk from the bosom of the mother or from a bottle from the nurse maid as to where the infant of a mermaid seemed to eat from the hands of themselves or from the hands of another merperson and they would eat solids and get their liquids from the water that they swam in as well as from any of the solids that may have had any liquids to offer. Once the discussion of feeding the twins was settled Jadellya changed the topic of conversation from the feeding of the twins to the housing on land for the merfamilies and shared her curiosity of why the angelic construction worker pale ones could not build the merpeople's homes close to the water's edge for a quick transfer from the lake to their room on land because it was already known that the infants could be out of the water for up to a half of an hour and with the new homes close to the water's edge it would not take near that long to get the infants transferred from home to home and just build large water tanks into the walls of the babies nurseries and make a beautiful décor with the tanks so when they were not in use for the children they would still look nice like a deliberate piece of decor and make the room resemble their home in the water and then if the merpeople had any more children they would already have the tanks and could build another nursery for the older child or children and keep the original nursery for the newborns. Jadellya's suggestion had created a long silence in the dining hall as every one in the dining hall was mulling the idea around in their heads and putting some deep thought into the idea and sincerely trying to add up all the pros and cons to figure out if it would really work without creating any issues for the infants or parents and if there would be any space problems with building so many homes in the area of the pond then the head angelic construction worker pale one broke the silence by suggesting that there be added a couple of more ponds to the community since the community was to be added to anyway for more homes for the angelic pale one coming of age to move out on their own and more shops and places of work being built that it would be a grand idea to put in a couple of new lake access areas and that would solve the problem of having too many houses in one area causing a congestion of buildings in one small area then the rest of the royal family acknowledged the suggestion followed by another session of silence for everyone to process the new idea then after ten minutes or so Darren broke the silence this time by sharing his concern that even though the plan to expand the number of lakes and different types of buildings there presented a complication and that was how to provide enough water and lake inhabitants of all sorts that would be necessary to make the lakes inhabitable then Andrew spoke up immediately and replied that God had always blessed them in the past when they were in need and usually before they could ask for the blessing so it was his suggestion that they all consult with God and find out if he would give his blessing and assist with the project or at least show them another way to go about making it safe to make the merpeople a part of their society without having to separate their infants from them for any amount of extended time and to top off the situation at hand and to wrap the situation up Jadellya got the attention of the royal family and explained that it would be a benefit to have every merpeople's home equipped with a nanny for each child just as was done for all the angelic pale ones and immediately, the rest of the royal family agreed with the plan set before the table so everyone agreed to consult with God as individuals and report to one another when they received any sort of answer or sign. Everyone continued with the consumption of their breakfast meal and had decided to retreat to the confine of their homes to call upon God for an answer to their prayers which was specifically an answer to their question of how to handle the situation of the merpeople's homesteads and security of the merinfant's medical stability so upon the end of the breakfast hour the entire royal family urgently verbally expressed their love for one another then darted to their homes to fall upon their knees calling upon God in favor of the merpeople and expecting some guidance in their favor. Melanie apologized the merparents about not being able to feed the twins this time but was glad to reschedule for another time for the moment at hand was for the better of the merpeople as a whole and it was imperative for her to address that at the moment than to just feed the twins and the merparents understood and replied that it was fine and they understood the emergence of the situation then went their way to their home to summon God as well. To no one's surprise the archangel Gabriel appeared to each angelic pale one of the royal family members as well as the merparents and relayed the same message to each and every one of them that the merpeople were in good hands with the angelic pale one royal family and to go ahead with their plans to make more lakes and homes in the community for them and God would make the lakes favorable for them to live in and would also bless the makers of the homes to build them in the likeness that would best suit them for the merpeople this was a grand blessing for the angelic pale ones to be able to partake in was even more of a blessing for the merpeople to receive and upon the end of the visit with Gabriel the archangel the royal family members started to call upon one another to reveal their visions of Gabriel to one another not yet realizing that the others had been blessed with the exact same blessing until they were all in the royal family room then they all were led into the royal dining hall by Andrew while Melanie brewed some of her special coffee for the royal family to enjoy while comparing their visits from Gabriel the archangel with the others and soon the coffee was finished brewing so Melanie brought out the coffee dishes and set everything up followed by all of the fixings to the big round table then joined the rest of the royal family members to compare her experience with the others and they were all exactly alike. Now everyone had their cups of coffee prepared and ready to drink so Andrew stood up from his chair and raised his coffee cup high up into the air and proposed an afternoon toast to the merpeople that their homesteads were a go and they would be close members of the royal family yet then the rest of the royal family engaged in the toast and all was well. Everyone had a busy afternoon as they saw it and they were ready for the unusual challenge so Melanie started her crew with the makings of the noon hour as she had the kitchen staff preparing the lunch hour meal in a hurry but to make it a celebratory meal with bonus dishes for the merpeople for this was a new dawning of an extraordinary relationship between the merfolk's and the angelic pale ones, species to species and it was the hopes of all involved so far that more of the merfolk species would come forward to join the combination of species for a life long relationship. Now that the lunch hour was at hand the royal family and merparent's were ready to consume their meal and move on to the construction of the new lakes and housing for the merfolk's and other angelic pale ones and with that Andrew called for the angelic head construction worker pale one to be brought to the castles dining hall immediately to join the royal family for the lunch hour and discuss the new construction project so it could take shape as soon as possible. No sooner than one of the castles runners heard the request he darted out of the castle and in a flash had returned with the set target and introduced the angelic head construction worker pale one into the royal dining hall then Andrew offered him a seat advising him to join them in consuming the lunch meal so he thanked the royal couple for their kindness then questioned them on how he could serve them then Andrew began to explain the situation with the mertwins and how the royal family wanted to keep the merfolk close but not at the expense of the mertwins or any other merinfant for that matter then Andrew went on to explaining that they had been visited by Gabriel the archangel getting the go ahead from God on the construction of several new ponds in the commune and building of homes specifically for the merpeople and homes for more angelic pale ones as well as more buildings for the various places of work that would be expanding then the angelic head construction worker pale one replied that it would be his honor to do the building of all the various types of dwellings that were in need to be done and he would start with the planning of what was to be where which included the lakes then after the royal approval he would start with the floorplans of the merfolk homes then move on from there and would be in close contact with the royal couple at all phases of the construction then he specifically and sternly stated that he was going to seek God's guidance throughout the entire process then added that he trusted that the royal couple would be doing the same and they assured the angelic head construction worker pale one that they had already sought God's approval and guidance and would continue to so. Now that they had an understanding that allowed them to have a verbal agreement the work would begin once they left the royal dinning hall and to wrap up the conversation the angelic head construction worker pale one informed Andrew that he was going to break his enormous staff into groups to do the work so things would run even more smoothly and quite a bit speedier then Andrew and Camillia whole heartedly thanked the angelic head construction worker pale one then the rest of the royal pale ones offered their services to the effort and they were told by the angelic head construction worker pale one that he would keep their offers in mind and would not be shy in requesting their help if needed and finally everyone had completely finished their lunch meal so everyone expressed their love for one another then scurried out of the royal dining hall to go about their busy afternoon and try to get as much done as possible. While the royal family and the angelic head construction worker pale one were all going their separate ways to start getting things started Melanie caught up with the merparents with a to-go package for the mertwins to get some of the lunch meal that they had gotten so the merparents took the package and gratefully thanked Melanie for thinking about the children then they went about their way so they could feed their children the fresh food and Melanie continued on in doing her job in the castles royal dining hall by cleaning off the big round table and resetting it for the dinner hour and overseeing the kitchen staff in the beginning stages of the dinner meal which started out with constructing a menu and that was to also include dishes specifically for the merpeople which were going to be first time recipes for the royal kitchen crew to prepare but they viewed that as a fun challenge rather than a bothersome task. While everyone was getting hard at work the commune was louder than usual due to more things going on than what was normally going on the noises just blended together so no one noise was heard over any other noise so it was no surprise when the merparent's panicked screams of horrific despair went unnoticed, it was their children they were lifeless on the bank and there was no way of knowing how they got that way and no one stopped to help because no one had heard their cries for help so the merman instructed his wife to keep the children wet and he would go for help then he darted off in the direction of the royal castle in search of the king and queen for some sort of help even though he was not sure what they could do for them and within five minutes he ran into Allen and Michael who were leisurely traveling on horseback to the hospital hall from the royal castle and when they spotted the merman in what appeared to be in a distressed mode they instantly stopped their horses to check on him and that was when he started to ramble on about his twins but he was not making much sense so Allen pulled the merman up on the back of his horse then Allen and Michael ran their horses hard to get to the lakes edge where they found the mermaid slumped over her twins crying hysterically and before the two angelic paramedic pale ones could get their horses to a complete stop they slid off of them and immediately each medic grabbed an infant as they were doing primary assessments then realizing they were not breathing they jumped into the water clothes and all then submerged the infants into the lake and proceeded to do cardiopulmonary resuscitation which they had never done on a creature that relied on gills to breathe but they were quickly running out of options so they just did the best that they knew how and after a few minutes the infants began to show signs of life then they fought to break away from the hold that the medics had on them so they released the infants and they healthily swam about rubbing around the medics legs as if to say thankyou and show their appreciation for what they had done then the mermaid splashed into the water grabbing her twins around their waists and questioning them as to how they managed to get upon the bank and the twins immediately stopped squirming and made some siren sounds that Allen and Michael could not make sense of because they had not learned how to interpret merfolk language or speak it yet but they as well as the rest of the royal family knew that it was important to learn how to communicate with the merfolk in their language anyway according to the mermaid the twins were playing with some of the other merchildren when another mermaid came to collect her child and used her tail to smack the twins out of the way so she could snatch up her child almost as if she did not approve of her child playing with the twins and when her tail hit the twins it was so powerful that it landed them on the bank and because the landing was so intense they did not have the strength to pull themselves towards the bank to be able to roll into the water and none of the other merparents that had witnessed that went to their rescue so the children were obviously left to die as if the other merpeople were shunning them for fraternizing with the angelic pale ones but they did not understand why because the angelic pale ones were friendly and there to cohabitate and help with anything that was needed and were going out of their way to make it comfortable to have the merpeople live on land with them for when they felt the desire to walk amongst the angelic pale ones then when the mermaid had made that knowledge clear to Allen and Michael they knew that was something they must report to the king and queen immediately so they could get to the lake and try to find the rest of the merpeople and make an attempt to help them understand their feelings of love and friendship for them and try to let them know that they too are welcome on land and that they were more than willing to build them a home on land that would have the special accommodations for their children to be safe out of the lake then wait for the merpeople's response and hope that they would reply in English if they could. After making sure the twins and their parents were okay Allen and Michael let the twin's parents know that they must rush to the royal castle to further handle the situation that nearly took the lives of the twins and that it was important to not give up until some sort of positive arrangements between the other merpeople and the land dwellers was accomplished then the medics mounted their horses, turned them around, and rode hard for the royal castle. Now at the castle the medics slid off their horses before they were even at a complete stop and the stable boy swiftly took their horses and headed toward the barn while the medics rushed into the castle and abruptly demanded that the butler take them to the king and queen immediately it was urgent and life threatening so the butler replied follow me then took off darting down the castles corridor the trio stopped at the doorway of the king and queens door that led to their home then the butler harshly knocked on the door like there was a great fire in the building or something so Andrew rushed to his front door and opened it asking what the emergency was then the butler announced to Andrew that Michael and Allen had a life threatening situation that needed to be dissolved as soon as possible then Andrew invited the medics into his home and thanked the butler telling him to go to Melanie and let her know that the king had sent him for some tea and biscuits then as the medics were entering Andrew's home the butler was heading up the hallway on his way to the royal dining hall. Jaden and the medics sat down in the royal day room as Andrew called out for Camillia to join them for some emergent business and in a flash without word Camillia appeared out of nowhere and took her seat at the right side of her husband then Michael proceeded to inform Camillia and Andrew of the events that had occurred on the pond's bank with the twins and how they responded to the mermaids cry for help and so on then Andrew's mind and heart grew to an extremely heightened level of concern but prior to any declaration Andrew mentioned to the medics and his wife that only Michael spoke and Allen stayed silent so now Andrew wanted to hear Allen's account of the occurrence of the twins and the mermaid so Allen spoke in his own words of the event from his own perspective and it was like hearing Andrews account all over again just with a different set of words but the important details were right on target. Andrew checked with Camillia on how she felt about the situation at hand and how she felt it should be dealt with if she thought it should be dealt with at all then Camillia spoke and with a soft yet firm voice she declared that the situation must be dealt with because there was not going to be crime in the land of grandeur on the new earth in the new garden of Eden and as far as she felt that incident was an evil attempt of murder that was foiled by Allen and Michael being in hearing distance of the merman and him being in the right place at the right time as far as Camillia was concerned that incident needed to be reported to God before doing anything else because they needed God's guidance for how to handle the situation correctly and everyone else had not looked at the outlook in that way because they were heavy at heart but they were thankful for Camillia's level headedness and all agreed to pray and speak of the incident to God and Camillia revealed that she was going to send for Gabriel the arch angel then Allen and Michael left the royal castle where the home of the royal rulers home was to go to their own homes and immediately Camillia and Andrew summoned for Gabriel the archangel to come before them for they had a terrible situation that needed to be handled by heavenly influence then several minutes after pleading their case God sent down Gabriel and he stood before the royal couple asking how he could assist them. Andrew and Camillia explained to Gabriel the relationship they had with the merparents and their twins so he had a back ground information for reference to better understand where they stood with the problem they were about to reveal to him then Andrew explained the terrible incident that had just occurred at the lake and stated that was why they summoned him because they felt that was a deliberate act of harm on the twins and the consequence would have been death for the twins and it was possible that the other mermaid may have known that and Andrew and Camillia did not want murder occurring in their land so they felt that divine intervention was necessary because trying on their own to assure that all the angelic pale ones wanted was to have a friendly relationship with the merpeople and allow them the opportunity to live on land comfortably for however long at a time and to make it safe for their infants was not something they felt they could relay to them for it seemed that they saw the angelic pale ones as enemies and they were shunning the merfamily that befriended the royal family due to their own selfish misunderstandings. Gabriel the archangel revealed to the royal couple that he already knew of the dilemma and God had sent him down with strict orders on how to handle the situation so the royal family was to stand down for now and they were not to have any contact with the merfamily unless they went to the royal castle and if there were to be any contact with any merpeople at the lake it would be only at the discretion of himself so Camillia and Andrew agreed to the terms and let Gabriel go so he could start on his appointed business. Gabriel went to the lake and transformed into a merman when he got into the lake and began to swim out where the merpeople primarily stayed and when he got there he did let them know who he was and that he was sent down by God to deal with an incident that had occurred then he proceeded to explain what the incident was and how it affected not just the merparents but the angelic pale ones also and that opened the way for Gabriel to disclose the involvement of the angelic pale ones with the particular merfamily that was being shunned and how that was not going to be tolerated any longer by God, there were going to be consequences and therefore the rest of the merpeople needed to start to investigate the angelic pale ones and make an honest attempt to get to know them and see them as they really were because they were a peaceful people and only wanted to share their lives with all creatures on the new earth in the second garden of Eden. The merpeople had a lot of questions about the angelic pale ones that they had asked Gabriel and as speedily as the merpeople inquired Gabriel gave his reply which was honest and positive. The question and answer session between Gabriel and the merpeople made the merpeople want to go and speak to the angelic pale ones after they approached the particular merpeople they had shunned and apologized and asked their forgiveness but they also wanted the original merfamily to accompany the group of merfolk's to greet the angelic pale ones. Gabriel felt that things were settled but he did have one more thing to address with the multitude of merpeople and that was that he wanted them to speak with the king and queen of the land to hear what the accommodations were going to be with the ability to stay on land for extended periods of time and to be accepted as family as equals to the royal family so after Gabriel spoke his final words he swam to the lakes edge and climbed out and got his legs back then his wings back and flew into the heavens. Now the work towards repairing things between the original merfamily and the angelic pale ones was now up to the group of merpeople so they got together and sought after the original merfamily and it did not take long to find them and upon approaching them they spoke in their language and apologized for their harmful acts and bade their forgiveness then pled for their assistance in meeting the angelic pale ones to hopefully have the kind of friendship with them that the small merfamily had with them and the small merfamily agreed to help them meet the angelic pale ones after they accepted their apology then the small merfamily swam to the lakes edge where the angelic pale ones met them at and the rest of the merpeople were there also so the merman that was from the small family that was close to the royal family climbed out of the water onto land and retrieved the cloak that he still had and put it around himself then left the lake side to go to the royal castle in search of the king and queen. As the merman was turning to leave the lake in search of Andrew and Camillia the patriarch of the merpeople firmly called out to the merman before he took a step away from the lake so he turned toward the lake and acknowledged the patriarch of the merpeople then the leader of the merpeople called the merman closer to himself and held out something towards him which he could not quite make out until he was within hands length to the patriarch of the merpeople then the merman knew without a shadow of a doubt that the patriarch was handing him the leadership identifier which was a grand necklace sent from the heavens and had been blessed by God so the merman knew that the tribe of merpeople were serious about becoming one with the angelic pale ones and as the merman was gently taking the necklace from the patriarch he whispered to the merman that he wanted to have the royal leaders before him post haste then the merman replied that he would work as speedily as his body and mind could allow then he turned and sped away. No more than eight minutes later the merman was at the heavy front door of the royal castle and knocking on the door impatiently waiting for the butler to answer his summoning and within two to three minutes the butler did open the door and greeted the merman asking what his business was and how he could assist the merman then the merman replied that he needed to speak with the king and queen on an emergent situation so the butler invited the merman inside and instructed the merman to follow him then the butler made room for the merman to enter then he closed the heavy door and turned to go further into the castles various rooms and the merman followed the butler as he picked up speed while going deeper into the castles structure then finally they were at the kings office room. The butler knocked gently on the door of the kings office room then Andrew called out to enter the room and the butler opened the door and let Andrew know that the merman was there with him on urgent business so Andrew urged the butler to let him move on into the office room and take a seat so that was just what occurred then the merman realized that Camillia was in the office room also and the merman sighed a sigh of great relief and Andrew noticed the merman's relief upon sighting Camillia's presence and questioned the merman's reason for his visit then the merman showed the necklace to the royal couple and right away Andrew and Camillia knew what it was so Camillia asked the merman how he had gotten the token of leadership so the merman explained the great break through with the merpeople wanting to put the past situations behind everyone involved and start anew to having a fresh start at an eternal relationship that was made up of love and trust so the patriarch of the merpeople sent the necklace to show his intent of peace, trust, love, and loyalty to the royal leaders of the new garden of Eden on the new earth then the merman reported that the merpeople expected that they may go immediately to the river bank to speak words of peace and clarity of both sides intent to be of one family. Andrew looked at Camillia and Camillia looked at Andrew then they both nodded their heads in an affirmative way then stood up off of their chairs and informed the merman that they were ready to go when he was ready for them to go so the merman thanked the royal couple and led the way out of the office room to the front door of the royal castle to go directly to the lake's edge and meet up with the merpeople especially with the patriarch of the merpeople. It was only approximately a ten minute walk from the royal castle to the lakes edge but Andrew felt a need for a dramatic arrival and for a lessened arrival time so he informed Camillia that he was going to transport the merman but she needed to follow his lead and they were going to fly to the lake and land right at the lakes bank edge where he would set the merman down safely then they could be right in the middle of the merpeople where they could do their introduction and get right down to business in a kind way and get to know each one of them and have some laughs along side of their business. Camillia did not like to fly because it was essentially a way of demonstrating their royal status in a bold way and she felt that it was essentially separating them from the other angelic pale ones in making it obvious that they were of a higher rank in the society they had when they wanted to make everyone equal to one another and show that it took everyone together to make their society to function smoothly and that was why everyone had different abilities and talents for what their specialties were therefore the only time Camillia would fly without hesitation was if it was a matter of life or death where some species in the new garden of Eden needed medical attention immediately or some situation just as serious as that but she agreed to follow her husbands request and put her heart into it so Andrew explained to the merman how he was going to hold onto him and the merman understood how he was to stay still but strong in the arms and to keep his body straight for a safe flight so now it was time to take flight. Now in the sky as the angelic pale ones call the surface of the underground portion of the old earth that sits above them the angelic royal pale ones and the merman flew for about two minutes then they prepared for landing by trying to spot a safe area where there were no merpeople that would get hurt by coming into contact with their fluttering wings as they landed and there did not seem to be such a space then the mermaid who was the mother of the twins figured out what the royal couple needed as they hovered over the lakes bank so she started to clear a spot for one of the angelic royal pale ones then once one of them landed then they could clear a spot for the other one to land. The first to land was Andrew due to the merman he was holding because he needed to be on land soon before he became fatigued so much that he could not maintain his rather rigid posture which could become somewhat dangerous for him and possibly for Andrew. Immediately the merman helped his wife the mermaid clears a space for her to land so she would not get injured while landing or become exhausted and simply fall to the ground which any of those situations could potentially harm some of the merpeople. Finally, there was enough space created for Camillia to land and she took the opportunity to land rather speedily before the space closed up by accident and who would know how long it would be before she got a clearing to land again. Camillia landed just fine then all the merpeople gathered around the royal couple, some on land and some in the lake that were partially on the bank this gathering of the merpeople was amazing to the royal couple for they were not aware of just how many merpeople were in the lakes Andrew started the communications and everyone grew silent then Camillia leaned over to her mermaid friend and questioned her as to weather or not the merpeople understood their language and the mermaid replied that they understood all languages that the old earth had ever had and then some which intrigued Camillia but that was not the time to inquire about it. Andrew first introduced himself and his wife and let the merpeople know that they were always available to the merpeople and wanted them as extended family that they were more than welcome to walk amongst the angelic pale ones anytime then Andrew got into the elaborate details of how the angelic pale ones were building homes that would accommodate them on land and a bank house to make their change comfortably before traveling about so they may be comfortable and not feel out of sorts amongst the angelic pale ones and how they were going to build more lakes around the city as it expanded and more merpeople homes as well. The merpeople were surprised at how the angelic pale ones were so welcoming to them and also how sensitive they were to their needs things were going well and all involved were content with their first meeting so Camillia made her statement which was more of a promise or treaty to the merpeople that they all were more than welcome to call upon them for anything at any time for any need or desire that they wished because as queen and king of the land it was their responsibility to assure everyone's happiness and safety so after making that clear Camillia virtually made the merpeople promise to go to her and Andrew with their needs and desires for that was their responsibility for the royal couple to be able to assist them. Now that introductions and clarifications had been done the royal couple announced that they had other business to attend to but they wanted the merpeople to meet them at the same place at the dinner hour so they could eat with them and the royal couple would supply the meal to share with the merpeople and supplying to meal would be the royal couples honor so the merpeople obliged then the merpeople expressed their respects for the royal couple and all angelic pale ones then the royal couple returned their respects to the merpeople and everyone went about their business. Within seconds of everyone leaving the bank the angelic construction worker pale ones arrived at the bank to start putting up the bank house for the merpeople to make their transition easily and comfortable and soon the seamstresses would arrive and start on the necessary needs of the house within their scope of duties and of course clothing for the families then the décor personnel would arrive and make the bank house appear as an extension of the lake. This process intrigued the merpeople as they observed the process of the building of the lake house and all of the hard work that the manual labor created as well as how many different types of specialists had to be a part of the process and that gave the merpeople a deeper appreciation for the angelic pale ones the feeling of love that the angelic pale ones must have had for them was amazing for they had not even met them when they had planned on doing the project but they did know the merpeople were out there somewhere The merpeople swam back out to their under water metropolis and held a meeting over how the angelic pale ones had trusted that the merpeople were of godly breeding and trust worthy and they had love in their hearts for the merpeople already so they decided that they must do something that showed trust and expressed love for the angelic pale ones as well and it needed to be done quickly so it could be presented at the dinner hour which was closing in speedily. The head of the merpeople recommended to make a crown for the king and queen of the angelic pale ones as he knew they did not have one and it was only fitting for them to have one, the kings would be a masculine version as the queens would be feminine. Those who worked with the king and queen as personal advisors and helpers would get special jewels to wear according to their attire such as the medics would have medical like jewels to pin onto their uniforms the security would get the same pins to place on the uniforms but they would be police type pins and the doctors would get pins as well but those of a doctor even the rest of the royal servants and workers as time went on they would spread the compliment to the rest of the community by making them simple necklaces but the royal family had to have theirs that evening at the dinner hour so as soon as the leader of the merpeople finished his statement the rest of the merpeople got to work for each merperson already knew who was to do what. Back at the royal castle Andrew hung out in the castles family room waiting for Camillia as she approached Melanie in the castles kitchen and informed her that the her and Andrew were going to eat at the bank with the merpeople and that her and Andrew were going to provide the meal so if it was possible for her to make a dinner meal for the merpeople to be taken down to the bank that would be greatly appreciated then the rest of the royal family would have to excuse them from the big round table and if she could would she give the royal family their apologies for not being there and let them know why then Melanie replied that she would have no problem in making a meal for them and the merpeople and a separate meal for the rest of the royal family and she would give the rest of the royal family their apologies for not being with them at the big round table with the reason as to why and Camillia hugged Melanie and thanked her then they expressed their love for one another and both girls went on their separate ways to attend to their business. Camillia made her way to the castles family room to get back to Andrew then they headed to their home but when they entered their home Gabriel the archangel met them in their family room with some information from God. Andrew and Camillia greeted Gabriel then questioned him as to what they could do for him then Gabriel replied that he was there on behalf of God and it was in reference to expanding the new garden of Eden. Andrew and Camillia sat on their couch and offered a seat to Gabriel so he too sat and the conversation continued with Gabriel informing the royal couple that God has commanded that the new garden of Eden should be expanded in every direction and continue to expand at a reasonable pace that the angelic pale ones could work with that would not cause any harm or discomfort to them until the entire underground surface was covered and the doorway to the tunnel leading to the surface of the old earth would be sealed and covered with plush greenery so it would no longer exist and the angelic pale ones would continue to replenish the new earth at a slower pace for they were not to have an overpopulated issue like the old earth had and if it was necessary God would pick individuals that had the pleasure of being parents and make them barren so that those who had not had the experience could have it once with giving birth to one child then become barren so the newborns could grow up find their mate then experience parenthood also and the cycle would continue. The royal couple acknowledged Gabriel then Andrew spoke up that he was in conflict with expanding the commune in every direction due to the destruction of the forest and the wild life being displaced both regular and mythological then Gabriel cut into Andrews words sharply saying that all the angelic construction worker pale ones had to do was to follow God's building plans and those would be sent down by one of God's angels to the royal couple since they were to monitor the building and progress therefore the regular animals and mythological creatures would still have an abundance of their natural habitats. It was extremely important to the royal couple that the various animals and mythological creatures have their homes also beings that they were friends of the angelic pale ones and even if it were not so they still needed to have their homes for it was their land before the angelic pale ones were ever there the only creature there who had not been familiar with the angelic pale ones were the merpeople and that has since changed so it was imperative to keep the land healthily divided for all involved to have their needs and luxuries met. Before leaving Gabriel asserted to hold back on building the homes for the merpeople but go ahead with the bank house and also hold back on the making of the lakes those plans would be provided by God as well and sooner than they thought so they needed to relay what pertained to the merpeople to them at the dinner hour and the royal couple replied affirmatively and were actually relieved to have God step in and take care of the building plans because for them it would have been a challenge and they were not really looking forward to that dilemma. At that point Gabriel let the royal couple know they would be seeing him soon then he disappeared and the royal couple hugged one another and romantically kissed. Andrew checked the time and discovered that the dinner hour was coming rapidly so he and Camillia went to the castles kitchen in search of Melanie to see how their dinner food was coming along and Melanie was there wrapping up the last of the things to go she advised the royal couple that the wagons were ready outside and she had a team of servants to go with them to help set up everything and they were ready to start getting the things they needed to eat and drink with out and once that was done they would take out the beverages then the meal and they would ride on one buggy and each one of the royal couple could drive one of the buggies one with all the things for the dinner hour and one with the kitchen staff and Camillia told Michell thankyou and that she was wonderful and that she would not have been able to do things like that if it had not have been for her then Melanie thanked Camillia for keeping her duties interesting and challenging that it kept her work great and she loved it that way. The two girls hugged and expressed their love for one another then the royal couple went out to mount the buggies and Michelle went on to taking care of the rest of the royal family starting with guiding them from the castles family room to the dining hall by giving them the message that Andrew said to give them and everyone was understanding so when all were seated at the big round table and had their drinks they proposed a toast to the success of the dinner between the royal couple and the merpeople to be a fruitful one. Out at the lakes bank the merpeople were finished with their gifts for the royal family and waiting for the royal couple so as the royal couple approached with the two buggies the merpeople started to wave at them and verbally greet them and the royal couple sent verbal greetings back. Now at the banks edge the royal couple and servants get off their buggies and the help started to unload the meal buggy while the royal couple moved into the crowd of merpeople giving hugs and pecks on the cheeks. By the time the royal couple and all of the merpeople had expressed their love for one another the help had gotten all the food and beverages set up as well as the dishes that were to be used all in a buffet style so the help could go down the line and prepare a plate and drink for each merperson and taking care of quite a few individuals at a time and the help would keep rotating until everyone had their food and a drink. Now that everyone including the royal kitchen helpers and all the merpeople as well as the royal couple has their plates of food and a drink it was time to feast and conversate but before discussing casual things Andrew took the chance to start the conversation with business by letting the merpeople know that Gabriel the archangel had paid them a visit before they had left the royal castle to the bank for their dinner hour to give them news of the expansion of homes for the angelic pale ones, the lakes, and the homes for the merpeople as well as some other building that was necessary. Camillia added that they were not there to speak about business but to not worry about the building project because Gabriel did close his visit by assuring them that God would be getting the layout of what he wants done and how and where to them through another angel soon so everyone would still get what they needed and wanted and no animals or mythological creatures would be displaced in the process of the expansion which was good news for everyone and everything. The merpeople were thrilled and relieved for they were a patient species who wanted what was best for everything and everyone also. Majority of the rest of the dinner hour was spent on eating and having casual conversation for the most part and the merpeople were impressed with the meal that Melanie had prepared saying that it was delicious and they appreciated her creating such a palatable choice of options for the menu then Camillia replied to the compliment by informing the merpeople that this was hopefully the first of many gatherings and the merpeople agreed that they would have many more gatherings but sometimes the royal couple had to allow the merpeople to supply the meal and the royal couple agreed to let them do so. The help that Melanie had sent from her kitchen staff had started to clean up the dishes from the meal and pack up the left over meal items and drink options while the leader of the merpeople took the opportunity to get everyone's attention to present the gifts that they had made for the royal couple and to let them know that the rest of the royal family must come to them on the bank to receive their gifts on the morrow. When the leader of the merpeople had presented the crowns to the king and queen of the angelic pale ones they were humbled and Camillia wept tears of sentiment and all that were there knew why she wept for all creatures in the new garden of Eden were telepathic and thus able to understand one another's language. Andrew made it known that on the morrow he would make sure to gather the rest of the royal family and bring them to the lakes edge to receive their gift and to properly introduce themselves so that when the merpeople set eyes on them they would know who they were in the event they needed their assistance or just wanted their attention for simple greetings they could get their attention right away and the leader of the merpeople questioned Andrew on when he would have the royal family there and he replied whenever was good for them. The leader of the merpeople answered Andrew and wished for them to meet after the breakfast hour so they would be certain to have everything prepared and then they could go on with their daily responsibilities but did want them back for the lunch hour stating that the merfolk wanted to treat the angelic pale one royal family a meal and while the entire royal family was leaving for the start of their day he did want Melanie to stay behind for a meeting of minds in reference to the menu options that the royal family usually feasted on so that would give the merpeople something to work with and Camillia giggled then Camillia and Andrew both let the leader of the merpeople know that would not be a problem and they would be sure to whisper in her ear to do so. Now the help that Melanie had sent with the royal couple had finished their chore they went to the banks edge to bid the merpeople a farewell and the merpeople gave them big hugs and kisses on the cheek as the help returned the gesture honestly and revealed that they would meet again so the merpeople responded that they certainly hoped so and when all expressions of gratitude and love had been expresses the royal kitchen help loaded up on one buggy and Andrew got upon the front of that buggy to drive the team and Camillia got on the front of the other buggy to drive that team home which carried all the dinner supplies and as everyone waved and said see ya Andrew and Camillia disappeared into the evening light so the merpeople went down into the lake to start the gift making process for the presentation of gifts to the royal family after the breakfast hour on the morrow. All the workers needed for the merpeople's bank house worked through the night so it would be ready for them as soon as it was time for the commune to awaken on the morrow. When the royal couple got to the royal castle and went into the royal castle the rest of the royal family was eagerly awaiting their return to find out how things went with the merpeople and the kitchen helpers that Melanie sent were busy getting the buggy that had the meal and dishes in it were busily working on getting it emptied and getting everything into the royal kitchen while the kitchen staff that stayed behind to wait upon the rest of the royal family helped to tend to things that were being brought inside from the buggy and soon everything was taken care of and the royal kitchen was clean but the royal couple and the rest of the royal family were still conversing. The royal family was awestricken by the crowns that the merpeople made for the royal couple and surprised to hear that they were to be at the lakes bank directly after the breakfast hour for their gifts and to officially meet the merpeople and now the merpeople would be walking amongst them and now they would have the means to easily transform to enable them to be on land for however long they so desired and the royal family was excited to have the merpeople amongst them and could not wait to be with them and now it was getting late so everyone retired to their homes to prepare for the sleeping hours and hopefully passing the time quickly. When Andrew and Camillia got inside their home and shut the door a bright light grew larger and larger in their family room right in front of them and the royal couple knew it was a good angel from God but they were not sure what the message would be but they did know it could possibly be in reference to the plans for building new homes and business and lakes and the sorts but the were going to just wait to see so they stood in their family room hand in hand until the bright light turned into an angel. The angel said he was a messenger from God and he held out a large roll of paper that was golden in color so Andrew reached out to take it gently then the angel spoke saying it was the plans for building up the new garden of Eden and expanding it. The royal couple thanked the angel saying that they would assure that the angelic pale ones followed the plan of God accurately then the angel replied if they did it correctly God would bless the work greatly and their work would be easy and God would do most of the work but if they did not follow the plan precisely they would be on their own and God would not bless the project and the new garden of Eden would fail just as the old earth did and this warning frightened both Andrew and Camillia so they plead with the angel for God to give them assistance as they worked closely with the angelic pale ones who would be doing the various tasks to guide their thoughts on the planning and approving of the various steps along the way for the success of the project essentially laid on the royal couples shoulders. The angel replied that he was that angel and he would be with them always throughout the project but only they would be able to see or hear him so be cautious about speaking to him so no one suspected that they were getting godly assistance or just plainly gone loopy and the royal couple agreed to be cautious then they offered their spare bedroom to the angel then they bedded down for the night. No sooner than they fell into a deep sleep their mini angels came and sang their wake-up song into their ears and awoke them for their nightly visit and it was a positive and informative visit. Their mini angels revealed that the new garden of Eden was going to be gorgeous and blessed by God then the royal couple questioned their mini angels on how they could say that the project was going to be blessed by God then the mini angels replied that if the royal couple could remember the mini angels could usually foresee the future when God allows them to and with that sometimes they were allowed to reveal their information and this was one of those times. That was wonderful news for the royal couple and so they were very gracious too their mini angels for revealing that information to them but it was time for their mini angels to return to the dinosaur tail and when the mini angels left the royal couple were so excited that they knew they were not going to be able to sleep after all so they got out of bed and did their morning routine to prepare for the new day then got the plans that the angel of God had given them and unrolled them across their bed and reviewed them carefully as they discussed the plans with one another so they both would have a clear understanding of what was what and what went where and so on but they also made sure they both knew what the other knew so they could work together in the absence of the other which would not be too difficult as long as each one had the same information and had an open mind to receive telepathic links to one another however their plan was to stay together at all times for this project so hopefully nothing could go wrong and neither of them made any decisions without the other. Because the royal couple had photographic memory it would not be necessary to haul the plans on the scroll around with them but they would have to move them to somewhere where the various workers could view them at their leisure to assure they could do their jobs accurately. After Andrew and Camillia spent a great amount of time looking over the plans that God had delivered to them they heard the angel moving about in their family room so they went out to greet the angel and thank him for his assistance and let him know what would be going on with their schedule but as they tried to explain their routine to the angel he stopped them in mid-sentence explaining to them that he already knew their full routine and if anything were to change he would know before they would because as an angel of God he had a direct link with God and therefore he would be as all knowing as God saw fit. The royal couple was pleased with the arrangement between the angel and God because it confirmed that they would be well taken care of which they already knew but now they knew how and it was a greater relief because it was essentially tangible. Andrew got a glimpse of what time it was and realized that the breakfast hour was about upon them so the angel followed the royal couple to the royal family room where Andrew would lead the rest of the royal family to the big round table in the royal dining hall for the morning meal filled with great conversation and expressions of love. Once everyone got settled in their chairs at the big round table Andrew got the royal families attention saying he had a major announcement and needed everyone's full attention then once everyone settled down and grew silent Andrew announced that God had delivered the plans for the building up of the new garden of Eden and everyone was to start the building that day and there would be no curfew they were to work around the clock and sleep only if it was needed and that decision was to be left up to each individual since angelic pale ones did not really need to sleep and if they did it was only about four hours every five to seven days and there was a gigantic need for the royal family to assist the royal couple to get each individual guidance on what they were to do and assure they were doing it correctly, the royal family expressed their full understanding and that they would commit to their responsibilities. Andrew then revealed that he needed some sort of large podium to place the plans on for all to see but the podium had to be movable to go from place to place and it needed to be covered with glass to avoid potential innocent damage to the plans that God had sent down with an angel then he asked for any ideas on how to construct some sort of podium such as that but before giving any ideas they needed to know that the plans were as large as their queen sized bed so it was a strange size for a podium then the family remained silent as they were thinking hard on how to construct such a podium. Melanie had the breakfast meal on the table and served everyone but the royal family was so focused on the podium construction that they mostly picked at their food while sipping their coffee. Suddenly most everyone started to speak at the same time with the same response of having the angelic head construction worker pale one figure the podium problem out because he was in construction and brilliant with things of that nature. Andrew and Camillia sort of giggled that everyone came up with the same idea at the same time and it was also what the royal couple was thinking so it was official Andrew would approach the angelic head construction worker pale one and see if he could take on the project and have a successful outcome. Camillia reminded Andrew that they were supposed to go to the lake's bank to be with the merpeople for a short time then Andrew made another announcement that the royal family could not let the merpeople down that after the completion of the breakfast hour they were supposed to go to the lake's bank to greet the merpeople and receive their gifts before the start of their day so the family agreed to keep their promised engagement. Now the breakfast hour was over and it was time for everyone to head out to the lake's bank including Melanie so the kitchen staff was left to clean up without her but she was most likely going to return before it would be time to plan the days menus and if not they would have to wait for her return. Everyone got their things ready to head out for their days work and their horses were saddled and ready to go so everyone headed out to mount their rides and off to the lake they went. When the entire royal family got close to the lake, they could see the merpeople waving at them and somewhat hear them vocally welcoming them out to them so the royal family waved back and within a minute or so the royal family was at the bank dismounting their rides. The merpeople were excited that the royal family was there and the leader of the merpeople got to the bank and actually got out of the lake and hugged the royal couple then verbally welcomed the entire royal family saying that they had gifts for the whole royal family but they would make the presentation quick because they knew that they had a busy morning that would be lasting for quite some time but to rest assured that if they would accept the merpeople's help they could assist with the expansion project they too were strong and able to do the same work as the angelic pale ones and had specialty talents to offer then Andrew thanked the merpeople and stated that it would be wonderful if they could help and if they wanted after they were finished with their presentation they could go with them to congregate at their religious hall to hear what needed to be done at that particular time and they could jump right in and volunteer themselves where they could best serve since Andrew was not familiar with who was best at what yet like he was the angelic pale ones and the merpeople were gracious that the angelic pale ones were going to allow them to help them and prove to them that they were a part of them as family and just like other species had been grandfathered in to be family they too wanted to be grandfathered in to be family. Now they moved on to the presentation of gifts from the merpeople to the angelic pale ones and the gifts were simply eloquent and fitting it was as though the merpeople had known the angelic pale ones for ever when they designed the gifts for each angelic pale one and it was the hopes of both parties that they would have an eternal relationship with one another and get to know one another intimately. The merpeople thanked the angelic pale ones for the lake bank house being done so urgently saying it was done in good time and it was then that the royal family noticed the bank house they were so consumed by their thoughts of the expansion project that they had not noticed the bank house but it was perfect and large enough to fit a lot of merpeople inside at a time so now that the gift giving was over the merpeople started coming out of the lake and entering the bank house to transform and get clothed with the clothes that were made just for them and placed inside the bank house. It was at that point that Andrew realized the merpeople knew what was going on with the expansion project but he was not sure how they knew about it for the royal family did not know until the royal family had revealed it to the royal family recently and the general population would find out within minutes when they would be summoned to the religious hall to be gathered by the sounding of the great bell and informed as a group by the royal couple so Andrew took the head merperson aside and questioned him about how he and the rest of the merpeople knew of the expansion project then the merman replied that he had the gift of foreseeing the future and the time frame of occurrence so when this happened he would inform his people and they would follow his guidance to help things work their way out in a positive way. Andrew was amazed by the merman's gift and thanked him for being open and honest about being put on the spot in the crude manner that he was then Andrew apologized for being so forward with the merman and the merman replied that it was okay that he understood it must have been a bit shocking to have witnessed the concern of a group of outsiders having knowledge that only the royal couple had been informed of. Now all the merpeople were transformed and ready to go to the religious hall to find out how they could best serve the others to get the expansion project fulfilled how God wanted it done. Camillia requested that all the merpeople follow her and Andrew to the religious hall and once they got there they would have the tower boys ring the tower bell to summon every one and every thing to the religious hall for the announcement of the expansion project and to be asked to do what they were best at and the animals and mythological creatures would divide to go where they could best benefit the workings of the project as well as the merpeople. It took approximately fifteen minutes to get to the religious hall but once there Andrew sent the tower boys to ring the large tower bell and when the boys rang the bell the angelic pale ones, animals of all sorts, and mythological creatures went charging toward the religious hall because they all knew when that bell rang that meant there was something that had to be addressed immediately and could not wait for even a second, now they knew it did not necessarily mean it was a negative situation but none the less it was still important. Everyone was there and Andrew was at the podium in front of the religious hall with Camillia at his side and the doors of the religious hall were open due to the simple fact that not all of the new garden of Eden's occupants would fit inside of the religious hall so that also meant that Andrew had to speak extra loudly into the microphone so he could be easily heard beyond the doors of the entrance of the building. Andrew and Camillia spoke loudly and clearly so everyone and everything could hear them and when disclosing all the information they had and the requests they had the animals, the mythological creatures, and the angelic pale ones all supportively spoke up in an organized fashion and offered their expertise and was willing to follow God's specifications so with no questions being asked all involved broke into groups and made their way to the royal castle to get a look at the plans that God had sent down then they went to where they needed to be and as they were on their way to where they needed to be they were conversating and getting to know one another's names and expertise as well as anything else that was relative to the project at hand. Within ten minutes of the great meeting ending all that could be heard was a township working hard with noises of machines running and people carefully working manually and putting their backs into difficult jobs and short talk of individuals hollering over the construction noises giving orders and other short talk in reference to the job at hand. So far the angel that God had sent down with the plans for the royal couple to put into motion was pleased with Camillia and Andrew so they felt that the way they had handled things so far was okay now what they needed to do was float from project to project and keep an eye on what was being done and how well it was being done. As the royal couple were floating from place to place they ran into the angelic head construction worker pale one who informed the royal couple that he needed them out to his shop because his people quit working and would not resume their duties so the royal couple appeared a bit confused but they did follow the angelic head construction worker pale one back to his shop and the royal couple was caught off guard to see the workers standing side by side stretching from one side of the shop to the other side so the royal couple started to speak but before they could utter a word the variety of workers hollered surprise then moved aside and there stood the podium that Andrew had requested for the floor plans that God had sent down for the expansion project, it was perfect. The angelic head construction worker pale one informed the royal couple that he would get a few of his crew together and have the podium placed where they wanted the expansion plans to be displayed then after careful thought for several minutes Andrew questioned the angelic head construction worker pale one where he thought the plans would best be displayed for everyone's convenience at that point understanding that after the immediate area was completed they would have to move the plans to a further location past what had been built to where they needed to be building and repeating that cycle until they were finished with God's plans for the expansion project. Before saying where to place the podium and extension plans Andrew's mind drifted to another thought and that was that now there were a few things that he was concerned about that God had not cleared with him but he had not asked God about those things and those things were new concerns so Andrew decided he was going to pull Camillia aside and speak with her about his concerns and find out what their current angel of God had to say and he and his wife could make their decision on how to handle the issue after the small meeting of the minds. Andrew ordered the angelic head construction worker pale one to place the podium and plans where he felt they would best serve the large variety of workers and then he took his wife by the hand and led her away in order to speak to her and the angel alone. Now alone Andrew informed Camillia that he was concerned about building in the area between the commune and the tunnel to the door leading above ground that even though the tunnel door would be blocked the area is desolate and not able to sustain life then Andrew also revealed his other concern about how far they were to build past their commune going in the opposite direction of the tunnel and door leading to the new earth's surface because they did not know how far the forest went and it would take a very long time to build from their home area around the earth and back around to their home area then populating the new earth would take time but that would happen naturally so that was not the concern but what was, was the distance between family members and how the distance would affect the relationships between the individuals. Andrew made it known that he was not against filling the new earth with life but he was concerned with the loss of the closeness that they had become accustomed to thus far and he did not want that to be lost under any circumstances. Camillia agreed with Andrew and then they both turned to their angel and questioned him as to whether or not God had prepared him for that kind of question and the angel denied having been prepared for a question such as that so it was decided by the royal couple to pray to God and go directly to the source himself so they went straight home and did just that. After reverently praying to God but before the royal couple could stand to their feet the archangel Gabriel appeared and took each one of the royal couple by one hand and raised them to their feet then began to speak starting by explaining that God had heard their words and that he Gabriel was sent as a messenger to respond to their plea for answers to their concerns about the expansion plans. Gabriel reminded the couple that the distance between them was not truly an issue because all life on the new earth had the ability to be from one place to another within the blink of an eye and some could even go to heaven in the same way and that ability would combat the missing of family and friends then Gabriel let the royal couple know that God was going to turn the barren land between the commune and the door to the tunnel that led to the surface of the earth into a plush vibrant land such ass the land that contained the commune then there was the concern of building beyond the forest's edge where the angelic pale ones went and Gabriel informed the couple that the forest did not go much further but God would turn the rest of the land into plush livable land and all life on the new earth would replenish the rest of the new garden of Eden and a gentle balance would be maintained of all species on the new earth. All of a sudden Gabriel looked deep into Camillia's eyes and urgently began t speak to her saying that he knew what she was about to say and that he had an answer then he simply said what her question would have been which was how were they to build a flourishing ongoing community to cover the entire new earth and not stop until reaching home to pick up on their life as if they never left and how were they to rule across the country and keep the people safe and comforted then Gabriel answered the queens questions that he spoke by saying that now that God had seen that they were going to take on the task that he had put before them even seeming impossible that instead of giving up the community banded together and turned to God for guidance God was actually wanting the job to be done but he was testing the earth bound species to assure their dedication for something so unbelievably daunting and since their response was far surpassing what it could have been but just what he already knew it would have been he will not have any of the species continue with the job for the job would be completed by God himself and Gabriel demanded that he needed the royal couple to call all living creatures to the religious hall so he could explain to all what God wishes of them and why then Gabriel told the angel that had been with Andrew and Camillia that he had done a good job while he was with the royal couple and he was needed in heaven for other things so he said his farewells to the royal couple who verbalized their love for him and wished him well then he disappeared. Gabriel and the royal couple immediately headed over to the religious hall and once they got there Gabriel took his place at the speakers podium while the royal couple went to the bell tower to ring the giant bell that calls all creatures to the religious hall then the couple joined Gabriel and all species started piling into the religious hall. It was not long before every living creature on the new earth was there and Gabriel started to tell the crowd of species just what he had told the royal couple then Gabriel could feel the questions every creature had and even though practically every creature was questioning something there were actually only a few questions that everyone shared so Gabriel answered them and all were okay with how things turned out and had an understanding of what God did and sort of why but everyone did not like being tested to such a magnitude and Gabriel knew that as he was picking up on the negative emotions surrounded with that thought so Gabriel smoothed things over verbally by sharing examples throughout the bible where God had tested individuals in harsher ways and other ways that were not as harsh but more frequent for some and they just needed to understand that they had easy lives and for that they needed to have trials to keep them in check to remind them that their way of life could turn them onto pride and that would be the very thing that would destroy them amongst other things as did the individuals on the old earth. Gabriel ended his address to the variety of lives with letting them know that upon the midnight hour their garden of Eden would be expanded and the entire new earth would be completely expanded so there was to be a curfew of eleven at night for all so God could see obedience and at the stroke of midnight he would make the changes and during that time there would be a few seconds of darkness then after the changes there would be the light back as usual and by one in the morning if so desired all living things may go about and look around to appreciate the works of God as well as to see what will be where. Gabriel verbally expressed his love to all then disappeared then they all expressed their love for Gabriel and one another then voiced that all praise be to God and then they left the religious hall to go prepare for the next meal time which was to occur at the community dining hall for all creatures to congregate and share the lunch hour together for they knew the next day was somehow going to be the first day of a new beginning of advantageous fortunes for the new garden of Eden on the new earth and all the various species were going to have moving experiences of positive natures that at one time they could only wish for and dream of and now it was coming to pass and it was to be even better than what they could have ever imagined. Everyone is at the community dining hall and Melanie's staff are serving all the different species their lunch meals as they were all communicating and discussing the changes that the new garden of Eden was going to undergo during the night hours and how excited they all were to get to witness a miracle of God once again. That was one thing that everyone agreed upon without a thought but there was one more thing everything everyone agreed upon and that was that they wanted to stay in their current homes if possible and keep their colony tight for they were the original settlers who had a special common bond that was practically unbreakable. Melanie overheard the conversation about no one leaving the commune to go to other parts of the new garden of Eden then she butted into the conversation and inquired about who would occupy the homes and work places throughout the rest of the garden of Eden then Camillia spoke up and said that she supposed that God would have to summon those whom he wanted to go or send down occupants then everyone else grew silent due to the fact that no one had thought of that issue and with no one wanting to go it would most likely come down to God appointing individuals from different species to go and it would not be wise to argue the matter with God so Camillia's reply to that was that she was going to fly to heaven and stand before God himself and plea for the commune's desires to stay where they were and try to come up with another way to find others to populate the rest of the areas that have been built then Andrew scolded Camillia pointing out that it was not right to advise God on what he should and should not do so Camillia politely excused herself from the table and went outside of the community dining hall and proceeded to fly into the heavens and once there she went to the angels that guarded God's throne room and requested to stand before her maker. Camillia was granted her desire to stand before God and she bowed before her father humbly and showed reverence then God told her to rise up before him so she did then he demanded to hear her reasonable plea for her commune and its inhabitants. Camillia softly spoke to God telling him that she knew that he already knew why she was there for he was all knowing but she was there because her commune had a close bond and much devotion to one another and wished to stay together but that may foil the plan to repopulate the rest of the land but she knew thru him all could be done then God replied in letting her know that he had no intent on separating the inhabitants of her commune per say in fact the adults would be staying right where they were it would essentially be the children that had met the age of accountability that would be moving to the next set of properties and their children would do the same at the right time under the right circumstances and the process would continue until the whole new earth's new garden of Eden was satisfactorily inhabited by all the various species. Camillia was relieved to find out what God's plan was and God had already known that so he had requested that she not say anything to anyone because he had planned to address the various species in his own way as soon as she returned to her husbands side so God excused her from his presence after expressing his love for her and she returned the gesture of love then within a couple of seconds she was back with Andrew. When Camillia appeared at the table at Andrew's right side and at the presence of the rest of the various species that were at their table they knew something was going on but did not know what for they saw her go outside of the great community dining hall then after a few minutes she just popped into the community dining hall at her seat, everyone grew silent from the conversation they were carrying on in her absence so Camillia started to try to think of something to say when Gabriel the archangel appeared at the entrance of the great community dining hall. Gabriel's voice was one of those voices that carried throughout a large amount of space and caught everyone's attention so when he spoke everyone grew silent and listened as was the situation this time. Gabriel announced that he had some very important information for them and they needed to hear him clearly with an understanding and forgiving heart and be sure to put themselves in the shoes of a teaching parent then he went on to make the various species aware that God had called off the expansion project that they were to be performing and that he was to retrieve the plans and that God himself was to do the expansion himself. Gabriel explained that the giving of the plans and specifications were a test to assure the various species commitment to one another as well as to their God and if their response was as expected where everyone was unified and willing to pull all their resources together selflessly towards a new common goal without asking the obvious questions God would call off the project and do the work himself as a miracle but if their response was just the opposite God would have made the task become one disaster after another and it would not have been able to have been accomplished and the community would have been divided many times over thus making the commune much like the humans just before the third world war and it would have been a stressful place to be but God already knew how it was going to turn out and was extremely pleased so now at the stroke of midnight the lightning bugs would not provide any light for a few seconds and during that time their miracle would occur then the lightning bugs would light up again. All God requested was for every species be in their homes by eleven at night and not go out until one in the morning then at that time all were able to go out to venture through the land and view the wonderous work of God and celebrate the miracle together if they so wished. Once Gabriel finished making his announcement he inquired if there were any questions or if anyone needed any clarity on the requirements that God had placed on them and no one stood up so Gabriel expressed his love for all the various species then congratulated them on a job well done and immediately disappeared. With Gabriel's announcement done Camillia stood up and made it known that she would like for everyone to arrive at the royal castle at one in the morning to venture throughout the land together then when they were finished she would like for them all to congregate at the community religious hall to praise God then they could go from there to the community dining hall for some wonderful together time and morning drink of their choice while Melanie and her crew made the breakfast meals for everyone then they could continue their together time while consuming their breakfast meal and then they could separate for their own time to do what ever it was that they needed to be doing for their daily tasks. For now it was time for everyone to exit the community dining hall to go take care of their daily tasks that needed to be done before the dinner meal which everyone would be eating in their own homes that evening so they could get settled down for the evening prior to when God would perform his miracle for the various species on the new earth in the new garden of Eden. As all the various species were exiting the community dining hall Armellya caught up with her parents Camillia and Andrew with a very important question so she pulled them aside and asked them if there was going to be other dinosaur tails with other queens of dinosaur tails so that other species that required mini angels could have them close by and Armellya's royal parents did not have an answer for their child but they did agree that Armellya needed to summon for God's clarification on that matter for they had an issue similar to that which needed God's clarification also then Armellya wanted to know what her parents could possibly need to know about for they usually know all that they needed to know then Camillia told

Armellya that they were not sure if her and Andrew would be king and queen of the entire New garden of Eden once it was constructed to go around the new earth or if there would be more royal leaders to watch over a certain amount of land which would make them only responsible for their commune and the other leaders and them would have to work together to keep the peace and devotion to God. As Andrew and Camillia saw it things could become difficult with many rulers but they would hopefully do things how God wanted things to be done. Jadellya decided that the three of them should summon Gabriel the archangel and see if he could help them with the information they sought and Camillia certainly agreed so Camillia suggested that they go to her and Andrew's home to do that then they moved onward to the door of the community dining hall and were the last ones to exit the community dining hall. As soon as the three of them were outside they took flight to get to the royal castle quickly and within seconds they were there so they landed and hurried inside of the castle to go directly to the royal's family room. It never failed, when Camillia and Andrew had something pressing to discuss with God that could usually be done through the archangel Gabriel or one of God's private messenger angels who would be waiting for them in their family room and that was what happened that time and it was Gabriel waiting for them when they entered their home. As soon as the royal couple's door to their home closed and the three of them got to the family room Gabriel stepped out of the shadows and started to speak immediately saying that he was there to settle their current concerns. Gabriel explained to Camillia and Andrew that their concern that having other rulers to tend to other parts of the new garden of Eden could create some unwanted situations was true and that was why God was not going to make things occur that way Gabriel then got specific in saying that Camillia and Andrew would be the king and queen of the entire new earth with the new garden of Eden and it was a tough job but God knew they could handle it and that was why they were chosen from the very beginning. As for Jadellya Gabriel informed her that the mini angels would have other dinosaur tails to be closer to their guarded target however she would be the only queen over them and just like the royal couple her job to supervise them would be harder and require traveling but with her gift like the royal couple they could be anywhere within a blink of an eye so there would be no competition over the mini angels and how they were to be handled. Now that Andrew, Camillia, and Jadellya received their answers they were more relaxed and the news that their jobs would be a bit more complexed they did not mind for they were already processing the information of how to handle the task in the most affective way and becoming more enlivened to standing up to the challenge for they knew the opportunity was a blessing and would hold many blessings within it as well as difficulties but the difficulties would not be in vain they would simply be lessons to be learned from and a way to gain strength in multiple ways. Gradually the tasks would become easier and feel more natural so they would not have the hardships that they would encounter in the very beginning so now that the three of them had been enlightened they expressed their love to Gabriel and thanked him for his immediate response then Gabriel returned the expression of love and instructed the royal couple to meet with him at the community religious hall immediately and be on the stage near the podium which was where they would find him so they agreed to do so then Gabriel disappeared and the three of them high tailed it out of the royal castle to go to the community religious hall as they had promised Gabriel they would upon his demanding them to do. As the royal couple and Jadellya were about half way to the community religious hall they heard the large religious meeting bell ring so they picked up their pace to getting to the community religious hall post haste. When Camillia, Andrew, and Jadellya arrived at the community religious hall it was just on time for them to be able to get through the crowd of other species as well as angelic pale ones to get to the front of the building where Gabriel wanted them to be so after being where they were told to be for about five minutes things settled down and grew quiet then Gabriel explained to all just as he had to the royal couple and Jadellya not so long ago that they did not need to continue with the expansion project and why then Gabriel laid out God's requirements for the curfew and the time when they could go out and about to admire God's creation and move on with their early day if they so chose to or just to go back home and catch up on some needed sleep if that was necessary because even though angelic pale ones and the other species needed little sleep they were all on different schedules. At the end of Gabriel's informative speech, the crowd was speechless yet relieved as the royal couple and Jadellya was after Gabriel had spoken the same words to them and

Gabriel could feel the stress lifting off of all of them also, he now knew his job was done. Gabriel expressed his love for all of them and reminded them that he would always be nearby if they should need him then the crowd expressed their love for him followed by a grand thanks for bringing them the message from God then Gabriel flew off like a ball of fire flashing across the sky headed for the heavens. Once Gabriel left there were a couple of questions on practically everyone's minds that they could not get themselves to ask about but through telepathy the royal couple knew exactly what the worries were that everyone was thinking about so Andrew took it upon himself to address the situations by getting to the podium where Gabriel was and letting everyone know that he knew what was on their minds and he could settle their curiosities so he let them know exactly what they wandered about which was their concern at one time also such as was there going to be other queens and kings and other mini angel queens and God's answer was a simple no. upon Andrew's answering those two inquiries everyone was satisfied and ready to go on about their business for they loved the community working just the way it was and they were hoping that the rest of the new earth communities would run as smoothly and Godly as theirs and they knew with other leaders it could create issues that may be extremely challenging. Now with every species leaving the community religious hall to go back to what they were doing before Gabriel called all species to collect together for an important message from God it was also time for the royal couple to return to the royal castle to complete their unfinished duties for that specific day before consuming their dinner meal then turning in for the evening just like everyone else. Melanie was at the point of preparations of the dinner meal of putting the finishing touches on each dish and having her staff running the meals to each royal family home within the castle so she had her staff first check to find out if her royal family members were in their homes and ready for their dinner and they were so she then had her staff run every royal family their dinner meal to their homes within the castle and they would all finish their meals in enough time for the kitchen staff to eat their meals then collect the dishes and the staff would be able to clean the kitchen before they were supposed to be in their homes on time for the curfew and that was just what happened. With everyone in the commune in their homes and settled down for the evening including the mini angels for even they were home bound for the night hours so that meant that the mini angels would not be going out that night for their nightly visits with their appointed recipients which was the first time this had occurred in the history of the mini angels existence on the old earth as well as in the new garden of Eden but it would be for the better of reasons as God put the curfew over the mini angels as well. All species felt it best for them to try to get some rest for two reasons, one was to pass the time a bit faster and the second was to be able to get through the new parts of the commune that God had bestowed upon them and enjoy the beauty and wonder of the new structures placed within the forest with the new lakes and channels connecting all of the lakes for the water dwellers to travel from one area of the new earth to another area no matter how far and for all species to be able to praise God whole heartedly without fatigue being in the way of their enjoyment and being able to be productive in their new days responsibilities and for however long past the next day that they could continue being productive in their small community before needing more rest. Now that all species were ready to bunker down for the night and the lightning bugs had found a place to settle down and wait for them to be darkened by God for a spell all were anxiously waiting for the time when they could go out and see God's miracle which made it a bit difficult to fall asleep but eventually all were sleeping in the new garden of Eden and finally it was time for God to perform his miracle. It took all of one minute for God to make his masterpiece and within five minutes after the miracle being completed the entire community was awakened by the brightness of the lightning bugs' glow reflecting off of all the gold that was already in the commune plus the new gold that had been placed there, it was so much brighter than before. All the merpeople raced to get out of the water to go into the bank house to undergo the change from merpeople to angelic pale ones comfortably and get dressed into the clothing that the royal family had made for them by the seamstresses and placed into the bank house for them. The rest of the inhabitants of the new garden of Eden did their morning routine super quickly to prepare to start their day by first admiring God's miracle all together and they were all gathered in the center of the commune which was not planned it just worked out that way and all of the inhabitants of the new garden of Eden felt that was just the perfect way to go about the new parts of the commune together instead of individually so they could worship God together and discuss the layout and beauty together it was surely going to be miraculous in the business structures and the new buildings for gatherings as well as homes for the population that would be being produced. Andrew and Camillia were to lead the entire commune through the wonderful addition of the new garden of Eden that God created and everyone wanted it to be that way since they were to be the king and queen over the entire land so Andrew took it upon himself to get the attention of all those gathered to announce that even though he and his wife were heading them through the new additional land growth set by God it was really for all of them not for the king and queen then Andrew suggested that the pastor come forward and offer some prayer time over the new land and praise be given to God as well as thanks before they were to step foot on the newly gold paved streets to observe the new variety of golden buildings that would serve the new various species to call home which many of the closest homes and a few business buildings would be occupied within the week as the pale ones would time it. The pastor had made his way to the front of the crowd and stood next to Andrew and Camillia then requested that all would change their postures into an reverent one and prepare for prayer then he gave a minute for all to regain their posture into a prayerful one then he began the prayer which was a beautiful one and a very fitting one at that. Upon the end of the prayer the pastor said amen then let the various species know they could regain their normal stance and relax so they all went back to their relaxed state and as the pastor made his way back through the crowd to his original place the various species were patting him on the back and letting him know that they felt his prayer was beautiful and fitting as they stood in awe for what they could already cold see of the new structures that God had blessed them with which was nothing compared to the whole work that God had bestowed on them and they knew it. Now Andrew announced that they were going to move thru the street slowly to take in as much of the wonder that they could however he realized it would take some time to really appreciate the blessing that was given to them then Andrew and Camillia turned their backs to the crowd and began to walk extremely slow, so slow that a baby could crawl by ten times faster than what they were walking. Practically as soon as the inhabitants of the new garden of Eden walked one half of a mile down the golden road through the new extensions of the commune the inhabitants went from speechless to making noises of awe for the additions were marvelous and there was no lack of forest nor lakes with paths to combining lakes with other lakes and bank houses for every lake and fully stocked with clothing and large tanks for the child merpeople to be in while they waited for their parents to undergo their change so they could undergo their change after their parents did. The houses were furnished with furniture but the décor was left up to the inhabitants and the animal world was happy for God even set them up nicely for their home structures and plenty of extras and the mythological creatures agreed that God had remembered them as well and had made beautiful places for them to live and play as well as do their work to contribute to the community even though they spent most of their time in the community for they loved to mingle with the animals and angelic pale ones. It was no surprise that God had thought of every species and provided for them in abundance in work play home and every other area possible and then some. Everyone had been walking for four hours and was not keeping track of time and was still wanting to keep walking the blessing seemed to go on forever and it did so Michael the archangel appeared right in front of Andrew and Camillia and held out his arms saying it was time to go back to their commune to engage in their tasks and enjoy their community for it too was a blessing to them and a gift from God to them then the species realized it was the breakfast hour and that they had been traveling for four hours and since the entire commune was on that trip there was no one in the commune preparing the morning nutrition so things appeared a bit gloomy because in another four hours they would just be arriving back to their own commune and it would be a bit late to have the lunch nutrition on the tables on time and Michael spoke to the species saying that he would get them back to their commune in a flash and God wanted them to go directly to the community dining hall for the breakfast hour so that was what took place then there was Gabriel again at the head of the building known as the community dining hall, he had more business with them so he rendered everyone quiet then explained to the various species that there would be some of the younger of each of the various species that would be inhabiting the extensions of the new garden of Eden and God would choose who would be moving there by touching the hearts of those who were to move on and those that were to be moving on would be in need of support from those who would be staying behind because even though it would be hard on those remaining it would be even more tough for those moving forward but they would only be a blink away for all species had the gift of bending time and being somewhere else in the blink of an eye and returning in the same fashion and as far as needing someone for more than a simple casual visit they all had the ability to focus on someone else and speaking back and forth telepathically. You see when Darren and Deanna came up with the idea to make the vaccine for making humans unaffected by the radiation of the weapons that were unleashed during world war three it had some positive side affects which God had a hand in because he knew ahead of time what was going to transpire later in the lives of the underground species as God was and would always be all knowing. That was not to say that God was through blessing the various species because he was going to always watch over his creations and would always bless them and help them along as long as they were willing to help themselves and remain God fearing creations. Once Gabriel made all that clear to the occupants of the new garden of Eden, he verbally expressed his love to all then disappeared to the heavens and everyone finished their morning meal then went out and about to complete their morning tasks in preparation for the afternoon meal and socialization time. Andrew and Camillia wondered about how the old earth became more and more toxic to live on as time went by and they became leery that the new earth may be at risk for becoming toxic also and they were appointed to assure that that did not occur but they could not control what others thought or did and should others become irresponsible and careless then the royal couple may have to come up with disciplinary actions to be set in place for certain things but they were not fond of that responsibility because they felt that it was God's place to punish individuals and they knew there were angels watching over them who had the responsibility to report transgressions to God directly so he could correct the situation by what ever means he saw fit. It was also Bridgette's obligation to report to God any transgressions that any individual from any species may have done and at that point it now became her responsibility to travel like the speed of light by using her ability to fold space and travel from space to space within seconds and observe the happenings and collect any data necessary to gain information on how the residents of that particular area she was in were doing and behaving and she would do so by telepathic readings of the minds of all species in that area and they could not block her from reading their minds for she and the royal couple had the ability to get through their ability to block their methods of blocking the reading of their minds. That ability enabled the royal couple and Bridgette to keep the variety of species walking the thin that God had placed before them and any straying could be detected right away especially with the mini angels who shared ne mind and communicated amongst one another so if one of their targets was out of alignment that mini angel could send the detailed message to Andrew and Camillia's mini angel and they would know within seconds and be able to witness the said infraction to confirm the said action then report it to the proper channel in heaven for God to correct in his own time with his own method prior to it affecting the surrounding commune through the various species that lived there. Camillia and Andrew knew they had the chief and Sharonna looking down upon them and protecting them and their purpose so they had no fear but they did have some concern for the others that lived in the new garden of Eden for they may not hold onto their faith like the royal couple did and the royal coupe loved the entire occupants of the new earth and did not want to witness any of them being chastised for transgressions that did not have to take place. With all the thoughts and wondering that Andrew and Camillia were doing and sharing telepathically between the two of them and blocking their thoughts so only the two of them could read their minds so they did not alarm anyone else the breakfast hour was completed and the others realized that the royal couple appeared to be in some sort of trance and did not touch their food or drink then one of the individuals at the table questioned the royal couple if they were okay and they replied that they were fine they just were not very hungry due to all the mornings excitement and the rest of the tables occupants were fine with their excuse and went on about their business by excusing themselves from the table and verbally expressing their love for one another then exiting the community dining hall to start their new day. As usual Andrew and Camillia were last to exit the community dining hall they were to return to the royal castle and it did not take long for them to get to the castle but instead of going into the main castle door to go down the major hall way to the door to their home they went down the outside of the castle to where their door was to their home from the outside and they noticed that a female wolf that appeared to have recently had pups was on their doorstep apparently waiting for them so they started speaking to her. Camillia was the primary interactor with the female wolf and when she asked the wolf what her name was the wolf said she was called blue star and had been named by the pale one known to them as the chief who was now an angel in heaven and had adopted one of her pups he called Deutaronomy. Camillia was touched by blue star and reached out one hand slowly and caressed the wolf's head then told her she was welcome to her home any time and if she was ever in need to not be ashamed to come to her and her husband Andrew for help she was a part of the family. Blue star lifted her head and locked eyes with Camillia then requested that her and Andrew follow her into the wooded area so the royal couple followed blue star and soon they were at Blue star's den and she had pups. Blue star urged the royal couple to get close to her pups and she explained that she had given birth to more pups than she had teats and therefore could not care for all of them and she needed for the royal couple to adopt two of her pups and they could pick which two to take then Camillia replied that the wolf must be heart broken to have to give up two of her pups but the royal couple promised to care for her two pups with the most care possible and with great love as if they were their very own children but they would make sure the pups knew their mother by bringing them to the den to see their mother and play with their siblings and love up to their mother and any time their family wanted to visit the castle they could. Blue star was moved and thanked her queen and king for their assistance and concern for her family then the royal couple picked out two pups a male and a female they were to call the female Brandy Alexandrea and the male Mister Mistofeles. Getting the pups at the time that the royal couple did was essentially great timing because Camillia had recently finished breast feeding children and was still producing great amounts of breast milk that she could pump and put into small bottles to feed the new pups and the royal couple would just have to go to the royal kitchen to retrieve Deuteronomy's bottles from when the chief used to feed him when they were earth bound. When Camillia informed Blue star of her plan to feeding the two pups Blue star felt that it was a good idea because it would help the pups to bond with her and Andrew plus it was healthier than the imitation milks that came from other sources unless they could get milk from an animal that was nursing a young one which as of now there were none. Now that Andrew and Camillia had picked out their pups and swaddled them in their capes and had made arrangement with Blue star to have time with her babies and had figured out how to best provide them with sustenance they let Blue star give her pups some loving nudges then the royal couple turned to head back to the royal castle they verbally called back that they would take the pups as their own children and would be seeing her very soon then Blue star howled into the morning air and went into her den to care for the rest of her hungry pups. Andrew and Camillia finally made it back to their home within the walls of the royal castle and after putting the wolf pups into a cozy spot Andrew and Camillia rushed into the royal kitchen and caught up with Melanie to have her retrieve the tiny bottles that were used to feed Deutaronomy when he and the chief were earth bound and Melanie went directly to where they were without hesitation and handed them to Camillia and she gave the bottles to Andrew then she got the breast pump that had been stored in the royal kitchen so she could provide some breast milk for the wolf pups. Melanie questioned Camillia about why she needed the bottles and breast pump so Camillia answered Melanie by simply motioning her to follow her and Andrew then the royal couple headed out of the royal kitchen going back to their home with Melanie in tow and when they got to the royal couples home sure enough right at the door to greet the royal couple were the wolf pups just carrying on because they were hungry so Camillia immediately started to pump milk while Melanie played with the wolf pups and pleasantly distracting the pups from their hunger pangs enabling Camillia to comfortably let down her milk and Andrew was filling bottles as Camillia was putting out enough milk to fill a bottle. Once there were four bottles per pp Camillia quit pumping milk and Andrew asked Melanie to pick up a pup while he handed the other pup to Camillia then he handed a bottle to each female and they proceeded to feed the pup they had in arm. The pups were certainly hungry as they drank quickly and wildly they actually drank all three of the bottles designated for them and still seemed to be hungry so Camillia handed the pup she had to Andrew and she began to pump more milk as

Andrew and Melanie played with the wolf pups then when she filled three bottles for both pups each they began to feed the pups again and they ate all three bottles each but did slow down and this time upon finishing their third bottle they were finally satisfied. Now that the pups were ready to sleep Andrew let Camillia know that he was going to go out and get the necessary items needed in order to make their home pup friendly such as beds for the pups dishes for them to eat and get water from and toys to play with and bones to chew on for their growing teeth and so on then Camillia agreed that was a superb idea and that she wished she could go then Melanie intervened and let the royal couple know that there was no reason why she could not go because the pups were napping and she had nothing to do right away so she could pup sit while they were gone and when they got back she could get back to her work then Camillia got excited so it was a plan and Andrew told Camillia that they had better go quickly because there was no telling how long the pups would sleep for so off they went after thanking Melanie and verbally expressing their love for her while she was verbally expressing her love for them. It was not long before the royal couple were back from their pup shopping and they were still in a deep slumber and Melanie was relaxed and comfortably admiring the sleeping pups Camillia was quietly showing Melanie all the things that she and Andrew got for the pups and it seemed that they bought out the shop they thought of everything and Melanie just knew that the royal couple would be the best fostering parents for the wolf pups that there could ever be. Now it was time for Melanie to get back to her duties so the royal couple gave Melanie hugs and thanked her for her help then she left to get back to her duties while Camillia and Andrew started to put their pups items in their place so when the pups awoke the royal couple could show them where their things were and hoped that they approved of their new things and once that was completed they wanted to have blue star over to examine the home for her to know they had a good home with adequate supplies and to also know she was always welcome there any time. Andrew was also going to put a doggie door type of set up in their front door that led to the outside for the pups to be able to come and go at will and for the pups family to come and go freely the royal couple felt that the doggie type door was a very necessary thing for the pups did have a wolf family and needed to have open communication with them to still have their roots being known to them. As Camillia put all the pups things in place throughout the home Andrew worked on the doggie type set up on the front door which would allow any wolf adult or pup to enter and exit at any time they should desire and the couple completed their task about the same time and right then the pups awoke so the royal couple got their pup and took them around their home showing them their special things and then last but not least the royal couple showed the pups their doorway to the outside and how to go through it and the pups seemed to be happy with everything so the next step was to bring Blue star to their home and get her approval for the pups set up. Now that the pups had eaten and taken a nap it was time for them to relieve themselves so the royal couple let them exit their home through the doggie type door to the outside then they opened the door for them to get out and the pups went to the wooded area to find a suitable area to relieve themselves and while the pups were taking care of their business Camillia howled very loudly into the forest calling for Blue star to come to the castle and then they would wait for her to howl back. After a couple of minutes Blue star howled back and was on her way to the royal castle so the pups finished their business and were on their way back to the royal couple who led them back to the doorway to their home but did not go back in yet they were waiting for Blue star's arrival first so she could experience the doggie type door with her pups. Within a few minutes Blue star emerged from the tree line and ran to the castle where the door of the royal couples home was and when she got there she bowed her head to the royal couple in respect so Camillia and Andrew caressed her head and told her that they had some things she needed to see and that they would like for her to examine their home for her approval of the things they had done for the pups and for her advice of anything they could change or add for their growth and comfort so Blue star lifted her head and locked eyes with Camillia and replied that she already knew things were perfect but she would look anyway and Camillia started with the doggie type door and explained that it was for all the wolves and Blue star was appreciative of it and thought it was well thought out and promised that she and her other cubs would use it frequently then once inside the home Camillia walked Blue star throughout the home showing all the other accommodations they had thought of and gotten and Blue star was quite impressed saying that the royal couple must have thought of everything and then some there was nothing that her two pups would be in need of. Once the show and tell was over Andrew butted into the conversation between Blue star and Camillia and asked Blue star if she would be offended if he and Camillia got gifts periodically for her and her other pups and Blue star said she would be honored to receive gifts from her king and queen but for them not to feel obliged and Camillia informed Blue star that the pack was family and that family took care of one another and expressed their love always and that they got the best gifts and expressions of love ever and that was to be graced with the care of her two babies. Camillia told Blue star that as a mother she could not imagine how much bravery it must have taken to entrust someone else to take care of two of her young ones and have to figure out which two to have to give up that she could not have emotionally have handled it. Blue star said it was difficult at first but when she and her other cubs were essentially taken in also it made things easier but the very thought of how things could have turned out differently brought with it great guilt. With what Blue star had just said Camillia received a great idea and that was for the angelic head construction worker pale one to have his crew build on an authentic wolf den onto the royal couples home so the wolf pack could stay together and they would always have the option to return to their original den when they wanted and when Camillia suggested that idea to Blue star and Andrew they both agreed that was a great idea so Andrew came back verbally that it would be completed by the end of the day and he was on his way to getting it started and the construction would start within one half of an hour so everyone was to get prepared and off Andrew went. Blue star was concerned about one thing and she brought it up to Camillia which was once the new den was completed and she and all her pups including the two that were supposed to be raised by the royal couple were moved into the new den how would they all be fed and Camillia chuckled then replied that she would pick the two that she and Andrew had picked out of the pack and she and Andrew would bottle feed them as planned but then they could still sort of feed with their brothers and sisters and that arrangement would allow her to essentially raise her own two pups and they could grow with their siblings and know about their heritage as they grew just like they should and the royal couple could be there only if needed and other wise she could be natural with her litter. Blue star admitted that she was blessed to have such a compassionate queen and king and to be an official part of the royal family was an honor and she felt that she had done nothing to deserve it then Camillia interrupted Blue star and insisted that she had earned the position to be a part of the royal family by taking care of her family and being selfless in the process of being a great mother and for that Camillia held a great amount of respect for Blue star and on that note Camillia informed Blue star that she needed to put the pups on a feeding routine so that it worked around the families meal times for she was to go to the royal dining hall in the castle and eat with the rest of the royal family and she would have her own place at the big round table then Blue star was surprised to hear that she would join the royal family for their traditional gathering three times a day and Blue star let Camillia know that she felt that the royal family may not accept her being with them for meals and private sharing time then Camillia replied firmly that the royal family would have things no other way and they would accept her with love and open arms so she was to be there by word of the queen of the land of grandeur and that was already discussed with and backed up by the king of the land of grandeur so Blue star accepted the invitation with honor and assured Camillia that she would put her pups on a feeding routine that would work around the families feeding and sharing time. With the living arrangements and a few miscellaneous things taken care of it was time for Camillia to move about the commune to make sure things were operating well then she was to find her husband and assist him in what ever he was doing so Blue star was going to go to her original den while leaving the two pups that the royal couple had agreed to foster at their home so she could make the necessary arrangements to move herself and her other pups into the new den once it was complete and ready to be moved into. As Blue star and Camillia were ready to leave the royal couples home Andrew and the angelic head construction worker pale one and his crew arrived to start the new den project that was going to extend off of the royal couples home for Blue star and her litter of pups so Camillia informed Blue star that she would howl when it was time for her to bring her pups to their new den and Blue star replied that she would howl back and they would be on their way then Camillia and Blue star expressed their love for one another and parted ways to care for their duties until it would be time to cross paths again.

Camillia gave Andrew a romantic kiss and let him know that she was going to check on things out in the community then she would be back at his side to help him with what ever he should need from her with then Andrew replied that he would see her soon and they went about their business. As Camillia became more and more exited over the royal castles changing she started to feel somewhat ill and tried to ignore it but the ill feeling was getting more and more defined so it was not as easily ignored and with that she decided to have the stable boy saddle her horse so she could put out less effort in moving about the community checking on everyone and socializing and if needed rendering any assistance to those who may be in need and she hoped no one would be in need for how she felt she probably needed to be resting in bed and not be out in the community but she felt if she was not dying she needed to tend to her responsibilities as everyone else did. Andrew and Camillia kept a close telepathic link with one another and could feel one another's physical state but to not allow Andrew to feel her current discomfort she had to block his link to her and he could tell that she was blocking his link which concerned him because she very rarely did that and when she did it was usually due to something being wrong with her so Andrew excused himself from overseeing the den project to go out to look for Camillia to assure her safety so he had the stable boy saddle up his horse to cover more ground quickly so he could hopefully catch up with his wife sooner and help her with whatever was going on and it did not take him long to find her and when he did he noticed that she appeared sickly so he rode right up next to her and dismounted his horse then helped her off her horse then she fell lifeless into his arms so Andrew called out to a passer by in the community to take their horses to the community hospital and have them placed in the stable there while he flew Camillia to the community hospital to get her medical attention and it took all of two minutes for him to get her to the nurses desk inside the community hospital. Just as the charge nurse was going to send for the head doctor and Jaden walked around the corner moving toward the nurse's desk and the nurses saw Andrew standing there with Camillia draped over his arms lifelessly so he picked up his pace and got to the doctor within seconds and he instructed Andrew to take Camillia to her regular room then the doctor called out to the charge nurse to gather the team of nurses to work with him as he was gathering the usual doctors tools that the nurses were not allowed to check out of the tool box then with a timely manner the whole staffing crew that the doctor had called for and himself were in Camillias room with her then the doctor assessed Camillia to get an idea of what may be going on with Camillia then the doctor started giving orders to each nurse and everyone was busy so the king still was not allowed in the room with his wife and that created a bit of anxiety for him for this was the first time he was forbidden to be in the room while the doctor was there so he believed that whatever was wrong was serious. An hour later the doctor made his way out of the room and took the king to the family waiting room and began to advise the king on what was going on with the queen, his wife starting by informing the king that if he had not have been with her she would surely have died then Andrew questioned the doctor about what could have been so serious that would have had no symptoms for the seriousness of the ailment then the head doctor simply laid it out that Camillia had what was called a silent heart attack and

Andrew was familiar with the diagnoses but pale ones were supposed to be healthy and free of disease and sickness the closest to any of that would have been child birth. The head doctor affirmed to Andrew that silent heart attacks happen without warning as they are called silent and the fact that he acted so quickly was what contributed to her survival for once the heart stops the victim only has about six minutes to getting the heart beating again before the victim is lost forever and as each minute that goes by it gets harder and harder to revive the patient. Andrew was beside himself when he came to realize just how close he was to losing his soul mate and love of his life. The head doctor informed Andrew that he could go to Camillia immediately so the king thanked the doctor from the bottom of his heart then ran off to be at Camillias side but one thing was stuck in Andrews mind and that was why did Camillias heart stop in the first place because God had promised the pale ones a healthy life ailment free and the only time any one was ill was when two of the pale ones offended God and they were punished as they knew better and they acted on their own free will knowing that there were going to be consequences but Andrew and Camillia had done no wrong that they could see so while Andrew was visiting Camillia he questioned Camillia if she could think of anything he or she could have angered their God and after some gentle thought she replied no so they decided that once they could leave the hospital they would go directly to see God and find out what they could have possibly have done to anger him and how they could repair the offense. By now the entire population heard about the incident of the silent heart attack but the commune also knew that the king and queen had not have done anything to have been punished for. The head doctor finally returned to the queen's room and informed the royal couple that they could go home now so they were set free. Now the couple went to the stable boy to retrieve their horses and ride to the edge of the commune so they could tie their horses to a tree and fly to the skies to present themselves before God. The trip to the edge of their city was short and the flight to the heavens was just as short so they had summon God's angel and made the request to appear before God for they needed to clarify an incident and it's meaning so the angel granted them permission. Now at the feet of God the royal couple bowed before their God until told to stand before their God and explain their presence so the royal couple timidly stood up then Andrew informed God that they were there because Camillia had a silent heart attack and they were inquiring about what they may have done to have a punishment such as that then in a gruff voice God requested to know why the couple thought that the incident was thought to be a punishment from him then Andrew replied that God promised a life of no disease illness or anything along those lines and God agreed that he had promised that then he admitted that he was responsible for the silent heart attack and that was not a punishment it was God using the royal couple as an example in front of the pale one members to realize that they are not free from being punished and prove that they were not free from being watched at all timed and now the pale ones have gotten the message God did apologize for making the couple go through the whole thing but there was no one else to use because only they would have survived the ordeal God let the couple know that they would be graciously rewarded then the couple thanked their God for using them and for clearing things up then said that they were at his disposal and that they considered their services a blessing. Now that everything was cleared up the angel that took the couple into God's room was back up to take them back to where they needed to be so they could fly back to their horses and return to their castle. The royal couple made a rapid journey back to their horses but once they were mounted and ready to head to their castle they decided to ride the commune for a while and try to cover the entire commune to find out if word had gotten around about what had happened to Camillia as well as why and try to observe if the pale ones had understood the true meaning of why the event occurred. As the royal couple traveled through the commune, they discovered that the word had reached everyone and they had a sound understanding of why it occurred and the pale ones had just had the fear of God placed in them. As the royal couple rode among the other pale ones the others could only drop their heads in shame and were at a loss of words. At that point the royal couple saw no point to continue to ride amongst the pale ones anymore so they turned away and headed for their castle at a trot. When the royal couple got to their stable the stable boy went to take the lead from the horses and steady the horses for the couple to dismount and the boy was feeling uncomfortable but the couple could feel it so Camillia called out his name before he could get too far and he walked to her so she quickly started to speak before he could speak telling him that was no fault of his and not to let the incident get to him then all three of them hugged as Andrew told the boy to keep his head up and ruffled his hair then they went their separate ways. As the couple were heading home various community pale ones some individuals and some couples with children and some without had the need to stop the royal couple to apologize to the royal ones for their mental indiscreptions, allowing their mental statuses to get to the point that God should have to step in and use them for an example of God's ability to be an angry God as well as a loving God then Andrew would respond to them to always be diligent, to watch their thoughts and desires both positive and negative then all would turn and go about their separate ways. Once the royal couple had gotten home and settled down they would be summoned by the stable boy for the couple could be presented with new and improved horses, two pegasus's and two unicorns had summoned God to get his permission to cross breed and when old enough present their young ones to the royal couple for the ultimate horse and God happily approved it so it was now time to do this, the babies were now two years old and ready to be ridden. Things went perfectly when the royal couple got home they gave their horses to the stable boy and proceeded to go inside the castle to unwind a bit before taking on another task and once the couple had just wound down there was a knock on the castles door the royal couple allowed the butler to answer the door and there stood the stable boy requesting that the royal couple come to the stable immediately for there was something they must take sight to. The way the stable boy played the surprise out the royal couple took it to be a slight emergency so the quickly got up and headed to the stable and they had a difficult time getting inside as they were being blocked by two Pegasus and two unicorns then the stable boy squeezed in and stood next to the babies and once the royal couple got to where the babies were the stable boy introduced them to them to their new rides and he also made mention that they were born with the grace of God and that there would only be half breeds if they needed no common pale ones would have one. The royal couple thanked the babies parents hugging them and giving kisses on their forehead then they went to their new horses and introduced themselves to their new ride and let the parents know that they were welcome to their stable at any time and if ever they needed or wanted anything just to let them know and it would be their honor to fulfil the request then the parents thanked the royal couple after confirming that if they had any needs or desires they would let them know. The stable boy interrupted and let the royal couple know that the new the additions had special care requirements outside that of a regular horse and that he was well equipped to keeping them healthy and strong. Through telepathy the parents to the baby's told the royal couple that they were honored to become part of such an honorable act and they would be just a whistle away and would definantly make their presents known for now they were definantly family then the royal couple offered to build onto the royal castle a new barn just for them and the babies parents replied that it would be nice for they too were at their use without question. While Andrew was still conversating Camillia urgently ran into the castles kitchen to grab some cubes of sugar for the special horses then she made it back to them on time to give each of them a yum-yum and all of the mythological creatures were surprised to get a long-loved treat and were greatly appreciative. Suddenly the mythological horses bowed after turning toward the entrance of the barn and with that the pale ones immediately turned to see what the creatures were looking at and at first there was nothing then suddenly there was Gabriel the archangel and he spoke to Andrew saying that Andrew was to call all the citizens to the religious hall for a commune meeting and he wanted Andrew to have everyone ready within the next hour so Andrew replied as you wish then Gabriel left but it was well known that he would be back in an hour so the business they were working with before the showing of Gabriel had to end and Andrew had to round up the commune. Before doing anything Camillia put out an idea she said that the receiving of the babies would shock the community's populations of pale ones since no one had never seen a creature such as this so the surprise was about to get out of the bag before the community. The couple mounted their new rides then rode hard to the center of the commune to start the roundup and just as Camillia had said their rides did attract many pale ones and they did gather all of them eventually it was easy to gather the commune into the religious hall for Gabriel to address shortly. Once everyone was inside the religious hall Andrew got everyone's attention to make them aware of why they were called to the religious hall saying that Gabriel the archangel had requested that he and his wife were ordered to get the entire commune into the religious hall for a message from Gabriel and that he should be arriving very soon. With the end of Andrew's words everyone remained silent then suddenly Gabriel appeared upon the podium thanking the residents of the new garden of Eden on the new earth then he continued on making sure that everyone knew about the health scare that queen Camillia had just encountered and everyone confirmed that they had known about it so Gabriel continued in informing the pale ones that the event was not to punish the queen for any misdoings it was actually God using her as an example for the commune residents to know that God was all knowing and if they did not change some of their miss doings they would perish so it was time for each individual to search their souls and deal with any negative things that may be in their hearts and do what ever they needed to be done because God had proven that he is a loving god but now he was displaying that he was also an angry god. Gabriel made sure that the communes pale ones knew that God allowed the shock that the doctor used was able to bring Camillia back because she was innocent of any transgressions however if anyone had received the same punishment there would be no way to bring them back with what Gabriel had to convey and now being done the archangel expressed his love for the pale ones and disappeared as quickly as when he appeared. Andrew and Camillia immediately got upon the podium and questioned the community members if they had any questions or needed anything clarified or just had to express themselves and no one needed to speak so all were excused and went on to think and process if they needed to repair something within their hearts or minds and most pale ones needed to repair something or another so they waited no longer and acted immediately by making an appointment to speak with the royal couple for guidance on how to address their transgressions and after what had happened to Camillia the communes residents could not get their business taken care of quickly enough the incident along with the meeting with Gabriel all of the commune pale ones were in a state of personal panic because they did not want to leave things any longer than necessary because they were afraid of dying if they did not get things under control fast enough. Andrew and Camillia already knew what the commune pale ones wanted so they came up with a game plan to get everyone taken care of in bundle rather than on an individual basis, they would just take them in groups of individuals that their business office in the castle could hold starting as soon as possible so Andrew spoke immediately to the commune residents letting them know that they needed to line up at the castle door and their business could be taken care of as quickly as possibly then the royal couple made their way home so they could start on providing relief to the pale ones. At the castles business office the royal couple were meeting with ten pale ones at a time and it took a lot of time going through the entire pale one species but it had been done and each pale one was able to start working on the things that had them in peril but twenty hours later things had been addressed and all was running with precision and no one was in fear of death and everyone's minds were clear the commune was like it had been given a reboot and ran with precision it felt like a rebirth and the pale ones appeared to be closer than ever. Now that things were running smoother and still having things to get done it was time for the royal couple to meet with the construction angelic pale one worker to see about getting the specialized horse stable built onto the castle for the mythological horses and when Andrew found him they discussed the project the head construction pale one worker agreed that the stable could be done and the construction pale one crew could start that day so Andrew agreed it would be done and made sure that the workers knew that they would be eating their meals with the royal family and the head angelic pale one construction worker acknowledged that he and his workers would be at the royal chow hall when it was to be time and then the worker left to go get his crew pulled together and start with the stable project. The head construction angelic pale one knew that the new barn would have to be much taller than others because of the wings on some of the mythological horses and that the stalls had to be wider since these mythological horses were much larger than a simple horse and since there were going to be six animals in the new barn it was going to be giant plus there had to be extra room for the things needed to care for the mythological horses but the workers were not intimidated by the challenges that lay ahead of them. The stable boy had been given heavenly instructions on how to care for the majestic mythological horses so as he did his job with those horses his knowledge with them will grow and things will become routine and the stable boy had concern over having too many horses both regular horses as well as mythological horses to properly care for them all so the stable boy went to the royal couple and voiced his concern and Andrew agreed so Andrew appointed the stable boy to care for the mythological horses and Andrew would seek out another boy to serve the couple as stable boy for the regular horses. Camillia advised the current stable boy that it would be an honor for him to accept the job because he had earned the position and there had been no one else they could trust their precious new rides to so the current stable boy graciously took the job and informed the royal couple that he felt that it was like they were family and serving them was more than a privilege then he advised the royal couple that he knew who would be perfect for the new position and he would vouge for the new stable boy who at that time had no job because he had just turned the age of accountability which was also the age of being able to get a job and be an adult. Andrew questioned the current stable boy about how long it would take to have the boy in question in their presence and the boy replied only a few minutes so Andrew replied for the current stable boy to have the new stable boy in front of them post haste and the current stable boy jetted out of the royal couples sight and had planned to be back in their sight with the new stable boy within five minutes. It only took the regular stable boy a few minutes to find the stable boy in question then the regular stable boy called out for the other boy and informed him that a stable job just opened and it was for them to work together to hurry and join him so the new boy followed and they traveled with the speed of light and within five minutes they were dismounting their horses in front of the royal couple and the original stable boy was introducing the new boy to the royal couple saying he could work the horse stable and the original stable boy offered to get the new stable boy familiar with things and the way they were done. Andrew looked over the new stable boy then asked the original stable boy why they should hire him then the original boy replied that since that would be his first job he had not learned any bad habits and because the boy was his brother he knew what his morals and values were and he was a grand worker and quite the perfectionist then Andrew turned to Camillia and questioned her as to what she thought about the matter and she replied that she would hire him but as king he had the final say so. Now it was time for the king to make the final decision as to giving the child a chance at real work or nipping the chance in the bud and extending the search for a second stable boy and Andrew's heart was saying to give the lad a chance and Andrew's mind concurred so Andrew knelt down to be face to face with the new boy and asked him if he was ready to move into the castle and start work immediately and the lad blurted out absolutely as he hugged the king and queen as his new employers. Andrew ordered the original stable boy to help the new boy to move in so they could get to work sooner. However, before they got to work after getting back, they were to check in with the king who had one more thing to discuss with the boys prior to getting back to work. Once the boys completed the job of getting the new boys belongings from his birth home into the new room at the royal home they sought out the king for any instruction needed and any other things that the king felt was in need of getting across to the boys and the boys found the king rather quickly and announced their presence immediately and when the king turned toward the boys he appeared to be in a rather laidback mood as usual. The king requested that the boys sit on the couch together while the king sat on the chair across from the boys and then the king started to speak in a low and calm voice which was calming to the boys until suddenly Blue star came sliding into the family room as she had been running so fast that the pads of her paws could not gain traction on the castle floor and it was obvious that there was some sort of emergency so Andrew got Blue star calmed down to be able to listen to what was going on then he was able to understand the urgency of things she had found one of her pups had stopped breathing and she had not known for how long or what was the cause so Andrew instructed the boys to stay put until further notice from himself then he instructed the butler to go out into the commune to find Jaden and get him to the wolf den as quickly as possible then the butler replied consider it done as he was rushing to get out of the door of the castle and Andrew headed to the wolf den to see what he could do and about the time Andrew found his way into the den he found Jaden working on the wolf pup so Andrew ordered the rest of ]the pups to go with him to the castle and meet up with Melanie in the castles dining hall for some *wolf snacks and of course beverages that are considered to be wolf treats also so the pups did as Andrew suggested and they hoped that their leaving their home would help things go better however Blue star stayed close to her sick pup and Jaden was okay with that. As the pups entered the royal dining hall the sick pup that was still in the wolf den began to choke and drool then Blue star made her way to her pup and began to clean his face and nudge him to get up and finally, he started to wince and get up then once he stood up he nestled with Jaden then with his mother and now it was time for Blue star and the now well pup to join the rest of the pups in the castles dining hall for some yum-yum's nobody knew what caused the ailment for the tiny wolf pup but things were back to normal again so it was time to return to work and the mighty king had to get back to the stable boys and check up on the pale one angelic construction crew in case they may have some questions or concerns for the royal couple about the new ultimate barn construction project. The king was now with the stable boys and explaining who does what it was simple actually the original stable boy would tend to the mythological horses and their barn while the new stable boy would tend to the original horses and their stable while the original stable boy taught the new stable boy all the ropes and the royal couple had full faith that the new stable boy will do just fine because their original stable boy was an excellent stable boy ant the boys were brothers who would look after one another. Now that the boys were settling in and ready to work Andrew suggested that he and Camillia go meet up with the head pale angelic construction worker to find out how things were coming along with the new stable and when the royal couple finally found him they questioned the pale angelic construction worker how things were going with the new stable and the angelic pale head construction worker informed the royal couple that they had a fabulous draft to build by and that it would be an easy job so it would be completed quickly most likely that evening and the royal couple were overjoyed. Camillia butted in and offered a financial bonus if the work were done that evening and done properly in fact they would try out the barn with all the mythological horses being put into their barn which would be the final test meaning if the mythological horses did not like something about it the workers jobs were not complete for the stable was to be their home and should be comfy and steady enough that God will see it worthy to touch it and turn it into gold as he had done for their commune and the rest of the communes. The pale angelic head construction worker gave his word that the barn would be done that evening with no flaws and they had been doing construction based on advice from the words of the mythological horses and have also been having various mythological horses step inside during different steps of the construction in order to keep things in proper alignment then Andrew acknowledged that the idea of using the occupants to keep the work satisfactory the royal couple excused themselves so they did not take up any more of the work man's precious time so for now all was well in the commune. Camillia suddenly got the idea to ride throughout the commune and greet the rest of the angelic pale ones to wish them well and encourage them to continue their wonderous work that together they work to make their lives a productive one and simply being there for one another was something that made the commune a beautiful place to be and Andrew agreed with Camillia so that was what they did for the rest of the day and once they got to finishing up they got word that the angelic pale lead construction worker was in search of the royal couple in reference to the new barn so the royal couple rode hard to the new barn and finally saw the new barn and the angelic pale one head construction worker and he began to speak to the royal couple while the royal couple dismounted their ride and the angelic pale one construction worker took the couple by the hands and walked them into the new barn for the mythological horses and the royal couple could not believe the splendid job and to the royal couple's surprise all of the six mythological horses were in their stalls and the angelic pale one head construction worker even went as far as to make sure that all the tools and gadgets were there and strategically placed for use the royal couple went from one end to the other asking each mythological horse how they liked their home and they all gave the same review saying that there was more than enough room and more than that they were together. It was nearing diner time so the royal couple instructed all the workers to go and clean up then meet back in the barn and make it quick so that was just what the workers did then eight minutes later the working men were all back at the barn then the royal couple paid the men their dues then the royal couple mad a second round the royal couple paid the working men their bonus then they went to the royal dining hall and had a merry dinner. Everyone at the dining hall wanted to meet the mythological horses and see the new royal barn so Camillia excused herself from the table and after being gone for five minutes she returned and she had six mythological horses with her Camillia introduced the creatures and as she gave their names they would bow then the angelic pale ones went around the table and introduced themselves and what their purpose was in the commune then ended their introduction with letting the creatures know that if they ever needed them for anything just to let them know then the creatures thanked them and the creatures went back to their stalls while the angelic pale ones continued to feast. In fact, all was well in the commune now as it would be from here on out the mythological animals and the angelic pale ones lived in harmony with one another That was how the earth was supposed to be but it failed and now it man had finally learned an easy lesson the worst way ever. The population grew very slowly and stayed simplistic as it should have but now will forever be.